He Had Just Stepped Onto the Sidewalk When He Saw Her.

He had no idea why his disinterested gaze should have focused so suddenly upon that particular person. But once it did, the street might as well have been empty.

She was walking away from him, her long raven hair swinging slightly with the rhythm of her stride. He watched as she emerged from a shaded area into a patch of sunlight. Her black hair came alive with a glimmer of silvery blue.

He walked on, but he thought about *her*. Not the woman he had just seen, but the one she had briefly reminded him of.

Could he, in this small Cotswold town, have found her again?

PAMELA LIND
loves to work with words and has always wanted to be a writer. Her hobbies include sewing, tennis, horseback riding and, of course, reading.

Dear Reader:

Romance readers have been enthusiastic about Silhouette Special Editions for years. And that's not by accident: Special Editions were the first of their kind and continue to feature realistic stories with heightened romantic tension.

The longer stories, sophisticated style, greater sensual detail and variety that made Special Editions popular are the same elements that will make you want to read book after book.

We hope that you enjoy this Special Edition today, and will enjoy many more.

The Editors at Silhouette Books

PAMELA LIND
Echoes of the Past

Silhouette Special Edition
Published by Silhouette Books New York
America's Publisher of Contemporary Romance

Silhouette Books by Pamela Lind

Past Forgetting (DES #30)
Shadow of the Mountain (DES #51)
Echoes of the Past (SE #197)

SILHOUETTE BOOKS, a Division of Simon & Schuster, Inc.
1230 Avenue of the Americas, New York, N.Y. 10020

Copyright © 1984 by Pamela Lind
Cover artwork copyright © 1984 Howard Rogers, Inc.

Distributed by Pocket Books

ISBN: 0-671-53697-4

First Silhouette Books printing October, 1984

10 9 8 7 6 5 4 3 2 1

Map by Ray Lundgren

SILHOUETTE, SILHOUETTE SPECIAL EDITION and
colophon are registered trademarks of Simon & Schuster, Inc.

America's Publisher of Contemporary Romance

Printed in the U.S.A.

BC91

Echoes
of the Past

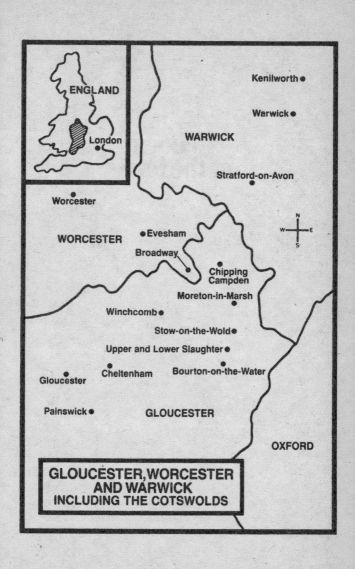

ENGLAND

London

Kenilworth •

Warwick •

WARWICK

Stratford-on-Avon

Worcester •

WORCESTER

• Evesham

Broadway

Chipping
Campden

Moreton-in-Marsh •

Winchcomb •

Stow-on-the-Wold •

Upper and Lower Slaughter •

Gloucester •   Cheltenham •   Bourton-on-the-Water •

Painswick •   GLOUCESTER

OXFORD

GLOUCESTER, WORCESTER
AND WARWICK
INCLUDING THE COTSWOLDS

Chapter One

$\mathcal{M}$ichael Bradford breathed deeply of the country air as he stepped through the stone-arch doorway of the inn. He still wasn't quite certain why he had come here when he should have returned to Washington, but he didn't regret his impetuous decision, either.

The truth was that he had no damned business being in England, let alone out here in the Cotswolds. When the meeting in The Hague had ended he should have gotten on the plane with the rest of the congressional delegation and headed home.

But he had talked himself into a side trip to England as a reward for having won the senatorial nomination, or perhaps more accurately, as a treat to take his mind temporarily off the grueling campaign ahead. England had beckoned, just as it always had for him. It seemed that anytime he went to Europe he always managed to find some excuse to visit this country he loved almost as much as his own.

So he had given himself a few days in London and Oxford to renew old friendships. It was at Oxford that the Cotswolds had begun to call to him. In the space of a few short hours he had slipped back into the ambience of his years there. Despite having attended several other very prestigious schools, Michael had always considered his two years at Oxford to be the high point of a very distinguished academic career.

But if Oxford had taught him to think, it had also given him a deep and abiding appreciation for the English countryside. A friend's casual reference to several biking tours of the Cotswolds had awakened in Michael a desire to see his favorite part of England again. Even the weather had conspired to draw him. He knew very well just how rare such beautiful weather was for England in May—or at any other time, for that matter. So, instead of returning to London and then Washington, he had come here.

Several long strides carried him away from the inn and onto the main street of Broadway, where the incomparable beauty of the scene tugged at him once more. He had not been here since his student days, twelve years ago, but the village had waited quietly for him, as he knew it would forever. To an American, accustomed to change, the simultaneous existence of past, present and future had a very strong attraction.

The golden Cotswold stone was burnished by the early morning sun, giving it a soft, warm glow. Steeply pitched roofs, some of them thatched, topped the small shops that lined the thoroughfare. And the flowers. How the English loved their flowers. One of his American friends at Oxford had once said in wonder, "Give an Englishman a cubic foot of dirt, and he'll turn it into a garden."

The flowers were everywhere, blooming ferociously,

wanton in their sensuality. Flowers in ancient barrels, spilling out of window boxes, growing with wild abandon in stone planters. How very different from the carefully planned gardens at home. Yet it was their very disorder that appealed to him, a strange thought for a man whose life was generally so well-ordered. And always had been, if the truth were known.

Sometimes it seemed to Michael that he had never really had any choices. His whole life had been neatly arranged for him at the moment of his birth—or perhaps even before. The schools he had attended, the choice of politics as a career, all had been preordained, and Michael had simply accepted them. Yet if he had to do it all over again he was certain that he wouldn't change anything.

He frowned slightly. If he was so blissfully satisfied with his life, why did these thoughts persist in coming lately? It seemed that cynicism had crept unobtrusively into his mind and taken root there. Certainly no one would ever have described Michael Tyson Bradford as a cynic. No, they would have said that he was intelligent— maybe even brilliant—after all, there were Exeter and Princeton and Oxford—forthright, strong in his sense of duty, and . . . The frown deepened. Damn, but he sounded boring. Was that really all there was to him, all there would ever be to his life?

Finally, when no answers were forthcoming, he dismissed the subject with an inward shrug. Probably it was no more than a sudden case of pre-campaign, pre-wedding jitters. Normal, he supposed. But even though he effectively banished the thoughts, that strange sense of unease persisted.

As he walked along slowly he thought with pleasure of the days he had just spent at Oxford. He had avoided the place for so long. Despite the happiness he had known there, he had been unable to escape the dark memories that also clung to those years.

The old sadness slipped over him, as it hadn't done while he was there. He saw in his mind's eye the anguish on his father's face that he hadn't understood then, and couldn't understand even now. His mother's pain he had understood, and even the suicide attempt. For a brief time he had hated his father—truly hated him. But time had allowed that emotion to recede to no more than a memory. His father was a good man, in every sense of the word. But he had slipped once, and it had very nearly cost him everything.

To a certain extent Michael had been shielded from the scandal by his absence from home. But he remembered very well the phone calls and the hurried trips back across the Atlantic.

Without realizing it, he had paused beneath a huge old tree that shaded a tiny park in the middle of the street. It took considerable effort for him to pull himself out of the dark past, but he finally turned his attention to his surroundings.

Broadway was beginning to awaken. There were few tourists as yet, so most of the people who walked purposefully along the street were natives. For a while Michael watched the scene, thinking that modern dress and a few cars were the only reminders that he was in the twentieth century.

He had just started back across the narrow strip of roadway to the sidewalk when he saw her. He really had no idea at that moment why his disinterested gaze should have focused so suddenly upon that particular body among all the others. But once it did, the street might as well have been empty.

She was walking away from him, her long raven hair swinging slightly with the rhythm of her stride. He stopped in his tracks, one foot on the stone sidewalk, one still in the road, and watched as she emerged from a shaded area into a patch of sunlight. Her black hair came alive with glimmers of silvery blue.

His eyes traveled assessingly over the body beneath all that hair. She was wearing a pair of heavy ribbed corduroys in a putty color, and a long sweater of the same hue. It wasn't a particularly enticing outfit, but something told him that there was a very attractive body beneath the loose-fitting clothing.

Only when she turned and entered a shop did he finally put his other foot up onto the sidewalk, and in that moment he knew why he had been watching her. It was ridiculous, of course, an illusion brought about by his reminiscences. Nevertheless, he started down the sidewalk in the direction she had taken.

And as he walked along he thought about her. Not the woman he had just seen, but the one she had briefly reminded him of. What had happened to her? His brow furrowed in thought. He hadn't seen or heard anything about her in years, not since her mother had died. That was unusual, now that he thought about it. Of course, he never read any of the tabloids that might have carried news of her. He could hardly expect to find mention of her in the *New York Times* or the *Wall Street Journal*. Nevertheless, it did seem strange.

He had almost forgotten the woman who had triggered those thoughts, so he was startled when she suddenly reappeared, coming out of the shop less than a block ahead of him. But once again he saw only the back of her head as she turned to speak to someone about to enter the shop.

Her arms laden with packages, she moved down the sidewalk in the opposite direction from him. Michael hesitated, then began to follow her, keeping his distance.

He tried to tell himself that he was headed in that direction in any event, but he knew that something was drawing him along in her wake. He watched as several other people greeted her, but even when she turned her head sideways he saw nothing of her face, since that glorious ebony curtain hid it from his view.

A smile flitted briefly across his face as he was suddenly reminded of a fellow student from his Princeton days. She had had gorgeous long blond hair and a voluptuous body—and a face that would have looked better on a horse. How many times had he seen men follow her on campus, absolutely entranced—until they caught up with her. Was this woman the same?

His curiosity aroused, he gave up any pretense about just going for a stroll and continued to follow her, even when she left the shopping area behind and continued up the slow incline past small cottages secluded behind stone walls.

He did, however, feel a certain amount of shame over his unusual behavior. What would his constituents say about his following some nameless woman around a small English village when he belonged back in Washington, tending to their affairs? But he wanted to see her—it was as simple as that. No, it wasn't really as simple as that, but he wasn't prepared to examine his reasons more closely.

After being momentarily distracted by the barking of a small dog, he turned back to see her disappearing between two high stone walls. Was that where she lived? He was just cursing himself for not having overtaken her when he had the chance, when a memory stirred. He quickened his step. As soon as he reached the path between the walls he knew that he had been right. The path led to a car park. No parking lot was permitted to blemish the charm of Broadway's shopping district.

Instead it was located at the edge of the area, hidden behind cottages and walls.

After standing aside somewhat impatiently while a woman with a pram came along the narrow part of the path, Michael hurried along. When he reached the edge of the lot, he stopped and swept the area with an impatient gaze. Then, catching a movement in the far corner, he turned in that direction just in time to see her lowering the trunk lid. Still he didn't see her face clearly, since she had her head lowered and that shining mane continued to obscure her features.

But then, just when he had begun to despair of ever seeing what she looked like, she opened the car door and, with an impatient gesture, tossed her head to send the long black hair swirling over her shoulders. A shock rippled through him and forced a strange cry from his lips. She couldn't have heard it, but for some reason she glanced briefly in his direction before sliding into the little car.

Long after the car had left the lot Michael continued to stand there, staring at the spot where he had last seen it. The shock still tingled along his nerve endings and paralyzed his muscles. His mind simply refused to accept what his eyes had seen. It wasn't possible. The words kept repeating in his mind, a rhythmic chant.

Reality washed over him finally when two women broke the stillness with their animated chatter as they came up behind him on the path. He shook away the remnants of the vision, then shot a quick glance at the women to see if they thought he was crazy. Fortunately for his peace of mind, he encountered no more than pleasant smiles.

Slowly Michael turned back to the center of the village, and by the time he had reached the shopping district, he had regained his sanity. After all, he had seen her for no more than a few seconds, and even then from a considerable distance. Also, she had been wearing over-sized dark glasses. He began to feel better. His mind had merely played a trick on him—merging past and present for a moment. Probably something in the air of this unique place.

Besides, she had seen him, and there had been no sign of recognition. That thought calmed him still more—until he realized with a start that she had no reason to recognize him. It wasn't very likely that she even knew of his existence. An unreasonable anger boiled up in him. At the very least it seemed to him that he shouldn't have to go up to her and shout his name before she realized who he was. And would even that do it? It had been a very long time ago, and his father had been only one of many—very many.

Once again confused about what—or whom—he had seen, Michael paused in front of the pharmacy, the shop he had seen her leave just before returning to her car. After a moment's hesitation, during which time he told himself that this would be better left alone, he walked in.

But as he did, he asked himself why he was doing this, and the answer came all too quickly. He needed to exorcise a ghost. Once he satisfied himself that it wasn't her, he would be able to let go of these thoughts.

He lingered in the shop for a few moments, finally picking up a bottle of aspirin he didn't need and grabbing several postcards he would never send. Irresolutely he approached the pleasant looking middle-aged woman behind the counter.

After paying for his unwanted purchases and receiving his change he asked in a carefully casual voice, "Would you know the name of the young woman who was in here about fifteen minutes ago? She had long black hair."

There was a slight pause while the woman closed the cash drawer, and he would have sworn that she seemed to hesitate for some reason.

"That must have been Miss Bromleigh. Jennifer Bromleigh."

The woman's voice was pleasant enough, but Michael heard the question in her voice. This was England, after all. If his accent hadn't given him away, his very American behavior certainly had. No English country gentleman would ever have asked such a thing of her.

Feeling compelled to explain his interest, he gave the woman his best candidate's smile. "I only caught a quick glimpse of her, but she reminded me of an old school friend of my sister's. Bromleigh, you said?" He shrugged. "I guess I was mistaken." He nodded pleasantly to the woman and left the shop.

Jennifer. Even though the last name was different, the fact that she had the same first name shocked him. Was it no more than a coincidence? It had to be.

Michael returned to the inn, determined to put the whole thing from his mind. But when he put in a call to an old friend in London whom he hadn't gotten to see, she was still there, a tantalizing and terrifying ghost.

Greg greeted him cheerily, and they made plans to get together when Michael returned to London.

"I'd expected to see you in The Hague," Michael commented, knowing that Greg, who was a reporter for one of the wire services, usually covered such events.

"I was supposed to cover the conference, but at the last minute they decided to send me to Rome to cover the latest political scandal. Just got back this morning."

As they talked it dawned on Michael that his friend might know something about the woman who continued to haunt him.

"Greg, do you know what ever happened to Jennifer Wellesley?"

"Jennifer Wellesley? My God, what are you trying to do, destroy me for the day?" Greg gave an exaggerated sigh. "No, I don't cover that sort of scandal, unfortunately. She dropped out of sight a long time ago, difficult as that is to imagine. I seem to recall that there was some mention of her being in New York a few years ago, and that she'd been living in France. Why?"

"Oh, I saw someone today who reminded me of her, that's all." Michael kept his voice neutral.

Greg laughed. "Isn't that kind of like saying that you saw a painting that reminded you of the Mona Lisa? I can just feel my blood pressure rising. I'll never forget that scene—you know the one I mean?"

Michael knew. It was burned into his brain. Jennifer Wellesley, with her almost waist-length midnight hair flowing across the gold satin of her shoulders, naked to her waist in a canopied bed. He even remembered the bed linens—pale pink with tiny roses, matching the canopy. The way she had looked. Innocence and awakening womanhood. He tore himself away from the image as Greg went on.

"My God. I just realized that that was . . . what . . . ? Twelve or thirteen years ago. She was only sixteen or seventeen at the time."

Seventeen. And it had been twelve years ago. He had good reason to remember. He didn't correct his friend, however.

After they had hung up Michael tried for a while to turn his mind to anything other than the woman they had been discussing. But now that the memory had surfaced, it refused to be put down again. Greg's mention of the film hadn't helped at all. That scene. He closed his eyes, and that only made the image clearer. The powerful, all-consuming sensuality of it swept over him once more, and with it came an echo of the other feelings he had had at the time. Disgust? Envy? Even now he couldn't bring himself to think rationally about them.

Suddenly it became of paramount importance to resolve the doubts in his mind concerning the woman he had seen. The voice of reason was warning him off, but he chose to ignore it.

Instead he went down and got his car, then drove slowly through the narrow streets. He remembered the direction she had taken when she left the village, and he knew he would recognize her car.

He left the village behind.

The phone rang just as Jennifer was climbing down from the small stool she used to reach the top cabinets in her kitchen.

"Jennifer, it's Mary. The bath salts you wanted came in this morning, just after you left. Would you like me to drop some off later?"

Jennifer smiled. Mary was so thoughtful. She was the closest thing Jennifer had ever had to a woman friend. "That would be lovely. Could you stay for tea?"

"I'll try." There was a small hesitation. "Jennifer, just after you left the shop, a man came in asking about you. He said he'd seen you come into the shop and thought you were an old friend of his sister's. But when I told him your name he said he must have been mistaken."

The image came all too quickly to her mind. The tall blond man in the parking lot. "What did he look like?"

"Very nice." Mary giggled appreciatively. "Tall, athletic looking, with blond hair. An American."

Yes, she had been sure of that the moment she had seen him. He might as well have had the Stars and

Stripes draped over him. Only during the years she had been living abroad had she come to realize just how distinctive Americans were. She could always spot them. And she always avoided them, even after all this time. She frowned.

"You didn't tell him where I live?"

"No, of course not," her friend assured her. "He didn't ask, actually."

That made her feel somewhat better. He couldn't have been too interested, or he would have tried to get that information from Mary. But after they hung up Jennifer continued to think about him. She had felt uneasy from the moment she had seen him watching her. He must have followed her to the parking lot from the shop, then gone back to ask about her. But if he had suspected, why hadn't he overtaken her? Considering the difference in their heights, he certainly could have done so.

She had been pacing about her small cottage while she thought about him, and now she paused in the bedroom to stare thoughtfully at her reflection in the mirror.

A friend of his sister indeed. Jennifer was very realistic about her beauty, and she knew full well that she didn't look like a friend of anyone's sister. Who was he? He hadn't looked like a reporter, but she'd been fooled before on that one. Still, something told her that she was right this time.

Perhaps he was no more than an American tourist on the make. But if that were the case, why had he kept his distance? The man disturbed her for reasons she didn't fully understand. His appearance and behavior didn't fit into either of the categories she was considering.

But the incident did remind her that the tourist season would soon begin in earnest. That was the only thing she didn't like about her home. The Cotswolds were popular with tourists, and among them were many Americans. She didn't worry much about British tourists, or even those from the rest of Europe. But Americans . . . Yes, she still worried about them. They were more inclined to ask questions, just as the blond man had done, and they had unbelievably long memories.

All she could do during this period was to lie low, shop early in the morning when they were still sleeping, and disguise herself as best she could. She just hadn't realized that it was time for that already.

The tall American stayed on her mind until she went into the room that served as her studio and lifted the cover from her typewriter. It was time to get down to work and forget about her paranoia. Her editor had called the day before and was pushing, as always, for her next novel.

Jennifer had been tapping away for several hours when she gradually became aware of the growing stiffness in her neck and shoulders. Glancing out the window in front of her typewriter, she pulled herself with difficulty back into the twentieth century. A perilous flight across the moors was put on hold for the time being as she switched off the typewriter and got up, stretching with feline grace. Time to go for a walk. She didn't feel like changing, so she would confine herself to the fields behind the cottage.

Jennifer was careful to affect a shapeless appearance in public, but at home she wore whatever she chose. At the moment that consisted of tight faded jeans and a bright orange tee shirt that fitted like a second skin.

She paused long enough to put on sneakers, grab a sweater and ask Chaucer if he wanted to join her. The large marmalade cat peered at her from his bed near the hearth, then got up, stretched ostentatiously and ambled

over to her. They left the cottage together, but when
Jennifer headed toward the fields, Chaucer struck off on
his own.

Jennifer had intended to use her stroll to work out a
problem with her current novel—a question of how to
impart some vital information to her hero without
straining her readers' credulity. But instead she found
herself thinking about the hermitlike existence she would
have to lead for the next few months. Not that she went
out much anyway—a few dinners or an occasional film
with her friend Mary. But when that was the sum total of
one's social life, it became very difficult to give it up.

Perhaps she was being foolish, even paranoid. But
habits of long standing were difficult to break, and
Jennifer had been avoiding publicity of any kind for ten
years, ever since her mother's death.

The blond American intruded once more into her
thoughts. How she wished that she knew whether he had
been a reporter or simply an amorous tourist. By the
time she turned back to the cottage she had opted for the
latter, although his failure to pursue her more aggres-
sively still puzzled her. The thought of him following her
at a discreet distance all the way from the shop to her car
unnerved her.

She paused to take off her sweater and tie it loosely
about her shoulders. The warmth of the sun and the heat
generated by her exercise had made it unnecessary. Then
she bent to pick up the small bouquet of wildflowers she
had gathered. She loved them, even if she never could
remember their names. Mary had named them all for
her, but by the time she found them again, she had
forgotten. They tended to wilt all too quickly, but for the
brief time they lasted, they added a special charm to her
home.

Jennifer was halfway around the side of the cottage

when she saw the car parked close behind hers. A chill went through her, and her breath caught in her throat. It was too early for Mary, and Mary didn't drive a Jaguar, in any event. The blond American filled her panicked mind.

She started to turn, thinking that she could just escape into the fields again, but the sound of footsteps brought her head around quickly. The man from the parking lot stood there, staring at her. She clutched the bouquet to her chest in an unconsciously protective gesture.

Michael had been knocking on the door for several minutes, and the only living thing he had seen had been a large orange cat. It had given him a distinctly unpleasant look before walking regally in the other direction.

He was almost relieved when his rapping went unanswered. What would he have said to her? Very clearly, he hadn't thought this matter through. That in itself was uncharacteristic of him. He had a sudden sense of having been prevented from making a fool of himself by a kindly fate. But as he finally returned to his car he thought he heard a sound at the side of the cottage. The cat had started in that direction, too.

Michael's long strides carried him quickly around to the far side of the driveway—and the living, breathing past stared him in the face. Nothing, not the pictures, not the three times he had seen the film, had prepared him for the stupefying impact of seeing her in the flesh. For there was no question of her identity now.

She was somehow more fragile than he had imagined, and that, combined with those huge, sapphire-blue eyes that were now wide with shock and darkened almost to violet, gave her a vulnerability he wouldn't have believed possible. With difficulty he reminded himself of just who and what she was.

She turned for a moment as the cat came up to her,

and he stared in what could only be called awe at her profile. My God, he thought, how can any woman be that perfect? The clothes she was wearing now revealed what he had only guessed at earlier in town: a stunningly perfect figure, every curve, every line, the product of male fantasy.

Chaucer rubbed against her legs as she continued to watch him for a few seconds. She was shaking badly inside, but trying desperately not to let it show. And she was suddenly very much aware of their isolation.

But when she at last turned back to him, she realized that he looked almost as shocked as she was. Something else fluttered briefly inside her. A memory, perhaps? She had no time to consider it.

"Have you lost your way?" she inquired politely, hoping foolishly that that might be the case.

He remembered that voice, too. The years had changed it very little. It was a surprisingly deep voice for someone so small, and had a husky quality that could send shivers of desire along a man's spine.

"No, I was looking . . . for you." His dark eyes never left her. He knew he sounded like a babbling idiot.

Jennifer sensed that she had caught him off-guard for some reason, and she allowed herself the hope that he didn't know who she really was. Her years in England had given her a slight British accent, and she used it now to its best advantage.

"Looking for me? I don't understand. You're American, aren't you?"

"Yes. I saw you in the village this morning."

Jennifer took a few steps, heading toward the door of the cottage. It was calculated to be a dismissive gesture.

"I see. So you just drove around until you found me." The very proper British accent was in full bloom now.

He looked slightly ashamed. "Actually, I asked the

woman in the drugstore for your name, and I saw the direction you headed in when you drove away earlier. So I just drove around until I spotted your car.''

For a brief second Jennifer felt flattered. It was a strange reaction for someone who was accustomed to being singled out for her beauty. But this man seemed so different from the others who had made passes. Why, she wondered, then felt something stir once more. What was it about this particular man? But there would be time enough to consider that once she had gotten rid of him.

''Isn't that a rather unusual way to be spending a holiday? Chasing after strange women?'' There was mockery in her tone. She hoped it would have the desired effect of putting him off. She suspected that he was already ill at ease with his unconventional behavior.

He was silent for a long moment as he continued to stare at her. She stared back. She couldn't really say that it was a lascivious look, and that too was unusual. She began to feel better. If he had known who she was, he would have said something by now. And furthermore, she was on her doorstep, with safety only a few feet away.

She had to admit that he was very attractive, and not at all the kind of man who would be forced to pursue strange women. He had a healthy, rugged appearance. She could see him in tennis whites, or at the helm of a sailboat, with the wind ruffling his dark blond hair. She guessed that he was somewhere in his mid-thirties. Faint lines were beginning to appear around his dark eyes, and there were suggestions of grooves on either side of his wide mouth. He looked like he smiled a lot. He was dressed casually in tan corduroy slacks and a light sweater, but even so, he exuded an aura of breeding and money. A preppie, she thought with a small smile. That was the term in vogue right now. Old money and good schools and yacht clubs. She had never really been comfortable with his type, and yet . . .

"I'm Michael Bradford."

Jennifer drew a sharp breath, then forced herself to release it slowly. The elusive memory that had stirred so briefly now flooded through her. Bradford. The name couldn't be a coincidence. She saw the resemblance now and wondered why she hadn't seen it before. But his father had been darker. As she looked at him again she saw the same square, determined jaw and the tiny cleft in the chin. And finally she saw the same calm self-assurance, as though the act of identifying himself had banished his previous uneasiness.

Jennifer searched her mind for something to say as a nerve-wracking panic stole over her.

"J.T. is my father."

There was nothing to do but brazen it out, convince him that he was wrong. "And I'm Jennifer Bromleigh, Mr. Bradford. You'll have to excuse me. I must get back to work now." She managed to sound amazingly calm as she turned to open the door. But she knew that her movements were jerky and stiff from the tension that gripped her.

"Like hell you are." His hand shot out to grab her upper arm in a viselike hold, forcing her to release the doorknob.

Jennifer froze—body and mind. For a moment she simply stared at the strong hand that held her, noticing irrationally the light sprinkling of golden hairs against his tanned skin. When she finally summoned up the courage to meet his gaze she saw a strange interplay of emotions cross his face. Hatred, which she had expected, but something else, too. He was once again unsure of himself. That gave her a modicum of courage.

"Please let me go, Mr. Bradford. I don't know who you think I am, but . . ."

"You're Jennifer Wellesley. Don't lie to me." His voice was tight, and he continued to grip her arm tightly, lessening the pressure slightly only when she winced from the pain.

She knew there was no longer any reason to deny it, so she lowered her head to avoid his eyes and murmured, "Please let me go."

"Only if you'll let me come in. I want to talk to you."

When she looked back up at him the anger had drained from his face, replaced by what almost appeared to be a pleading look.

"What would that accomplish? We have nothing to say to each other."

"I want to know what you're doing here." He still held her arm securely.

"Why?" She gave him a puzzled look.

"I don't know why, but I want to know."

His confusion was plain in his voice. But she also heard a firmness there.

"If I satisfy your curiosity, do I have your promise that you won't tell anyone about me? About where I am?"

He seemed somewhat surprised at her request, but he nodded and let go of her arm. She rubbed it gingerly and saw the red welts where his fingers had dug into her soft flesh. Then she opened the door and went into the cottage without turning to see if he had followed.

He had, of course. She heard him close the door behind him. When she turned to face him, he was looking with interest around her small living room. She had furnished it for comfort and not as a showplace. But over the years she had collected some fine English and

French antique pieces, then added her own touch with hand-crocheted pillows and macrame hangers for her collection of plants. The result was a cozy, feminine decor that suited her well. It crossed her mind as she followed his gaze that it undoubtedly wasn't at all what he had expected. Considering what she suspected his opinion of her to be, he would have anticipated an atmosphere of blatant sensuality—the type of thing her mother had favored.

She broke the heavy silence. "Would you like some tea?"

"Yes, thank you," he answered distractedly, glancing briefly at her, then back at his surroundings, as though he still didn't quite believe his eyes.

She sensed a return of the good manners that she knew must always be a part of him. But her bruised arm reminded her painfully that something more primitive lurked beneath that civility. She hurried off to the kitchen.

Putting on the kettle, she considered her situation. For all the emotions she *did* feel, what she *didn't* feel was fear. True, this man had forced his way into her home—but how could she be frightened of J.T.'s son? Memories of him came flooding back, and a warmth mingled with sadness washed through her. She had suppressed them for so long. And Michael Bradford was already reminding her of his father. Didn't that make him dangerous?

She decided that she would find her way through this journey into the past and then consider the matter later, when he was safely out of her life.

Remembering her wildflower bouquet, which she had dropped onto a living room chair, she filled a delicate Sèvres vase with water and returned to the living room.

He was gone. Surely he hadn't just walked out. But no, she could see the impressive silver Jag still parked outside. The bathroom door was open, so it wasn't likely that he was in there. Frowning, she crossed the room to the small hallway where her studio and bedroom were located. And there he was, standing with his back to her as he bent slightly to read the page in her typewriter.

He heard her approaching and turned with a surprised look on his handsome face. "You're a writer? Jennifer Bromleigh is your pen name?" He glanced toward the wall near her typewriter, where she had hung framed covers from her novels.

"Yes," she said simply. "I write historical romances, as you can see."

"Do they sell well? I don't know anything about them."

"I'm scarcely starving, if that's what you're thinking, Mr. Bradford. Yes, they sell well, both here and in the U.S."

He came toward her then, and she backed away from the doorway. It bothered her when he came too close, though she wasn't quite sure why. The longer she remained in his presence, the more she saw his father in him. It was both unsettling and oddly reassuring.

Michael followed her back to the living room and watched as she carefully arranged the flowers in the vase. Concentrating on that simple task allowed her a few moments' respite, but when she had finished and looked over at him, she saw him watching her with an odd expression.

"Why are you writing, instead of acting?"

Jennifer gave him a level look. "Because writers can remain anonymous. Actresses can't."

"And that's what you want—anonymity?"

She heard the disbelief in his voice, and knew the reason for it. Just as he reminded her of his father, so she must remind him of her mother. And no one would ever have suggested that *she* had wanted anonymity.

"Yes, Mr. Bradford, that is exactly what I want. Now do you understand my request for your promise not to reveal my whereabouts?" She took a seat on the flowered sofa and looked up at him. "I've lived here in peace for the past four years, and I want to continue that way."

Michael had remained standing in the middle of the room, his presence dominating without being threatening —except perhaps to her peace of mind.

"But the critics said that you could have a career just like . . . your mother's." He hesitated before the final two words, and his distaste was plain.

"I have no desire to emulate my mother." Her voice was both firm and very cold.

Suddenly his mouth curved into an unpleasant sneer. "Do you really expect me to believe that?"

At that moment a shrill whistle from the kitchen told her that the kettle was boiling, so she got up, her movements very stiff and formal.

"You may believe what you like, Mr. Bradford. I'll make tea. Please excuse me."

In the kitchen, she strove to calm herself. Her hands were shaking, and she had a queasy feeling in the pit of her stomach. She was sure now that he hated her. She glanced toward the phone. Should she call the constable? No, she couldn't do that. First of all, there would be too many questions to answer. And secondly, J.T. Bradford's son wasn't exactly a nobody, and that could mean publicity.

Quite suddenly she remembered that J.T. had once mentioned his sons—two of them, if she remembered correctly. He had told her about them that day when they were on the beach, the day the photographer . . . She hurriedly turned her attention to the preparation of the tea.

Then another thought struck her. What if J.T. had never told his family the truth? Surely he had at some point. But if he hadn't, then Michael Bradford thought . . . Another thought was left unfinished.

The china rattled on the tray as she carried it with shaking hands, so she set it down quickly on the table before he could notice. He had sat down on the sofa, so she took a chair facing him and concentrated all her attention on what she was doing.

For a few minutes they behaved like two very civilized people. The pouring and serving of tea was an eminently civilized activity, and Jennifer was reminded briefly of an ancient tea ceremony she had witnessed as a child, traveling with her mother and . . . Fill in the blank, she thought. There had been so many of them that now they tended to blur together. Or most of them, at any rate. J.T. had been different.

Then, the task completed, she raised her eyes to find Michael Bradford watching her intently. How she wished he wouldn't do that. She had long ago grown accustomed to men staring at her with barely disguised, or even undisguised, lust. But Michael Bradford simply stared.

Unfortunately, he also resumed the conversation just at the point where they had left off. "Just as a matter of curiosity, if you had no desire to . . . ah . . . follow in your mother's footsteps, why did you make that film?"

She gave him the full force of her remarkable eyes for about thirty seconds before asking in a quiet voice, "Why do you want to know?"

He shrugged his wide shoulders, returning her look with that inscrutable dark gaze. "Curiosity, that's all. Just as I said."

"Very well, Mr. Bradford. Since you appear to have me at a disadvantage, I'll tell you. But I don't expect you to understand." Jennifer leaned back in her chair, trying to relax.

"I was all of sixteen when it began. My mother was probably the finest actress of her time. She was also all I had—literally. And she was a good mother, in spite of . . . everything. Perhaps she should have tried to shelter me from her life. Many famous parents do that, sending their children off to school in Switzerland or here in England. But she didn't. She wanted me in her life and kept me with her. Because we were together all the time, people began to comment on the resemblance between us.

"Mother wanted the role of Simone in *Two Loves* very badly. You see, her last two films prior to that had been no more than vehicles for her. That happens sometimes, when someone gets to be as big as she was. Producers know that they can have the star spend two hours reading from a catalogue and still have a box office success, because people will come just to see that star.

"She believed that the role could be the finest of her career, and she was right, as it turned out. When she got the role, the producer and director met me, and they decided that I would be perfect for the role of the daughter. I've never really been certain that she wanted me to do it, but she didn't try to dissuade me. And I was so caught up in her enthusiasm over the film that I agreed, and it was done. I hadn't even read the script before I accepted the part, and I'm not sure it would have made any difference if I had."

Jennifer stopped for a moment and got up, carrying

her delicate teacup with her as she moved about the room. A remark of J.T.'s came back to her. He had teased her that she seemed able to talk and think only when she was in motion. It was true. She often paced about the house or went for walks while she sorted out her plots. She turned back to J.T.'s son.

"I can't expect you to understand acting, since I assume that's not your profession." He was still watching her, and she began to wonder if he ever blinked.

"Any actor or actress sees every role as a challenge. I've known some who deliberately choose roles as far as possible from their true natures just to stretch their talents to the limit. In fact, Mother did that on several occasions.

"One gets involved in the character, of course, and depending upon one's training or inclination, one may even to some extent become that character for the duration of the role. But it's still another person; morality doesn't enter into it. One of the chief attractions of acting is the opportunity to do or say things one would never do or say in real life. Am I making any sense to you?"

She stopped, seeing that he hadn't moved since she'd begun.

"I think I understand what you're saying, but it doesn't answer my question. And why would any mother—any good mother, as you describe her—allow her daughter to . . . to take such a role?"

"For the reasons I've just described to you," she said impatiently. "It's a matter of perspective. I don't expect anyone who has grown up on Philadelphia's Main Line, with all the advantages that life has to offer, to be able to understand a woman who literally grew up on the streets of a Chicago slum, the illegitimate daughter of a prostitute. Those two worlds are light years apart."

"That story was true, then?" Skepticism and surprise showed in his expression and his voice.

"Yes, it was true. She used to tell me about it, when I was old enough to be told. Her mother hadn't the vaguest idea who her father was. It could have been anyone. I'm afraid that my family tree—on my mother's side, at least—is rather sparse."

Jennifer gave him a wry smile, almost enjoying the shocked look he gave her. Was that why her mother had told anyone and everyone of her origins?

Michael was badly shaken by this confession. Here she was, seemingly every inch the lady, calmly discussing her unusual grandparents. She was right. He couldn't possibly understand. He was angry that she could see that, and he retaliated harshly.

"So you excuse what she became just because of her background?"

"And just what did my mother become, Mr. Bradford?" Jennifer asked in a dangerously quiet voice.

"Exactly what her mother was."

She turned away from him and said nothing for a long while, long enough that he began to regret his words.

"My mother was not a prostitute. She had five husbands and numerous affairs between—and occasionally during—her marriages. But money wasn't involved in any of them." Her voice dropped, becoming almost inaudible. "And I really think that she loved every one of them."

Then she whirled on him, suddenly angry that he had forced her to talk about all this. "If my mother was a prostitute, what does that make your father, Mr. Bradford? He was a married man. Mother, at least, was free at that point."

Michael winced. He had been wrong to come here, and he knew it now—too late. He was learning that there were still things he didn't want to face. He set down his cup and quickly stood.

"My father made a mistake—a mistake that cost him . . . cost all of us . . . a great deal. He was forced to give up a political career that meant everything to him. It might have survived the affair with your mother, but when you . . . came into the picture, that was the end."

Jennifer stared at him. He didn't know. She was sure of it now. How could J.T. not have told them the truth? She was standing near the window in the far corner of the room, and she kept her back to him.

"Did you ask your father if he had an affair with me?"

"No, of course not. How could I?" Michael's response was harsh.

She turned then, giving him a humorless smile. "Of course you didn't. Generations of fine breeding simply eliminate such sordid questions from the brain, don't they? One simply doesn't discuss affairs between seventeen-year-old girls and fifty-year-old men." The saccharine smile vanished as quickly as it had come.

"I would suggest, Mr. Bradford, that the next time you ask that question, you ask it of your father. He *is* still alive, isn't he?"

Michael nodded slowly, almost in a daze, then turned and strode out the door. She stood by the window until she saw his car back out and roar away. Then she closed her eyes and let a pent-up tear trickle down her cheek.

Michael poured himself his third straight Scotch. It was late, and he knew he should be in bed. He had gotten through the evening by accepting a dinner invitation from a M.P. and his wife, then joining them and their other guests in the television lounge to watch the news. As soon as it had become known to the assemblage that he was an American congressman, the discussion had turned to politics and continued until less than an hour ago.

Since then he had been trying to get to sleep. He felt a strong urge to call home, but he quelled it, knowing that there was nothing he could say. Then he thought of calling Sandra, his fiancée, but she seemed terribly remote at the moment, part of another life.

He could close his eyes and relive every moment he had spent with Jennifer Wellesley. In time he might forget some of their discussion, but he would never forget her calm, cultured voice describing her prostitute grandmother and unknown grandfather. He felt confused, angry, hurt—all that and more. Worse, he was filled with self-loathing at his behavior toward her.

Had he ever really believed that his father had been involved with the child she had been then? He didn't think so, but he wasn't sure that he might not have *half*-believed it at some point, especially after seeing that film.

Two Loves had been the story of a mother and daughter who became involved with the same man, a man not much younger than his father had been at the time. And the pivotal scene had been the one he remembered so clearly—when the young daughter lost her innocence to that man.

Worst of all, the film had opened to critical raves at the time when his father's name was being headlined in all the scandal sheets because of his involvement with Jennifer's mother.

But the final straw had been the photograph. He could see it as clearly now as though he held it in his hand. True, it had been taken from some distance away, but there had been no doubt about the identity of the two figures on the beach, entwined in an embrace. Two days after that photo had been published in all the tabloids, his mother had taken an overdose of sleeping pills and barely survived.

Actually, a part of her hadn't survived. Sometimes she seemed to be only a shell of her former self, outwardly polite and pleasant, with that very sincere smile almost perpetually on her face. But Michael suspected that there was very little left inside.

And his father? Something had died inside J.T. the day he learned of Jennifer's mother's death. Until that day ten years ago, he had been regretful both at the loss of his political career and at the grief he had caused his family. But he had been very much alive in spite of it all.

Michael had been with him when they heard the news. They were at their club, and had just finished a tennis match. His father had a small transistor radio with him as they sat at a table near the courts. He was waiting for the Wall Street closings when the news came over the air that Diana Lansing had died in a private plane crash in the Swiss Alps. And J.T. Bradford had become an old man in a matter of seconds. Both of them had sat in a stunned silence, until J.T. had finally excused himself. Michael found him later sitting in a quiet corner of the club bar, an empty bottle nearby.

Michael had never seen his father drunk before. All the way home he had listened to J.T.'s drunken ravings, most of them unintelligible. But he had said quite clearly, again and again, "Diana, I love you. I'm sorry."

Somehow Michael had gotten his father into the house and up to bed without anyone seeing them, and the matter had never been mentioned again.

That kind of passion was then, when he had been twenty-five, and now, when he was thirty-five, something he couldn't understand. It was so different from the quiet, dignified affection and respect Michael had always seen between his parents and most of their friends. And it bore no relation to what he himself had felt for various women, including Sandra, his fiancée.

Sandra. He tried very hard to conjure up her image. But all that would come to his mind were the perfect face and midnight hair of Jennifer Wellesley.

Michael was at a loss to explain his reaction to her—even to himself. He had assumed that she would be no more than a carbon copy of her notorious mother. But now that he had met her, he found himself questioning that assumption. Or was he merely bedazzled by her beauty? Perhaps for the first time he was beginning to understand what might have happened to his father. What Michael was as yet unwilling to admit was that he was afraid of Jennifer Wellesley. But he was also curious. And he knew that he had to see her again.

Chapter Two

*J*ennifer awoke the next morning convinced that she hadn't slept at all. She felt drained, as though everything had somehow been sucked out of her. Everything except for a deep, aching sadness. How well she knew that feeling. But she had managed to cover it for the past few years with her writing and her various crafts projects. It had worked—until Michael Bradford had found her.

She stumbled into the kitchen and made some coffee, then dug through the drawers until she found a half-pack of cigarettes that Mary had left behind at some point. Another brief search yielded some matches, and she lit a cigarette with hands that were far from steady. Jennifer hadn't smoked in years, but she took a long drag on the cigarette, then coughed. They must be stale. They'd been lying around for months. But she needed something at this point.

What she felt now, more than anything, was a sense of

betrayal. It was obvious that J.T. had never told his son the truth about his relationship with her. Why? Michael Bradford had scarcely been a child when it had happened. And she had gotten the impression that J.T. was very close to both his sons. Had he simply been unable to discuss the matter with them? Had they been afraid to ask?

Jennifer's open—sometimes too open—relationship with her mother had always made it difficult for her to understand how other families kept secrets from each other.

As to her relationship with her own father, it simply hadn't existed. Her parents had divorced when she was less than a year old, and her father had died two years later. Perhaps mothers and daughters were just closer than fathers and sons. She had no way of knowing, but in her heart she wanted to forgive J.T. for his failure to set the record straight.

Jennifer thought about the effect the affair must have had on J.T.'s family. It was strange that she had never really considered that before. But she supposed that she had simply been too wrapped up in her own turbulent life at the time to think about it. Seventeen-year-olds weren't noted for their perceptiveness, and Jennifer had been no exception.

She knew something about the Bradford family, of course. They were about as close as anything America had to aristocrats: possessed of great wealth, enormous power and a long tradition of public service. She knew that despite J.T.'s position as Senator the family had lived quietly, shunning publicity.

How terrible it must have been for them to have been subjected to such a scandal. In a sense Jennifer had become inured to scandal as a result of being the daughter of a woman whose every move was chronicled —and sometimes exaggerated—by the press.

But her life since her mother's death had made her very much aware of the value of privacy. She could well imagine the effect upon the Bradford family of J.T.'s name being linked with that of a notorious film star and her teenaged daughter.

It was obvious that the scandal had affected Michael Bradford deeply. She had behaved horridly toward him. Of course, he had deserved some of it, with his superior attitude and his deliberately vicious attack on her mother. But she had certainly retaliated in kind, and she was ashamed of that.

Well, he was out of her life now, gone as quickly as he had come, and everything could return to normal. Still, she regretted that she hadn't told him the truth, and that she hadn't been more understanding of his feelings.

Finally she got up from the kitchen table, determined to put the past away once more. Or at least, she told herself, she would put her own past away. The trials of her seventeenth-century heroine beckoned. She went off to her studio.

Writing was an escape for Jennifer, and she knew it. But the results were good enough to provide a comfortable income and allow her to lead the quiet life she cherished. She particularly enjoyed the research that was a large part of historical writing. She was painstaking, and the results showed it.

Jennifer often lost herself in her characters, sometimes to such an extent that she wondered if she really had a life of her own. Might she not awaken one day to find herself an old woman who had never really lived?

Lately that thought had crossed her mind more than once, and today it persisted for quite a while, making it difficult for her to settle into her heroine's mind. Had the thoughts of the past dredged up by the appearance of Michael Bradford brought her mind by some circuitous route to thoughts of her future? She thrust them away.

By the time the knock on her door roused her an hour or so later she had succeeded in traveling back through time and immersing herself completely in her story.

For just a moment she stiffened warily, then realized that it was undoubtedly the postman. Her mailbox wasn't large enough to accommodate her bulky manuscripts, and she was expecting the copy-edited version of her latest novel. She couldn't see the driveway from her studio window, but she went to the door without fear.

Jennifer opened the door with a smile on her face, and the smile simply froze in place when she saw Michael Bradford there. Conflicting emotions wreaked havoc on her senses. Part of her was actually glad to see him again, but the rest of her resisted the thought of being immersed in the past once more. By the time she thought about closing the door, he had put out a hand to hold it open.

"I need to talk to you."

"In case you've forgotten, Mr. Bradford, we had our talk yesterday." Her response was cold, even though she had decided that she was glad he had returned.

He simply stared at her for a few moments, then twisted his mouth into a wry, self-deprecating smile.

"I'm afraid I wasn't really myself yesterday. Actually meeting you gave me quite a shock, you know. Until I saw you here, I hadn't really believed that it was you."

In the face of his candor, Jennifer relaxed a bit, thinking that he hadn't been the only one who wasn't quite himself. There was something very disarming about Michael Bradford, she decided, recalling that she hadn't really been frightened of him the day before. Her fear had stemmed from who he was, and not from the man himself.

"And now you've gotten over that shock?" She didn't quite smile at him, but the corners of her mouth relaxed a bit.

"Yes, I think so," he replied evenly, knowing it to be a lie. Would he ever be able to look at her without experiencing a mixture of emotions that he didn't want to think about?

She exhaled a soft sigh, then moved back from the door. "Very well. Come in. It's time I took a break anyway."

"Do you write every day?" he asked conversationally as he stepped through the door.

She shrugged. "It all depends. When I'm starting a new novel I often work ten or twelve hours a day, and probably would work more if my back and shoulders could stand it. But then, when I'm finished, I sometimes don't work for weeks at a time. Writers are generally very erratic people, I'm afraid." She was wondering just how long they could continue the polite conversation this time.

They were standing in her living room, about two feet apart, when he suddenly grasped her arm gently. Caught by surprise, she offered no resistance. He used a pleasantly rough hand to raise her upper arm, then stared down at it.

"I'm sorry. I did that, didn't I?" He was frowning at the purplish bruises on her skin where he had gripped her so painfully the day before.

She followed his gaze. She had noticed the marks earlier. "I bruise very easily, and I accept your apology." She looked up to see real anguish on his face; she was certain that he had never done such a thing before.

He dropped his hand rather self-consciously, and she

thought how pleasantly gentle his touch had been. To ease the situation she asked if he would like something to drink, and he grinned rather shamefacedly and said that anything tall and cold would be fine.

"I'm afraid I had too much to drink last night, and I feel dehydrated. I'd forgotten just how bad a hangover can be."

She made no comment, although she guessed at the reason for his overindulgence. She might have been tempted to do the same if she'd had anything strong enough in the house.

A few moments later she brought him a large glass of lemonade which he drank very quickly. She had turned her attention to the already wilting blossoms of her wildflower bouquet and was wholly unprepared for his sudden question.

"Did you have an affair with my father?"

Jennifer became angry. She might have enjoyed his company for a while if only he would have stayed away from that subject. But she reminded herself of how important this must be to him, and her voice wasn't harsh when she answered.

"I told you to ask your father about that."

Michael shook his head. "I just can't do that. I know I should have, long ago, but it just seems that it's too late now. Besides, his health isn't all that good anymore. He had a stroke about a year ago."

Any lingering anger at son or father melted away at his words. The thought of that very vital man incapacitated in any way hurt her deeply.

"I'm sorry to hear that. I had no idea. Is he . . . able to function?" Painfully, she was picturing J.T. bedridden or in a wheelchair.

Michael nodded. "Oh, he recovered very well, considering the severity of the stroke. His speech is very slightly slurred, and one arm is a bit weak, but otherwise he's fine. He still goes into his office, although not every day.''

Jennifer breathed a sigh of relief. ''I liked your father. He was very kind to me. It was a difficult time in my life.'' She searched for the correct words, wanting very much for Michael to understand.

''The film had just been released, and the publicity rather overwhelmed me. There were many other film offers and . . . well, just the usual problems of being seventeen, compounded in my case by who I was.''

She looked at him then, her gaze unwavering as she met his eyes. ''Your father was, for a short but very important time, the father I'd never really had. And that was all.''

Jennifer sensed that he wanted to believe her; she could hear it in his voice when he protested, ''But that photograph . . . ?''

''That picture showed a man holding a teenaged girl in his arms. I'd like to think that if it hadn't been for the film and the affair between J.T. and my mother, the public would have accepted it for what it was—a gesture of comfort.

''I'd just had a really bad argument with my mother over my refusal to accept any of the film offers. Even though she hadn't pushed me at first, she said that I was too talented to throw it away.

''We screamed at each other in time-honored mother and daughter fashion, and I left the bungalow in tears and went running down to the beach. J.T., who had been there the whole time, followed me. He told me later that he must have been more strongly affected by the film than he had thought, because he was afraid that I might commit suicide—like the girl in the film. Also, I don't think that he was accustomed to such emotional outbursts between parents and children, even though Mother and I used to have them regularly.

"If that photographer had just continued to watch us, he would have seen that we spent over an hour there on the beach, just talking. And then Mother joined us." She stopped, then added quietly, "Now you know the truth, Mr. Bradford—if you're willing to believe it."

"I believe you," he said finally, then gave her a sad smile. "I don't think I ever really believed that anything had happened between you two, but I suppose that the film had an effect on me, too." And that, he knew, was an understatement. Later he would have to think about that. Why had this perfectly logical explanation never occurred to him before?

"Mr. Bradford," Jennifer said, searching for the right words, "I really am sorry about . . . everything." She gestured helplessly. "I guess I really never thought much about how horrible all of it must have been for you and your family. Your mother . . . is she . . . ?" Jennifer hesitated, not at all certain that she should be pursuing this.

"Mother is alive and well." He too seemed to be reluctant to continue, but finally he did. "She's not the same, and probably never will be. But sometimes I almost get the impression that she actually enjoys making Dad pay for the rest of his life for that one . . . mistake." Michael glanced away from her, surprised at his own words. He had had the thought for some time, but he'd never voiced it before.

"I think that's understandable, in view of what it must have done to her. And maybe it's a price your father's more than willing to pay."

He nodded slowly. "What I don't understand is why it ever happened in the first place. Please don't get me wrong. Your mother was a very beautiful woman. But how could someone like my father ever have gotten involved with . . . someone like her?''

Jennifer felt what she always felt when called upon to defend her mother: a mixture of resentment toward and sympathy for her detractors. But she stifled both reactions and said calmly, ''Mother had a way of making any man feel that he had her undivided attention. That ability, combined with her beauty, was a very potent force, believe me. If she'd been born in an earlier age, she would have made the perfect courtesan. In a sense, that's what she was. I really can't imagine any man being able to resist her once she decided she wanted him.''

''Did she love my father?'' Michael was thinking of his father's drunken words after her death.

Jennifer nodded. ''Yes, to the extent that she loved anyone. I've come to realize that we learn to love by example, and Mother never really had the benefit of example. She didn't know how to love, strange as that may sound.''

In her own mind Jennifer added, ''And neither do I.'' It wasn't the first time she had thought about that, but never before had the knowledge come with such aching sadness.

Michael was silent for a few moments, remembering his own thoughts of the previous night on the subject of love. But he was also thinking just what Jennifer had been thinking, and that led him to the further realization of just what an unusual woman she was.

He asked, ''What kind of life did you have with her?''

Jennifer smiled a strange smile that reminded him of his friend's comment about the Mona Lisa. It was an enigmatic smile, perhaps the smile of a survivor.

''A very interesting one, believe me. I never went to a regular school until I was nineteen and studied for a while in France. Before that there was a succession of tutors. You see, we never really had a home. Mother loved luxury hotels, so that's how we lived most of the time.''

A vision of his family's estate in Philadelphia came into Michael's head. The grand old house had been in the family for nearly a hundred years now. It was difficult for him to imagine a life without a place to call ''home.''

''It sounds lonely,'' he said simply, although the word didn't begin to convey what he meant.

''Loneliness is a state of mind,'' she answered. ''I don't believe in it.''

In that moment Michael became aware of the change in his attitude toward her. Jennifer Wellesley, who had been no more than a disturbingly beautiful source of information to him, was slowly becoming a person. He thought about her seemingly isolated life and couldn't believe that she might have deliberately chosen to shut herself off from the world.

''Surely you have friends . . . a man in your life?''

''I have one friend—two, if you count my paternal grandmother—and no men in my life.'' Her tone continued to be almost unnaturally calm, but being forced to confront her lifestyle made her apprehensive. She should have lied.

''But that isn't natural.'' The sentence burst out without thought.

She smiled, recognizing the spontaneity of his words. ''No, it isn't. But then, neither am I.'' Jennifer had long since accepted that fact.

Michael stared at her and suddenly saw her as she must see herself: the notorious daughter of a notorious mother, too beautiful to pass unnoticed in any crowd. He felt a rush of tenderness and protectiveness toward her quite unlike anything he had ever experienced before.

Jennifer saw the emotions flicker across his face, and even as she felt a strange kind of response to them, she sought to change the subject.

"Are you married, Mr. Bradford?"

He shook his head. "No, I'm . . . not." He had started to tell her that he was engaged, but the words stuck in his throat. Sandra seemed very far away at the moment. It had to be a reaction to Jennifer's situation— the overwhelming loneliness that she seemed to accept so calmly, as though she intended to spend the rest of her life punishing herself. For what? Michael felt strange things stirring within him, dangerous things. He wasn't sure why they were dangerous, only that they were.

"Please call me Michael. That's what everyone calls me."

"Not Mike?" she asked teasingly, seeing that he was upset about something. For a moment she considered the possibility that he might be lying about not being married, but she discarded the thought. He didn't seem like the lying kind, and besides, what possible reason could he have for lying to her?

"A few people call me that, but I've never liked it much."

Both of them had become silently aware of the long pauses in their conversation, of the undefined undercurrents in the room. Jennifer's response was to get up to refill his glass, which sat empty on the table before him. He followed her to the kitchen, aware only of a desire to stay close to her.

As she got out the pitcher of lemonade he was struck by the irony of seeing a woman he regarded as one of the most beautiful in the world performing a simple domestic task. He looked about the small, neat kitchen, noting the shelf full of cookbooks and the wealth of herbs and spices in neat racks.

"Can you cook?" It never occurred to him to find that a strange question, since he was simply following his line of thought.

She laughed, a true laugh for the first time. She had guessed the general direction of his thoughts, and his spontaneous outburst amused her. She suspected quite correctly that this was unusual for him.

"Of course I can cook. Actually, I'm very domestic. I cook, do my own cleaning, sew, knit—everything. You see, it's a reaction to my mother's inability to do any of those things." She handed him his glass.

He laughed, too. But he thought again about her other reactions to her mother's ways. Such as not having any men in her life. He couldn't quite accept that one. Perhaps she just didn't want to talk about it. Undoubtedly she still spent time with old friends in the playgrounds of the international set. But if so, how was it that there had been no mention of her in the press for many years? That crowd certainly didn't lead invisible lives.

He shot another glance at her. No, there was just no way that this bucolic life she seemed to be leading could be true. But it really wasn't any of his business, after all.

When they returned to the living room they began to talk about England. Michael told her how he got to London every chance he had, and she said that she went there several times a year to visit her grandmother.

"So you've kept in touch with your father's family?" He recalled that her father had been titled—an earl, he thought.

"Only with my grandmother, really. Once a year, at Christmas, I'm invited to the family home in Essex. But that's only because Gram's there then, and she insists that I be included in the family's holiday. Except for her, it's not very pleasant. I only go because she would be terribly upset if I didn't.'' She wrinkled her nose in distaste, making her look like a very young girl.

Michael thought about his own family's Christmas celebration and felt once more that strange tenderness. He wished he could give her . . . what? Cursing his sudden inability to put his thoughts into words, he turned instead to the immediate future.

"Would you have lunch with me?"

She glanced at her watch. "I hadn't realized how late it is. Would you like to have lunch here?" Then she smiled. She hadn't intended to prolong this visit. Perhaps his spontaneity was catching.

"Yes, if that's what you'd prefer. But I thought we might go somewhere nearby."

Jennifer got up. "It's such a lovely day, and I'm sure you know how rare that is here. Why don't I make up a picnic lunch and we'll dine *alfresco*—that is, if you don't mind cows for company?"

He nodded his agreement and once more followed her to the kitchen. "I don't mind at all—just as long as there are no bulls." Then he proceeded to regale her with a greatly embellished tale of a picnic long ago with a girl he had been trying to impress, when a cantankerous bull had interrupted them at a very inappropriate moment. Michael was an excellent raconteur—like his father, she recalled—and he had her laughing heartily by the time he had finished.

He leaned casually against the refrigerator while she worked, moving when necessary. As he watched her unaffected laughter, he began to wonder if he could break through the wall of reserve that she had built around herself. It was an unlikely thought, since he knew that he would never see her again. But something was tugging at him, something that was becoming increasingly powerful.

Chapter Three

$\mathcal{A}$ short while later they were strolling across the fields behind the cottage, with Michael carrying a wicker picnic hamper. The warm sun smiled benevolently down on them, and Jennifer realized quite suddenly that the earlier tension between them had vanished completely. The past they had shared so strangely had formed a bond between them, and she felt surprisingly close to Michael.

She glanced up at him briefly, struck once again by what an attractive man he was. Somewhere along the line the preppie image she had initially had of him had vanished. There was an openness to Michael's nature that she liked, and an honest vulnerability. Michael Bradford was a man who had no need of male posturing. He was secure with himself, and it showed. She envied him the background that made such security possible, knowing that she herself would never escape entirely the scars of her own upbringing.

The more she got to know Michael, the more he reminded her of his father, who had played such a brief but very important role in her life. It would be nice if she and Michael could be friends, but she suspected that that was only wishful thinking.

They circled a herd of grazing Jersey cows and headed for a small rise on the far side of the field. After spreading a blanket on the ground, they sat down beneath a huge old tree that crowned the hill.

Spread out to the horizon was a giant rolling checkerboard of greens, interspersed with occasional fields of golden mustard. Each square was tinted a slightly different hue. Above all this beauty was a sky of deep blue, where small, puffy clouds hung suspended.

They drank wine, and ate the cheese, fruit and bread that she had brought. And they talked. Michael continued to amuse her with his stories—about his years at Oxford, his political career and his many travels.

He encouraged her to talk, too, and she did. She said that her life was far less interesting than his, and missed the considering look on his face.

Jennifer drained her wineglass and leaned back, first resting on her elbows, then sinking to the blanket with a contented sigh. Michael was lying on his side next to her, propped up on one elbow.

"You're really telling me the truth about your life, aren't you?" He gave her a very serious look.

She turned her head to him in surprise. "Yes. Didn't you believe me?"

"No, I guess I didn't," he admitted, his dark eyes roving slowly over her face. They reminded her of brown velvet, soft and deep.

"I don't blame you. It's not exactly the kind of life most people would expect someone like me to lead." There was no rancor in her voice, and he was bothered by its absence as though she accepted the image the public had of her.

She had turned away from him, her lovely face in profile once more, surrounded by the ebony cloud of her hair and accentuated by delicately arched black brows and a thick ruffling of sooty lashes.

"Jennifer," he said very softly, and bent to her as she turned back questioningly.

His kiss was the lightest of touches against her lips that parted slightly in surprise. No more than a few seconds elapsed before he withdrew, but in those few seconds she almost raised her hand to entwine it in his dark blond hair. She could practically feel its springy thickness against her fingertips.

Then she wanted to touch her own lips, lips that tingled from that feathery touch. She sat up abruptly. She was making entirely too much of a mere kiss. More than likely he felt sorry for her. That bothered her, but she could understand it.

Michael had sat up, too, and as they glanced toward the western horizon, then checked the time, they realized that they had talked away the entire afternoon.

"I've kept you from your work." He grinned unrepentantly.

Jennifer was still disoriented by her reaction to his kiss, and she merely shrugged to show that it didn't matter, then asked if she had kept him from anything.

"Not at all," he said, then reached out to grasp her hand. "I've enjoyed this afternoon very much, Jennifer. In fact, I don't want it to end. Since you wouldn't let me take you to lunch, will you have dinner with me?"

She looked down at the hand that held hers lightly. It was pleasantly callused, strong and square. He was stroking her palm softly with his thumb, and she liked the feeling. She hesistated, not because she didn't want his company, but because it had been so long since she had gone out with anyone. Have I really become that set in my ways, she asked herself, then accepted his invitation.

He stood and extended a hand to help her up. They stood close together for a moment, his hand still holding hers. Jennifer felt very strange, not at all herself. She tried to examine the feeling, but it eluded her.

"I'm staying at the Lygon Arms. Would you like to have dinner there?"

She shook her head. It was a place favored by affluent Britons and Americans, and she didn't want to risk being seen there. Instead she suggested a small inn just down the road. She had gone there several times with Mary, and she knew that it catered mostly to a local clientele.

Michael agreed readily, and she guessed that he knew the reason for her lack of interest in the Lygon Arms. He dropped her hand, and they gathered up their things and returned to the cottage, where Michael took his leave, saying that he would be back in two hours.

As soon as he had driven away she felt both bereft and relieved. All her emotions seemed to be diametrically opposed to each other. She shouldn't have accepted the dinner invitation, yet she was glad that she had done so. She was bothered by this break in her routine, yet she welcomed it. She felt like the helpless victim of an emotional tug of war.

Finally she decided that she would enjoy the evening for what it was—a welcome diversion. They had passed beyond the trauma of resurrecting the past now, and could both enjoy the present. Of the future she thought nothing at all.

She did a few chores, including feeding Chaucer who lived up to his name by haranguing her with a lengthy tale while she prepared his favorite meal. She smiled at his ability to purr and eat at the same time, then wandered into her bedroom and opened the closet.

The inn she had chosen was a relatively informal place, which made things easier. In a flurry of house-cleaning about a year earlier she had gotten rid of five big boxes of designer clothes that she hadn't worn in years and knew she would never wear again. Her life was so simple now that she just hadn't bothered to replace them. Only when she went to London on her infrequent visits did she need anything other than jeans and slacks and various tops. The few dresses she now owned were definitely conservative. In fact, her grandmother had declared that she looked "dowdy" and grumbled that the granddaughter dressed entirely too much like the grandmother.

Jennifer pulled out several dresses, paying close attention to them for the first time. Gram was right—they were terrible. But what else did she have? Then she remembered. She had bought it some months ago, when her grandmother had talked her into accompanying her on a shopping trip to one of the elegant stores in Knightsbridge.

She searched through the closet and couldn't find it, then went to the closet in her studio that she used for storage. There it was. She had never even removed the tags. She held the dress up to herself approvingly. It was of silk paisley in shades of blue and violet that Gram had said complemented her eyes perfectly. It was, of course, modest, but it was still stylish, and the full skirt whispered softly about her legs.

By the time she had bathed and dressed she was feeling very good indeed. But she was somewhat ashamed at the thought of a woman her age being so excited over a dinner date. She had missed so much in life—either by force of circumstances or by her own choice—and she was now keenly aware of that fact for the first time in a long while. Sadness slipped over her briefly before she banished it abruptly. She wanted nothing to intrude on a pleasant evening.

After adding an exquisite gold chain and delicate gold earrings, she looked at the impressive array of perfume bottles on her dressing table. Jennifer had so little opportunity to wear them out that she frequently wore very exotic fragrances around the house just because she liked them. She sniffed at several, then finally chose a delicate floral scent because it seemed appropriate for the dress. She slipped her feet into high-heeled sandals, then stood back to survey the results.

She was considering the possibility of putting her hair up when she heard a knock at the door. Suddenly she was very nervous. Once again she thought about what a recluse she had become. It had happened so slowly over the years, and so deliberately, that she really hadn't been aware of how far she had withdrawn from the world.

For just a moment, when she opened the door to him, she was almost frightened. Michael seemed to devour her with his eyes, yet she felt none of the lust she usually associated with such looks. It was disconcerting.

She smiled up at him. "Would you like some wine before we leave? I'm afraid I don't have anything stronger."

He nodded, still not taking his eyes off her. At that point he would have agreed to anything she suggested. He finally forced himself to look away from her when he realized that he was upsetting her in some way. Something was definitely stirring inside him, and it wasn't hunger for the dinner he had promised her.

Later, as they sat at a small table in a secluded corner of the inn's dining room, Jennifer began to sense a subtle shift in the atmosphere. Currents fraught with an indefinable tension were running between them, threading their delicate way through the conversation. She didn't want to think about it at first, but finally, when their eyes met once more as they sipped their after dinner drinks, she knew she had to face it.

"Michael, please don't look at me like that. You're making me nervous." Her voice was barely more than a whisper.

Her candid remark startled him, but he recovered quickly. And he didn't stop looking at her. "I can't help it, Jennie. You're so incredibly beautiful."

"I don't like the name 'Jennie' any more than you like the name 'Mike,'" she said reproachfully, hoping to change the subject.

He laughed at that, then signaled for the check. "But it seems right for you, somehow. Before I got to know you, I would never have guessed it could."

"And what does that mean?" she asked, glad for the shift in the conversation.

But he didn't answer, because their waiter had approached. Only when they were back in his car did he resume the line of thought.

"Jennie is an old-fashioned name. It conjures up images that, before today, I would have thought couldn't possibly apply to you." He turned to look at her briefly before pulling out onto the road.

She guessed his meaning, of course. Impulsively she reached out and touched his hand that rested on the gearshift.

"Thank you, Michael. I'm very glad you believed me." For the first time in her life, she actually liked the nickname Jennie.

In the confines of the car she felt his presence very strongly. In fact, she was even more aware of him than she had been when he had been staring at her. She lowered her eyes and watched his competent hand on the gearshift, remembering its feel, then remembering his kiss. Reality was beginning to blur a bit at the edges. She was sinking into herself, feeling strange stirrings that didn't bear close examination.

When they reached the cottage she hesitated in confusion. She didn't really want the evening to end but she felt a need to be alone, to sort out what was happening. It was still early, however, and she saw no graceful way to avoid inviting him in. She knew that it wasn't likely that she would see him again, so she would have plenty of time later to consider everything that had happened between them.

Once they had settled themselves, he began to ask her more about her writing. She wondered briefly if he had chosen the topic deliberately because he was aware of her confusion. But she told him about her research and how she had discovered to her delight that many of the ancient landmarks still existed, some of them almost totally unknown outside the local area. She told him of finding landmarks still called by ancient names, even though the reason behind the name might now be quite unknown.

All this served to put her at ease with him once more, and later, when she thought about it, she decided that perhaps the tension hadn't really been there in the first place.

Then she asked him about his upcoming Senate race, which he had mentioned briefly that afternoon.

"Well," he said slowly, "I think my chances are fairly good. My opponent is also a congressman, but from a more rural district. So that gives me an edge—a bigger power base. In a sense it's not really a fair race, since he and I hold pretty similar views on the major issues. He's probably a bit more conservative—at least on social issues—but he's a good man.''

She smiled at Michael's description of his opponent. His attitude was a refreshing change from those demonstrated during most American political campaigns, which were so often acrimonious and filled with personal attacks.

"Once you've won the Senate seat, I assume that the next step is the Vice-Presidency . . . and then the Presidency?'' She regarded him with a slightly amused expression.

For a moment he said nothing, and she thought that perhaps she had offended him in some way. But when he did speak, his tone was musing.

"You know, just yesterday I was thinking about how my whole life seems to have been laid out very neatly from birth. I know that probably sounds strange to you, but it was a foregone conclusion that I would go to certain schools, then into politics. And no one ever goes into politics without seeking the ultimate prize—despite their protestations to the contrary.

"But there's something very . . . unsettling about realizing that you've just been following a preordained path all your life.''

"When I think like that, I just ask myself if I'll be satisfied when I look back at my life thirty years from now.'' In fact, she had done just that earlier in the day, but she hadn't found the answer.

"Will you?'' His question caught her off-guard, since she had expected him to apply it to himself.

"I don't know,'' she answered honestly.

"Neither do I,'' he agreed. "But it is a good question. I suppose that I'm just resenting the fact that I seem to have had no say in all this, at least in the beginning. But if I had, I doubt that I would have chosen any differently.''

Then he looked at her thoughtfully. ''In a way you've been far more a prisoner of your circumstances than I ever have.''

Jennifer nodded slowly, not at all happy at the pity she thought she heard in his voice. ''Yes, I suppose so. But I've made some very deliberate choices along the way, and I think they've been good ones.''

''You mean locking yourself away from the world? I can't think of that as being good.''

Jennifer tried to think of a way to explain to him that it had been good in the sense that she had avoided pain and ugliness by isolating herself. But she didn't know how to express the thought without making him pity her even more. She had begun to sense that Michael Bradford was one of those people blessed with eternal optimism, and she doubted that he could understand a situation where all the choices were bad ones.

''Have you ever been in love, Jennie?''

His sudden question made her very uncomfortable, but the honesty that had characterized their conversation up to that point compelled her to continue in the same vein.

''No, not really.'' Her tone was neutral. ''Except for teenaged crushes, and really there was only one of them. But I don't think a crush on a fortune-hunting beach bum can qualify as being love.'' She smiled in an attempt to lighten the conversation. ''I do write about it all the time, though.''

''You're afraid of it, aren't you, afraid because of your mother?'' As soon as he had asked the question Michael regretted it. The look on her face told him that he had struck a nerve, a very raw nerve.

''I'm sorry, Jennie. I shouldn't have said that.''

Jennifer had the discomfiting impression that she was quite transparent, and she quickly got up and asked him if he would like a cup of tea or coffee.

Michael merely nodded, saying that either would do, then watched as she disappeared into the kitchen. He sat there for a moment, staring after her, then got up and followed.

Michael's question had indeed struck a nerve. But it was far more than the accuracy of his guess that had unsettled her. It seemed to Jennifer that in the very brief time she had known Michael Bradford, he had gotten to know her too well. For someone who had shied away from closeness for so long, it was very frightening. She tried to tell herself that it was no more than the common bond of a painful past, but she wasn't sure she believed it. Now she wanted him to go, even though something told her that she would regret it when he had.

Jennifer had her back to the kitchen doorway, but she spun around when she heard a sound behind her. Michael was standing there, watching her intently, his hands jammed into the pockets of his slacks.

She said nothing, since she could think of no words that seemed appropriate, and turned back to the stove. But a few seconds later she heard the sound of footsteps as he came across the kitchen to her.

Two strong hands gripped her shoulders gently, and she started as she felt his body touch hers lightly. She willed herself to remain calm, but she was already thinking about his kiss. Something stirred deep inside her.

"Jennie, I'm sorry. I didn't mean to upset you."

More than anything else she responded to the soft plea in his voice. "You haven't upset me, Michael. I've enjoyed this evening."

Her words had the hollow sound of a lie, even to her.

But they hadn't been a lie. She *had* enjoyed the evening; in fact, she had enjoyed the whole day. Only at times like this, when he probed too deeply into her inner self, did she feel uncomfortable with him. And even then, something in her wanted to respond.

She sighed involuntarily and let herself relax against him, liking the feel of his strength. That fluttering deep inside became more noticeable, but she found it pleasant, rather than disturbing.

"So have I," he murmured as he lowered his head, causing his warm breath to rush lightly against her ear.

Michael's hands slid very slowly down from her shoulders and cupped her elbows briefly, caressingly, then finally settled against her waist as he drew her more closely against him.

Warm, undeniably masculine lips brushed softly against her neck, sending little tremors down to meet the languid warmth that was spreading through her.

Jennifer's body was poised for flight, but her feet remained glued to the floor. He had curved his supple body about her, trapping her between the hardness of his shoulders and the lean muscularity of arms that crossed just beneath her breasts. His lips and tongue teased the soft skin of her neck, gliding, nibbling.

She could have fled easily from a sudden, aggressive assault on her senses, but what defense did she have against his gentleness? The experience was so new to her that she reacted with total immobility.

Even when he turned her around to face him, it was accomplished with such tantalizing slowness that she did no more than follow his urgings. His hand slid slowly up along her spine as he lowered his mouth to hers.

There was wonder and beauty in this moment for Jennifer, and she quickly gave up trying to understand her reactions to him, reveling instead in the myriad sensations that his touch sent skittering through her body.

Jennifer had written a lot over the years about kisses—hard, demanding kisses, kisses that spoke of tightly controlled passion—but Michael's kiss was none of those. His gentleness left her breathless. Their lips were barely touching, and yet that touch was far more erotic than if he had plundered her defenseless mouth. Even the tongue that probed lightly at the softness of her inner lips was almost ghostly in its touch.

Jennifer was so overwhelmed by this delicate assault on her senses that she paid no attention to the increased clamoring of her own body. She moved still closer to him, fitting herself easily to his lean frame. Their bodies began to communicate in a wondrous language she had never heard before. Need, so long denied, made its presence known, shocking her with its assertiveness.

"Michael," she said in a strangled tone as she pushed herself away from him. But as she did so, she knew that it was herself that she was trying to escape.

He loosened his hold on her immediately, allowing her to move an arm's length away. She looked up to see her own confusion mirrored in his face. Had his reaction surprised him as much as her own had shocked her?

They stared at each other as though the answers they sought could be found within their suddenly vulnerable eyes. Silent questions flew between them in a kind of sensual shorthand. Then he abruptly shifted his gaze to a point behind her as the tea kettle began to hiss. The moment shattered around them.

By the time they returned to the living room, both of them were trying very hard to return to the easy conversation of what now seemed to be the distant past.

Michael said nothing at all about his plans until he was ready to leave and they were standing at the door.

Jennifer's mind was a volatile mixture of conflicting emotions. She wanted him out of her life, and yet she didn't want to face life without him.

"I was thinking of driving down to Stonehenge tomorrow. Will you come with me?"

She almost shook her head; in fact, she was sure that it had started to move in a negative direction. But the word "yes" came out of her mouth as though it had been lurking there, just behind her lips.

As soon as she had closed the door behind him, her composure cracked and she leaned weakly against the wall. One hand came up to touch her mouth absently. What was happening? She was certain that she had been thinking of him as no more than an interesting companion, a diversion, she had said to herself.

The closeness she had felt to him she had ascribed to the strong, if unconventional, link between their families. She had been certain that it was no more than that.

Michael Bradford wasn't even the kind of man she had thought she could be attracted to. Had she merely assumed that the lusty, aggressive heroes of her novels were the kind of men she herself would find appealing? She had learned very quickly that those were the kind of men her readers wanted, so she created them without difficulty. But now that she thought about it, they had a very limited appeal.

She knew, too, that the macho, dominating types her mother had generally favored had never appealed to her. Diana might have found their flashiness and blatant maleness stimulating, but her daughter had found them distasteful. In fact, much of Jennifer's lack of interest in men could be traced directly to the type of men her mother had always associated with.

But Michael was so different from both the heroes of her novels and the men from her mother's life that he seemed to be an altogether different species. He was closest perhaps to the grandsons of her grandmother's aristocratic friends, men that her grandmother had once pushed gently at her—well-mannered, well educated, sophisticated in their tastes. But as far as Jennifer had been concerned, something had always been lacking in them. They were all form, with no substance.

Michael Bradford, she decided, had both form and substance. He made the heroes of her novels seem like just what they were: the larger than life creations of a fertile mind. And he made the men who had surrounded her mother seem like crude caricatures.

This man had done what no other ever had: He had reached into her, into that part of her that she had suppressed out of dark, irrational fears. Could he also prove those fears to be groundless?

As she drifted off to sleep, still thinking about him, not once did it occur to her to remember just who he was.

Back at the inn, Michael tried to relax in the big, flowered wingback chair in his room. He stared at the half glass of whiskey he held in his hand, wondering if he should badger the staff for some ice. Only in England did they treat frozen water as though it were a precious mineral. He took a gulp of the warm Scotch and grimaced.

He was trying to make the difficult transition from a secret fantasy that he had suppressed from the first time he had seen the film to the reality of the woman he had held in his arms.

It wasn't really the knowledge that he wanted to make love to her that was bothering him. What man wouldn't want her? No, it was something else—a cataclysmic awakening of feelings he hadn't known he possessed. Powerful as the desire to possess her had become, he knew that something entirely different was happening here. He had been through all that hot-blooded lusting after women years ago. This time he sensed that he wanted more—far more.

It never occurred to him that Jennifer Wellesley was the last woman on earth with whom he could afford to become involved.

Chapter Four

"I think you've adjusted better to English driving in a few days than I have in four years," Jennifer commented as she watched him maneuver the rented Jag with ease.

"That's because I'm left-handed," he replied, turning to her briefly. "At least that's the conclusion some of my friends reached when we were at Oxford."

"You may be right," she said thoughtfully. "It's the gearshift I can't deal with, and you have to use your left hand for that."

"Maybe people who regularly shuttle back and forth become ambidextrous," he said lightly.

They were on their way south through the storybook countryside, headed toward Stonehenge. Each of them seemed to be making a determined effort to keep the conversation light and impersonal, but there were dangerous undercurrents beneath the surface calm.

Jennifer couldn't forget his kiss. She was sure that she was being quite silly; after all, at her age a mere kiss shouldn't be such an earth-shaking event. But was it accurate to call it a "mere kiss"? All she knew was that it had reduced her to a bundle of raw nerves.

She couldn't help noticing that Michael, too, seemed to be slightly wary, almost jumpy. Certainly he had far more experience in such things than she had, so if he were affected, too, something must have happened.

She tried hard to think of him as a pleasant companion and nothing else, but it was very difficult. She had become entirely too aware of him as a man, though she didn't really feel threatened by his maleness. In fact she was drawn to it, and finally admitted to experiencing a strong sense of sexual awareness for the first time in her life. She slid a quick glance in his direction, almost afraid that he might have tuned in on that startling revelation, but his head was turned toward his side of the road as he watched the scenery. She did the same, but if a parade of polka-dotted elephants being ridden by little green men had happened by, she wouldn't have noticed.

As the miles passed with no new surprises Jennifer at last began to relax. The weather was cooler than it had been the previous day, and there were dark clouds on the horizon. They passed a small cluster of thatch-roofed buildings close to the road, and Jennifer recalled aloud the first time she had seen them.

"I was about eight or nine, I think, when Mother decided that we should see some of the countryside. I'd been to England several times, but we'd never gone farther from the city than the zoo. When I saw my first thatched roof I was shocked, and I blurted out, 'Mother, they have hairnets.' They do, you know."

He glanced at the buildings they were passing and laughed. "So they do. I would never have thought of calling them hairnets, though. You must have been a budding writer even then."

A short while later they reached the village of Ave-
bury. Though not nearly as well known as Stonehenge,
the village was encircled by the same prehistoric monoliths. Glad for the opportunity to get out and stretch their
legs, they walked slowly around the village, continuing
their easy conversation.

"What made you decide to settle in England?"
Michael asked as their hands touched accidentally and he
wrapped his big hand softly around her much smaller
one.

Jennifer was busy trying not to react to the touch of his
fingers, but she kept her voice matter-of-fact as she
wondered why Michael's moves toward intimacy didn't
repulse her as others had done.

"There were several reasons," she said. "First of all,
my grandmother is here, and I like being near her. And
secondly, I've always liked England. Perhaps it's in my
blood. I was working on my first novel then, and it was
set in this part of the country.

"But I must admit that a part of it is the British nature.
People are polite and helpful, but never nosy. And that's
very important to me. Do you know that it took two
years of weighing and stamping my manuscripts before
the village postmaster finally asked me if I were a writer?
And even then I'm sure he only asked because I had
already broached the subject by commenting that I was
happy to be finished with that particular one."

Michael nodded in understanding. "Very typical.
That reserve is one of the things I've always liked best
about this country, too. The British may not have
invented the word 'civilized,' but they certainly exempli-
fy it."

Jennifer agreed with him, then went on. "Another
advantage is that the press is so busy tracking down the
royal family and keeping up with them that almost

anyone else can go unnoticed. I considered Lady Diana's appearance on the scene to be a godsend, although I do feel very sorry for her.''

"Your father was titled, wasn't he?"

"Yes, an earl. A very old title, too, and unlike so many others, a very wealthy one. That would entitle me to use 'Lady' before my name, you know.'' She gave him an amused look. "Mother always encouraged that, but my British relatives would have been very upset, and I felt that their sensibilities had suffered enough during my parents' brief marriage. I know that they would prefer to forget about me entirely—something Gram won't let them do.''

Michael was indignant. "How can they treat you that way just because of your mother?''

"Michael,'' she said gently, "you were very willing to do that, too. I don't blame them, just as I didn't blame you.''

She knew that her words had struck home when he was silent all the way back to the car. But he continued to hold her hand and didn't let it go until he had helped her into her seat. After he had gotten in on the driver's side, he took her hand once more and carried it briefly to his lips.

"I'm glad you don't hate me for that. I would have deserved it, you know." He kissed her fingertips lightly before releasing her hand.

Jennifer was silent, having fallen once more under the spell of his gentleness. Her hand lay in her lap, still tingling from his touch. As they drove on to Stonehenge her mind grew adrift with vague but lovely thoughts.

"There it is." Michael's voice startled her.

They were both surprised how suddenly Stonehenge appeared. A lovely country road, and then, without warning, it was there. It stood quietly in the middle of a

field, with cows grazing placidly nearby, oblivious to the
fact that they shared the scene with one of the world's
great mysteries. In recent years a single strand of wire
had been strung about the periphery of the giant stones
to prevent vandalism, but otherwise they stood as they
had always stood, an unnoticing part of a world that
continued to be awed by them.

They pulled into the parking area on the far side of the
road, then crossed under the roadway to the monument.
The dark clouds they had seen earlier by now covered
most of the sky and hung very low. A raw wind had
sprung up. Nothing could have been more appropriate as
a backdrop to a mystery enshrouded in ancient mystical
rites.

"When I saw them the first time," Jennifer said, her
voice hushed, "I really expected to feel some kind of
supernatural presence. I actually wanted those ancient
Druids to reach out and say something to me—and I still
do." She added the last with a slightly ashamed smile.

Michael grinned at her. "My first thought was that
they just weren't real. I'd seen them so many times in
pictures that it almost destroyed the reality." He didn't
tell her that he had suffered the same kind of shock when
he had first seen her—and he wasn't over that yet.

They circled the monoliths twice, pausing to read the
tablets set up at intervals to describe what was known of
their construction and purpose. At one point Jennifer
made some comment about what was on a tablet, and
Michael leaned close to hear her, his hand resting against
the back of her waist.

Jennifer turned to repeat what she had said and almost
forgot her words. The awareness that swept through her
wasn't unlike what she had told him she had expected to
feel there, but the cause wasn't the age-old stones. Their
eyes met, and she knew that he felt it, too. In that

moment they were alone in a windswept world, apart from time.

But the world intruded in the form of a group of Australian tourists, and they crossed back under the roadway, passing the snack bar–souvenir shop that had been carefully hidden from the road by having been built into the road bank. When they had reached their car they turned back for one last look at the eerie monument.

"I've always had the feeling that if Stonehenge had been discovered in America, by now someone would have built a domed stadium over it, then surrounded it with luxury hotels and condominiums." Jennifer gave him a wry smile.

Michael laughed. "You're right. And there wouldn't be any sneaking up on it, either. There'd be gigantic billboards beginning at least fifty miles back. Those Druids knew what they were doing when they built here."

They drove into nearby Salisbury and visited the famed cathedral, whose spire was visible from anywhere on Salisbury Plain, and strolled through the town until their wanderings were cut short by the beginning of the rain that had been threatening for some time.

"I thought the weather had been too perfect," Michael grumbled as they reached the car.

"You should know by now that there are two things one does not come to England for—the weather and the food." She quoted an old tourist maxim.

Their return trip was slowed considerably by the sheets of rain that blew across the road, pushed along by gusty winds. It was late afternoon by the time they reached her cottage, and their clothes were still damp from the soaking they had gotten in Salisbury.

"Do you mind if I light a fire?" Michael asked, eyeing the fireplace.

"I was about to suggest it," she replied. "I'll put on the kettle for some tea." She shivered slightly against the chill and dampness, then decided that she'd better change clothes.

By the time she returned to the living room Michael had gotten the fire started and was standing before it, unbuttoning his shirt.

He glanced over at her. "It's still damp. I hope you don't mind."

It was a very practical thing to do, and if she hadn't walked in just as he was actually taking the shirt off, she might have paid it no attention at all. But as it was, she felt her pulse quicken, and the tenseness that she had felt earlier in the day now returned more strongly than ever. How could such a simple thing produce such a reaction?

Not trusting herself to speak, she merely shook her head and went to get their tea. In the kitchen she remonstrated with herself over such silliness. She was behaving like a naive teenager. In fact, she suspected that most teenagers would have handled the situation far better than she was doing. Still, she braced herself for a further onslaught against her senses as she carried the tray into the living room.

He had brought a chair from the small dining area and draped his shirt over it near the fire. She kept her eyes turned in that direction for as long as she could, cursing herself silently for her juvenile behavior. Finally she was forced to turn to him.

Ridiculous, she thought. Absolutely ridiculous. How could the sight of a bare-chested man—even a very attractive one—tie her up in knots like this? And Michael was very attractive; there was no denying that. Broad-shouldered and slim-waisted, he had the perfect athlete's physique: muscular without being brawny. There was a light dusting of golden hair on the smooth skin of his chest, and the strands gleamed against his deep tan in the light of the fire.

Perhaps he guessed her reaction, because he broke the taut silence. "You wouldn't have anything that would fit me, would you?"

She shook her head, wondering if she could trust her voice. "I'm afraid not. Even my biggest sweaters wouldn't stretch that far. But I can give you a blanket if you're cold."

"No, I'm fine." Then, as if to belie his words, he got up as she poured the tea and went back to the hearth, were he squattted down and held out his hands to the warmth of the fire.

Jennifer poured their tea with unsteady hands, then sat down quickly, trying desperately to calm herself. A moment later he came up to her, but instead of sitting down on the sofa he knelt before her and took her face softly between his fire-warmed hands.

The heat from his hands spread slowly through her, bringing a flush to her fair skin. Their eyes met, hers darkening to violet and his already dark. A sensuous languor followed in the wake of the warmth he had brought. By the time his lips met hers, she was ready to accept his kiss.

Gentleness. The featherlight touch of his mouth on hers softly demolished her resistance before she could even consider the possibility of it. Jennifer wanted to deepen the kiss just as he moved from her mouth to her chin, then her neck, and finally to the hollow at the base of her throat, where his tongue brushed exquisitely against the throbbing pulse point.

She was wearing a cardigan-style sweater and had left the top two buttons undone. His lips followed the vee opening, then paused when they reached the third button. He lifted his head to look at her as he reached for the button. It did occur to Jennifer that it was time to stop, or at least to talk about what was happening, but the thought was fleeting. The slow wonder of it had completely undone her. It lent a quality of inevitability to this lovemaking that drew a desire she had never before known from some secret hiding place.

Even so, she sensed that Michael was giving her time when he stood and extended a hand to her. Jennifer knew the importance of the moment, and knew also that her decision had already been made. The consequences of that decision were buried deeply beneath wondrous new feelings. She gave him her hand, ready to step into a new world.

He led her over to the rug before the hearth and drew her down beside him, pausing when they were both on their knees to kiss her once more. She was barely aware of it when he dispensed with the remaining buttons of her sweater. Instead of removing it immediately, he slid his hands beneath it to caress her, even as his kisses subtly deepened their demands.

Jennifer wondered how he knew the exact moment when she decided that her sweater and bra had become an unwanted barrier between them. Her own hands were finding his smoothly muscled skin marvelous to the touch, and she ached to know the feeling of his body against hers.

The firelight played flickeringly over their bared skin as they caressed each other, each soft brushing of skin against skin raising them to a new plateau on the breathless ascent into passion. With lips and fingertips they savored every contour, every angle and curve. Hardened nipples, the curling hair on his muscled chest, the soft undersides of her breasts—each became an erotic way station on their journey.

It was a long time before Michael's hands dropped to

the waistband of her jeans, then hesitated. Their eyes met, and her breath caught in her throat with a small sound. What she saw in the velvet darkness of his eyes was a desire so pure that it made a mockery of all desire she had seen before.

The word "yes" was just rising from her throat when she saw his eyes cloud over with bewilderment, then finally widen in shock.

"No." The word was wrenched from somewhere inside him as he stood abruptly, then moved jerkily to retrieve his shirt from the chair. Jennifer stared at him in disbelief. Her mind was simply unable to comprehend what was happening, and she was still sitting there as he strode to the door before he had even finished buttoning his shirt. Her first movement was to shiver in the raw air that filled the room briefly as he opened the door, then slammed it shut behind him.

She strained to catch the sound of the car's engine, and when she didn't immediately hear it, she began to believe that he would return with some explanation that would restore them to each other. But then, just as she thought about reaching for her sweater, she heard the car roar to life. She sagged and withdrew into herself, fighting a chill that not even the fire's warmth could dispel.

Despite his protestations to the contrary, he hadn't believed her. As the tears began to trickle down her cheeks, she knew there could be no other explanation. He had only pretended to believe what she told him about her relationship with his father. He had wanted to believe it, so perhaps he had convinced himself that he had—until the moment when he had to face his own desire for her.

But she didn't feel any hatred for Michael. Rejection was all too familiar to her, and she had long since learned to accept it in all its unfairness. Her mother had alternately loved, then rejected her, and her father's family hadn't shown any ambivalence about it.

But strangely enough, this hurt even more. Not since her teens had she sought anything from any of them, but she had been ready, even eager, to give Michael all. Her pitifully small world began to shrink even more. She had allowed herself to reach out, only to encounter emptiness.

There was, however, a great strength within her. It wasn't a natural strength, but rather one born of pain and disappointment that could only have had one of two results: either her total destruction or the slow building of defenses. Fortunately for her, the latter had resulted. Now she drew upon that strength and got up, then calmly put on her bra and sweater, and collected the untouched tea things.

But even such strength as hers had a limit. Two hours later she had given up an attempt to read a novel, covered her typewriter after turning out several pages of rambling nothingness, eaten some soup and brushed the obliging Chaucer, but still the pain persisted.

Dusk had arrived, and she was considering the possibility of taking a walk, although the rain showed no signs of abating. Just as she reached to turn on a lamp there was a flash of light through the partially drawn drapes of the living room windows. At first she thought it was lightning and changed her mind about going for a walk. But then she heard the distinctive sound of a car door slamming. Panic came quickly, immobilizing her even when she heard the insistent knocking at the door.

She looked wildly about the room, certain that he must have left something behind in his rush. But she saw nothing, and the knocking grew even more insistent.

She opened the door to find him standing there with

rain pouring over him and running in rivulets down the front of his raincoat. His hair was plastered to his head, giving him an almost waiflike appearance—if waifs wore expensive trenchcoats.

Even though she had no intention of turning him away, he reached out to prevent her from closing the door. "Please let me come in, Jennie."

She nodded silently and stood back as he passed her, then reached behind her to close the door.

"Can you understand why I left like that?" He pleaded for her understanding, making no move to take off his wet coat or brush away the water that streamed over his face.

"Yes," she said in a small voice. "I understand, Michael. I don't blame you for not believing me."

He frowned, and the expression remained on his face as he shrugged out of the raincoat, then ran a hand through his dripping hair.

"Let me get you a towel," she said, and didn't wait for a response.

He thanked her when she gave it to him, then dried his face and hair. That accomplished, he seized her hand and drew her to the sofa with him.

"Jennie," he began, catching her face between his hands, which were chilled this time from the rain. To her it was a sad reminder of the difference between this moment and the gesture he had made a few hours ago.

"I do believe you about Dad. That wasn't it at all."

She looked up at him, puzzled. "Then what . . . ?"

He silenced her with a finger drawn lightly across her lips. "Jennie, when we talked about *Two Loves* you said that the suicide scene was your best. Maybe in the sense of drama, it was. But no one who saw that film is likely to forget that love scene. There was something so . . ." He paused, trying for words that he had never been able to find in all these years. ". . . so innocent, yet erotic, about you in that scene." Again he stopped, then cupped his palms once more about her face.

"Jennie, I saw that film three times, and it affected me just the same each time. You have to remember that this was right at the time of the affair; try to understand how I felt about both you and your mother. I don't know if I believed then that you'd had an affair with Dad, but at the least I had to admit to the possibility. I knew that I should hate you, should see you as being evil. And each time I went back to see the movie I expected to feel that way. But I couldn't. Worse still, I had the same fantasy every male who saw that film had—I wanted you for myself. Can you understand how that made me feel? Knowing that I should despise you, but wanting you instead?"

She nodded finally, thinking only that he had believed her, after all. But she knew that this was important to him, so she focused on the film.

"Do you know that we worked an entire week on that scene? What you say you saw is exactly what the director was trying to get: innocence combined with a growing sexual awareness. Mother had me rehearsing that scene day and night. At one point she got so mad at me that she suggested that I go out and have an affair so I'd know what it was all about. I got terribly upset and ran away, just to go for a walk. And when I came back she was beside herself, because she thought I'd done just that." She smiled, remembering.

"Somehow I finally managed to get it right, I guess. But I never expected it to get the reaction it did."

Michael smiled down at her. "Speaking as one who still recalls that scene very clearly, I'd have to say the director got exactly what he wanted."

Then he tipped her chin up and covered her mouth

with his, banishing all thoughts from her mind. But then he withdrew, even though he still held her chin firmly in his grasp.

"When I saw you there earlier, and you looked up at me, it was like reliving that film, Jennie. The memories just overpowered me. I was watching a fantasy come true before my eyes, and I couldn't deal with it."

Long moments passed, marked only by the ticking of her antique French clock and the beating of their hearts. Earlier Jennifer had been ready and willing to give herself to Michael, but it seemed that that moment had passed. Or had it?

He rested one hand lightly along the side of her face, the fingers caressing her neck and ear, the thumb tracing slow circles over her cheek. It seemed to her that it took forever for his mouth to reach hers, and by the time it did the heat of desire was radiating all through her. He made no attempt to close the space between them in any other way, though her body cried out for that contact. But rising swiftly out of that need came the knowledge that she couldn't stand to be rejected again.

"Michael, please don't do this to me," she said, pulling away from him. "I don't think I could take it if you stopped again."

"I won't stop this time, Jennie—unless you want me to." His breath fanned warmly against her ear. "And if you intend to tell me to stop, you'd better do it right now, while I still can."

She answered him by lacing her fingers through his hair and pulling his mouth to hers. Together they stood up and glanced toward the rug on the hearth. Then they both burst out laughing. Chaucer was curled up in the very center of the rug, and gave them a look that said quite clearly that he did not wish to be disturbed.

The brief moment of unease that Jennifer had felt

vanished in the laughter they shared as Michael led her to the bedroom. Briefly she thought of telling him of her continued innocence, but she was afraid that he might not believe her, or that, if he did, the revelation might send him away again. She suspected that the thought of a twenty-nine-year-old virgin might prove rather daunting for some men. And she wanted Michael, wanted him to help her break free of the past that continued to haunt her.

Undressing was a long, drawn-out affair, with neither of them in a hurry as they explored each other's bodies, renewing their brief acquaintance. As the final barriers of her clothing slipped away, Jennifer felt that along with them went a large part of the guilt and fear she had carried with her for so long. She was shedding a burden, moving into a new world that might have terrified her if Michael, with his gentleness, hadn't made it seem so right.

He had switched on the soft bedside lamp, and in its light he stared mutely at her with eyes that left no part of her untouched. Jennifer's eyes were filled with the naked magnificence of him, and they both stood for a long time, their hands clasped, drinking in the wonders of each other and letting the force of their desire flow around them.

Then Michael knelt on the bed, drawing her with him until they were lying side by side. His hands glided slowly down her back, pressing lightly, until she was brought against the full force of his desire.

Jennifer answered the insistent pressure by moving instinctively against him and arousing them both still further. Their need for each other was already building to a point of mindless abandon, but neither of them wanted to rush, lest they miss some smaller sensation along the way.

They floated together in a timeless sea of passion, coaxing from each other every precious drop of beauty. Lips and hands touched, teased, stroked.

Then the moment came when they could postpone the glorious end of their journey no longer, and Michael slid into her with the first fierceness he had shown. She welcomed him with her softness, wrapped herself about him and rode with him on the crest of passion's wave to an explosion of brilliance and beauty. She was surrounded now by that new world she had sought, and she found it more dazzling than she had ever believed it could be.

Michael was very quiet as he lowered himself down beside her, and she had just begun to feel rejection once more when he curved an arm around her still trembling body and drew her close. She was casting about in her mind for something to say when he suddenly rolled over on his side and propped himself up on one arm to look down at her with a frown that didn't quite banish the tenderness in his gaze.

"Why didn't you tell me, Jennie?"

She knew he wasn't angry, only puzzled, so she met his eyes without difficulty. "I was afraid you wouldn't believe me, or that you would run away again."

He traced the outline of her face softly, then dropped his hand to the curve of her hip as she shifted onto her side to face him.

"I wouldn't have run away, but I would have been more gentle, taken it more slowly."

"No man could have been gentler," she answered, touching his mouth with her fingertips.

He grinned suddenly. "You're hardly in a position to judge that." Then the grin faded. "Why?"

"At first I was just turned off by the way men always leered at me. It made me feel like an object, not a person. I knew that it wasn't really me that they wanted, only the body I live in. Then as I got older I knew that it was more than that. I had a fear—a very real fear—that if I let one of them have me, I would end up like my grandmother, or like my mother. I know how irrational that sounds, but we aren't always rational about things that are important to us.''

She stopped and saw from his expression that he understood. ''I think I'd pretty much gotten over that fear in the past few years, but with my life as it is now, there just wasn't . . . anyone. I couldn't very well go out and advertise my availability.''

Michael's mouth set grimly. ''Are you saying that I was the one only because I was available?''

''No,'' she said gently, surprised to find that he, too, could be vulnerable. ''You looked at me differently from anyone else. You wanted to talk . . . and you believed what I had to say. Before I really knew what had happened, you had tiptoed around all my defenses. I don't know a better way to describe it. You just sort of sneaked up on me.'' She smiled at him.

Michael threw back his head and laughed. He felt better than he had ever felt in his life. ''Tiptoed, did I? And here I was, worrying that I was rushing you, afraid that I was coming on too strong.'' He shook his head as he continued to chuckle.

''I guess I was never cut out to be a playboy. There was a time when I worked at it pretty hard, but it just isn't in me.

''Can I stay here tonight, Jennie? I assure you that I have excellent manners. I don't snore or steal blankets.'' He grinned down at her.

''I want you to stay, but I can't vouch for my own manners. I have bad dreams sometimes.''

He drew her to him softly. "Then I'll be here to kiss them away."

Throughout this lighthearted exchange they both sensed that there were things they wanted to say, things that needed to be said. But both of them were reluctant to venture any further into this new territory. It was a time for resting after a journey that had carried them very far, very quickly. They ignored the questions as they lazily explored each other, caught between sleepiness and desire.

Michael watched her tenderly as she lay sleeping beside him. He was filled with a lingering sense of magic—the magic they had shared during the night just past. But more than that, he felt within himself a fierce possessiveness that had never been there before. It was more than not wanting to let her go, it was a certainty that he *could* not let her go.

He tried to tell himself that it was only because he had been the first. It would be easy to believe that, except that he was sure it wasn't true. Leaving now was out of the question, even though he was scheduled to return to London tomorrow, then depart for home the following day.

He watched as her long lashes fluttered slightly and she moved the hand that lay on her pillow, reaching instinctively for him. He fitted her hand to his and bent to kiss it. No more thoughts about the future entered his mind.

Jennifer awoke with a feeling of pleasure. She was sure that when she opened her eyes she would find herself bathed in a wondrous new light. When she finally did, she saw that she was right. Her whole world was focused on a pair of velvet brown eyes that drew her immediately into a memory of the night before.

She smiled at him. "It's not fair, you know, watching me while I sleep."

He bent over to kiss the tip of her nose. "Maybe it's time you learned that I don't play fair. Anyway, it's your fault. If you weren't so beautiful, I wouldn't be watching."

"Michael," she said, finally asking the question that had been on her mind when she fell asleep the night before, "when do you have to go home?"

He gave her a rueful grin. "I was supposed to have been home four days ago." Then he grew serious. "I'll have to leave in another few days. But in the meantime, can we make the most of what we have?"

She nodded, then drew him to her. He was already too much a part of her to be given up. What would it be like after a few more days? But that thought, along with all others, was driven quickly from her mind as they lost themselves in each other. Desire awakened slowly due to their still slumberous state, and they took the time to seek new and delightful ways of pleasing each other.

Jennifer was surprised that she could learn so quickly how to please him. She found that his nipples grew taut and sensitive just as hers did, and teased them with her tongue. She stroked his muscular thighs lightly, knowing what he wanted, and almost shocked at her desire to give it to him.

Michael slid himself very slowly down over her body, pausing at every pleasure point along the way. A small cry of pure delight rose from her as he caressed her with tongue and lips, drawing her to the very brink of ecstasy.

Finally they were forced to abandon their intimate games as their combined passion grew too strong to be controlled, and they came together with both ferocity and great tenderness. Michael knew how very special their joining was, and even Jennifer guessed that only a very lucky few ever shared what seemed to come so naturally to them.

Later that morning Michael returned to the inn long enough to pack up and check out, then hurried back to her as though his life depended on being with her. In his absence Jennifer had begun to fear that what they had might be destroyed by too much closeness, but when Michael reappeared, she knew she had been wrong.

They fit their lives together just as easily as they fit their bodies together—two parts of a single whole. For the next three days they were never apart. They showered together, playing with happy abandon until the water ran cold. They cooked meals together, with Michael relegated to the tasks that he grumbled could have been better performed by a food processor, a gadget she disdained. They played chess, and he won every time because, as she pointed out, she hadn't played in years. They went for long walks through the fields and woods, and they learned each other's minds, threading their way through all the fears and hopes that lay hidden there.

But the one thing they didn't do was talk about the future. The future, to them both, was a vague but menacing void waiting implacably just beyond their vision. So they ignored it, staying safely within their special world.

Michael had at first avoided any discussion of his family, but when Jennifer began to ply him with questions, he began to talk about them. At one point he even told her about the painful days during his father's affair with her mother.

Jennifer listened quietly, and when it was over she realized for the first time the anguish his family had suffered, and understood, too, how very much Michael must care for her to have overcome his initial feelings about her.

He had also tended to avoid any serious discussion of his political career, assuming that Jennifer would find it of little interest. But here, too, she drew him out and learned just how much it meant to him. Michael, she decided, was one of those exceedingly rare people who actually believed in being a public servant, instead of a self-serving politician. She shared his views and applauded his common-sense approach to problems.

As Michael watched Jennifer he could hardly believe that such a beautiful face and lush body could be accompanied by a warm and generous nature, a wry sense of humor and a keen mind. When she was with Michael, Jennifer blossomed. Where before she had been a perfect bud, beautiful but closed, now she bloomed into the vibrant woman who had remained hidden all these years.

Both of them knew they were in love. To say the words seemed somehow superfluous; it was evident in every gesture, every look, every moment of their precious time together.

There was, of course, another reason that neither of them said those words. To say them aloud would mean facing the future, that dark monster that menaced them from the horizon.

But the future quickly became the present, and the monster could no longer be ignored. Both of them were forced to face it when they awoke the morning that Michael had to return home. The dream had ended, but they clung tenaciously to that ending, holding and loving each other.

"Jennie, I'll be back as soon as possible." Even as he spoke the words, he wondered how and when.

She merely nodded, already beginning to face the pain of life without him. She knew that she should tell him no, that they had to let it go. But the words stuck in her throat.

Later she followed him to his car, and they stood there for a long time, holding each other tightly, committing to memory the feel of each other. Then he was gone.

Chapter Five

For the first few days after Michael's departure Jennifer kept herself very busy. The copy-edited version of her last novel had arrived the day before he left, and she went over it with even more care than usual as she attempted to stave off the pain of separation.

Chaucer resumed what he regarded as his rightful place in her life and on her bed, giving her a welcome sense of continuity. She told herself that her life had returned to normal, and nothing more.

But within several days something happened that forced her to the realization that her life would never return to what she had once considered "normal."

She went into the village to do some shopping and to mail off the revisions to her manuscript. She entered the small post office to find a fellow writer there, with an equally thick manuscript in hand. They knew each other slightly from having met at the post office and in the small shop where they both purchased supplies. She had for some time been aware of his interest in her, but had never encouraged him in any way.

But this time, she found herself chatting pleasantly with him, and when he suggested that they have lunch she accepted without hesitation. After they had made their plans and parted to run their respective errands, Jennifer was shocked at her behavior. But by the time she met him at a small restaurant she was beginning to understand the reasons behind this dramatic change.

She was lonely. Where before she had been alone by conscious choice and had only rarely felt the pangs of isolation, now she craved company. Chaucer was a good enough listener, but he really didn't contribute much to a conversation. And her friend Mary had family responsibilities that prevented them from spending much time together. Michael had brought her back into the world, only to leave her there, alone but still wanting to be a part of it.

Brian Welles proved to be a bright and charming companion. Jennifer had read his novels, which were brilliantly allegorical and had been well received by the critics. He confessed to her over lunch that unfortunately critical approval didn't necessarily translate into commercial success. If it hadn't been for a private income, he told her, he would have been forced to go out and earn a living to support his writing.

As they lingered over lunch Jennifer decided that Brian would never force himself on her, and that she did enjoy his company. The plain truth was that she now needed someone in her life as she never had before, and Brian would do very nicely. So she accepted his invitation to dinner the following evening and smiled to herself at his obvious pleasure.

That evening, Jennifer finally began to come to terms with her love for Michael. Already she was subconsciously relegating him to her past. She cherished her memories of him and knew that she would never find such love again, but she had a strongly developed sense of reality—even if the life she had led was in many ways unreal—and she knew that the most they could have would be a few days here and there. Even if Michael hadn't been involved in politics, there would still have been his family to consider.

He had come into her life, changed it forever, then gone. But she had no regrets. She had never really expected to find the happiness she had shared with Michael, and she would have to be content with those memories.

Michael could not be content. In fact, he couldn't recall a time in his life when he had been more discontented. The work that had piled up during his prolonged absence kept him busy far into the evening, but when he finally fell exhaustedly into bed Jennifer was there, waiting for him.

Michael knew what Jennifer knew—that they had no future. But knowing it and accepting it were two different things. Unlike Jennifer, he had no experience with pain and disappointment, except in a secondary way with his father's affair, and he was blessed with a boundless optimism. They would work it out somehow. He never doubted it; only the details were vague at the moment.

After two days in Washington he returned to Philadelphia to face his fiancée. Sandra wasn't at all happy over his extended stay in England, since they had made arrangements for that time. Worse still, he hadn't even called her to tell her of the change in plans; the truth was that he hadn't even thought about it.

But it wasn't Sandra's nature to remain angry for long, and she accepted his apology without question, then launched into a lengthy discussion of their wedding plans. The date had been set for mid-December, when Congress would be in recess.

Michael finally broke into her monologue to tell her what he had known virtually since meeting Jennifer: There would be no wedding. He sidestepped her questions, knowing that she had a right to know the reason, but unwilling to discuss his feelings for Jennifer with her.

Then he went home and told his parents, who were if anything even more incredulous than Sandra had been. Again he gave only the vaguest of reasons and was enormously grateful for their reluctance to pry into his personal life. He was tempted to draw his father aside and tell him the truth, but by that time he was so drained emotionally that he just couldn't face it.

On the way back to Washington the doubts began to invade his battered mind. He was shocked to realize that his feelings for Sandra hadn't changed at all. He both liked and respected her just as he always had; but he didn't love her, nor had he ever. Their families were close, and Michael had known her all his life. She would make an excellent wife for a rising young politician, but he knew that he could never be happy with her.

He called Jennifer as soon as he returned to Washington, even though it was very late for her. There was so much he wanted to say to her. He wanted to convince her that they could work everything out. But the trauma of the day he had just lived through had left him less certain, so instead he talked about his work, rambling on at length even while he wondered why he was unwilling to say what he really wanted to.

After he had hung up he thought she had seemed very distant, almost the way she had been when he first met her. Was that her way of coming to terms with the future she couldn't believe they would have?

When he finally closed his eyes he wondered if at long last he understood what had happened to his father. Was Jennifer no more than an obsession for him, a temporary aberration? The echoes of the past followed him into sleep.

Jennifer curled up in her favorite chair with a cup of hot chocolate. When he realized that she was not returning to bed, Chaucer stalked resignedly into the living room and jumped onto her lap. The late night phone call had disturbed him, too.

She stroked the cat absently as she replayed the telephone conversation with Michael, seeking a clue to his frame of mind. He had sounded tired, distraught. But he had talked at length about his work, and she guessed that he had been very busy. Still, his conversation had been oddly formal. The only personal note in the whole exchange had been his final words: "I miss you, Jennie." And even then there had been something in his tone that belied the words, as though they had been an automatic response.

Was this Michael's way of coming to terms with their impossible situation? She could never deny her feelings for him, but she could see that he might be taking this way to put her from his mind. It could be that he found denying his love for her easier than facing the fact that it was impossible. She had learned enough about Michael to know that he believed that anything was possible if one worked hard enough—or loved enough.

Should she have been more encouraging, told him of her true feelings? No, it was better this way.

She finally went to bed with the painful thought that she had heard the last of Michael Bradford.

As the days passed without further word from him, Jennifer grew ever more certain that she would never hear from him again. She worked at her latest novel, began to knit a sweater and spent several pleasant evenings with Brian Welles.

Two weeks had passed since Michael's late night call, and Jennifer had invited Brian over to dinner. She was just clearing away the dishes when the phone rang. Brian had been in the kitchen with her at the time, but he discreetly withdrew to the living room when she answered the phone.

To her shock it was Michael. She wondered if her surprise communicated itself to him, but it was impossible to tell. She thought that he still sounded very tired and somewhat distracted, but there was something else in his voice this time. She couldn't put a finger on it.

"Jennie, I'm coming over to see you—this weekend, if it's all right with you."

She swallowed with difficulty. Every part of her rational self was screaming "no," telling her that it would not only be pointless, but also painful. But she couldn't do it. She simply could not bring herself to say no to him. So she said that the weekend would be fine and realized only after they had hung up that she had sounded less than enthusiastic. Had he noticed? He must have. But he was coming anyway.

She was both confused and unbalanced by having him reappear so suddenly in her life when she had thought she had him locked safely away in her memory.

Following her usual habit of pacing when she was

thinking, she wandered into the living room and started nervously when she saw Brian sitting there. He half rose in alarm at her expression.

"Jennifer, what's wrong? Was that call bad news?" He was full of concern.

She shook her head. "No, just startling. An . . . an old friend from the U.S." She sat down as she stumbled over her lie. It wasn't a lie, really. Michael was a friend, but he was scarcely an old one.

Brian accepted her explanation without question, then asked her to accompany him for a weekend with his family in Essex. Jennifer knew that while his family weren't members of the aristocracy, they were wealthy and very social. She was certain that she had heard their names mentioned by a member of her father's family, who also lived there.

"I'm afraid I can't, Brian. The friend who called is coming to visit this weekend." Then, seeing his disappointment, she decided to level with him, so that he would understand that she couldn't have gone, in any event.

"Brian, when you said once that I looked familiar to you, you were right. Bromleigh isn't my real last name—it's Wellesley." She held her breath, awaiting his reaction.

Realization dawned slowly across his somewhat ascetic features. "Jennifer Wellesley! Of course. How could I have forgotten? I saw *Two Loves* at least twice. But you never made any other films?"

She shook her head, wondering what else he remembered. "No, I found writing more to my liking."

Brian was still struggling with his newfound knowledge. "But you were so good, Jennifer. I'm sure that you must write very well, too, but why did you give up such a promising career?"

Jennifer was beginning to suspect, with considerable relief, that he knew nothing about the scandal. Still, she had to know for sure. She shrugged. "I just couldn't handle all the publicity, being followed all the time."

"Hmm. I do seem to recall something. And of course your mother . . . she died a few years after that, didn't she?"

Jennifer nodded, then decided to bring it out in the open. "Brian, there was a very unpleasant scandal involving my mother and a U.S. Senator."

Something flickered briefly before he schooled his features into impassivity. "Yes, I remember it all now. But that was so long ago. Surely you don't think that people would still hold it against you?"

"I really don't know, and I don't want to find out. And just for the record, there never was an affair between the Senator and me. He was like a father to me, and that's all."

Brian frowned. "Speaking of fathers, wasn't yours British?"

She told him more of the story, then said that since her father's family disapproved of her, she wasn't at all sure that his would welcome her, either.

Brian dismissed her objections. "Nonsense. They'll love you. We'll just make it another time, that's all."

But he seemed distracted, and after he left she wondered if his changed attitude were due simply to his having found out that she was Jennifer Wellesley, actress, or because he was thinking about the scandal. If someone like Brian, whom she was certain paid little attention to such things, could be so affected, then she still wasn't safe.

To Jennifer it wasn't so much that people might hold it against her. Brian was probably right about that. Too much time had passed. But they still remembered—or they would remember, if given the slightest chance. If only she hadn't made that film. If only that photographer hadn't been there at that exact moment.

She stopped, disgusted with herself. It had been a long time since she had played that self-indulgent game. Why was she doing it now? The answer was plain, if unwelcome: because Michael was back in her life.

Jennifer spent the next few days caught in a net of ambivalence over Michael's impending visit. She wanted desperately to see him, but she also felt a strong sense of futility. If ever there were two people who had no future together, they were Michael Bradford and Jennifer Wellesley. Hopeless love was a theme she had used in her novels, and there it held a certain perverse appeal. But in real life, she realized, all it brought were pain and anguish.

Not only was Michael the son of a man with whom the public believed she had had an affair, but he was also in politics, with what appeared to be a very bright future ahead of him. If the press ever got wind of their relationship that future would vanish just as surely as his father's had. And if Michael's family ever found out . . . That didn't even bear thinking about. Even J.T., who had been so kind to her, would be adamantly opposed to any relationship between them. She knew how very dear politics had been to J.T.'s heart, and guessed that he was now pinning all his frustrated hopes on Michael.

By the day of his scheduled arrival, Jennifer had decided that if Michael were not prepared to see the truth and end their affair, she would have to do it. How she could possibly hide her feelings for him and tell him that she wouldn't see him again, she didn't know. But she would do it. *My finest role,* she thought ironically. *Mother should be here to see the performance.* Then a conversation with her mother, forgotten over the years, came back to her.

Jennifer had asked her mother if she didn't regret all the adverse publicity that had cost J.T. his political career. By that time the affair had ended, and J.T. had returned to his family and announced that he would not stand for reelection.

Diana had fixed her daughter with her brilliant eyes. "What you're really asking is whether I regret the affair."

Jennifer had nodded, feeling uncomfortable.

"I would only regret it if he did—and he doesn't."

Those words rang through Jennifer's mind now, laden with fresh meaning. Should she feel the same? No, she couldn't. Unlike her mother, who rarely gave thought to the feelings of other people, Jennifer was always aware of the consequences her actions could have on those around her.

That had been the reason, or at least one of the reasons, she had told Brian who she was. She was aware of his feelings for her and had wanted him to understand the consequences of taking her to visit his family. Her mother would have had no such qualms.

As though welcoming Michael, the weather, which had been cool and rainy, was gloriously sunny and warm. By early afternoon Jennifer could remain in the cottage no longer, but instead of trekking through the fields behind her home as she usually did, she decided to walk along the narrow country lane that ran by the cottage. There were wildflowers to be found there, and she wanted some for the table.

As she walked along under the warm June sun the fatalism that had been her constant companion for days began to evaporate, blown away by the playful breeze that carried the soft scents of damp earth and sweet flowers. She felt lighthearted and almost giddy, and a smile hovered about her lips. If life had been less cruel she might have been a woman happily awaiting her lover, dreaming the dreams lovers shared. For those moments, she was such a woman.

She was on her way back to the cottage, clutching a large bouquet of flowers, when she heard the sound of a car approaching from behind. It was still too early for Michael, so she paid no attention other than to move as closely as possible to the steep bank beside the narrow road.

Only when she heard the driver gearing down as he pulled alongside her did she finally turn around, sweeping her black hair from her eyes. The car had come to a stop, and she heard the door open as she turned to see who had come.

"Michael!" The flowers dropped from her hands.

He said nothing as he ran to her, swept her into his arms and kissed her hungrily. Their greedy lips clung to each other for a long time before he finally loosened his hold and she slid slowly down to touch the earth once more.

She saw it in his eyes. He had not come to end their affair; he had come instead to reaffirm his love for her. She was both happy and fearful at the same time.

"Stealing more flowers?" he commented with a chuckle, recalling something she had said once about feeling guilty at taking the lovely blooms inside to die.

He bent to pick up the scattered blossoms, and she knelt to help him. Their eyes, then their lips, met once more. She felt such joy in that moment that it was burned forever into her mind—the breeze that whipped her black mane about her face and ruffled through his golden hair, the mingled scents of the flowers and Michael, and the benign warmth of the sun that seemed to caress them both. It was a moment of pure joy, untouched by reality.

He drove her back to the cottage, then drew her to him as soon as they had closed the door behind them. The warmly welcoming kisses they had shared now became an eloquent expression of their mutual need. Hand in hand they turned to the bedroom, anticipation quickening their pulses and sending glissandoes of desire along their nerve ends.

They undressed each other, their hands fumbling with eagerness, and fell into bed already locked together in an erotic embrace. Jennifer moaned with delight as Michael found once more all the ways to inflict a sensual torment upon her. No part of her was left untouched by his hands and lips—the pounding pulse point at the base of her throat, rose-tipped breasts, the small hollow of her navel, the mysterious beauty of her womanhood.

Wanting him to feel all that she was experiencing, Jennifer ran her fingers and lips over him, teasing his nipples, tracing a line of nibbling kisses down across his golden chest to the flat plane of his stomach and beyond. Her hands moved lower, stroking his hard thighs with their curling hairs.

Michael's groan was a plea as he pressed her to him and she caressed him intimately. Her own desire was growing rapidly, burning her, filling her with a need that was almost painful.

He drew her on top of him, welding them together with the white-hot flame of their combined passion. They moved quickly into the incomparable rhythms of love, rising to a dazzling beauty that shuddered through them both. Small tremors persisted long after they were spent, tiny echoes of ecstasy that kept them together.

"Ah, Jennie, how I've missed you." Michael lifted

her off him, then curved her against him, brushing a hand through her tangled hair.

"Sometimes I hurt so badly with wanting you that it was all I could do not to walk out of some meeting and hop on a plane. I suspect that some of my colleagues and campaign staff think I've gone off the deep end."

"You know, it's funny," she mused. "I had accepted your absence, almost as though you had been no more than a lovely ripple in my life, disturbing it for a short time." She stopped as he sat up suddenly, pulling the pillow up behind him. He was frowning, and she was angry with herself for having spoken without thinking.

She sat up, too, facing him cross-legged in the bed. "Michael, please don't misunderstand. It was just my way of dealing with the pain. It was just so easy, so reassuring, to slip back into my old life."

"Jennie, don't torment me this way. Don't make me think you don't love me."

"I do love you, Michael. I really do love you." Saying the words terrified her, but she knew they were true. And she also knew that she would never say those words to another man.

"You know," he said wonderingly, "those words can come so easily sometimes—almost like campaign promises. But until I met you, I never really understood what they meant. Now I wish there were something more I could say. I love you, I adore you, I need you—and I'm not going to give you up. Understand that now, Jennie. I know that's the reason you tried to forget me, but it won't work."

She was awed by Michael's tone. Never before had she heard such firmness in his voice. There was cold, implacable determination there. She was seeing this side of Michael's nature for the first time.

"Michael, it's . . ."

He cut her off with a finger pressed lightly against her lips. "I was engaged when I met you, Jennie. I know I should have told you, but Sandra was so far from my mind from the moment we met that she didn't seem real."

He watched shock widen her glorious eyes and open the mouth that was swollen from his kisses. Then he went on. "I've known Sandra all my life. Our families are friends, and we were thrown together constantly. I don't really know how to describe my feelings for her. I like her and respect her, and I know she'd have been a good wife—but I couldn't marry her. It bothers me a lot to think that I might have . . . if you and I hadn't met. So I broke it off right after I went home."

Jennifer's emotions were in a turmoil. She wasn't really angry with Michael for not having told her about his fiancée. She too knew how quickly they had slipped into a world where reality didn't matter. But she could tell that in some way he really cared for the other woman. And there was no doubt in Jennifer's mind that he was right: Sandra would have made him a good wife.

Tears began to sting her eyes as she realized that she might well have destroyed Michael's chance for happiness. The irony of it struck her almost like a physical blow. Her mother had very nearly destroyed J.T. Bradford, and now she might well be guilty of the same crime against his son. Never had she felt so much her mother's daughter.

"Michael," she said, making a concerted effort to keep her voice calm, "don't you think you should have waited to think things through?"

"I did think things through, Jennie—very carefully. I won't be pushed into marriage with someone just because it's expected of me."

Jennifer was startled by his tone, but she plunged on.

"Michael, do you remember what you said to me once about having doubts about your carefully planned life? I think you may be rebelling against that, and Sandra is the one you chose to rebel against."

He took her upper arms in a grip that was almost painful. His face was surprisingly harsh. "Jennie, what the hell are you trying to say? Do you want me to marry her?"

She shrank away from his fury, and he let her go reluctantly.

"That isn't what I meant at all. I just don't want to see you throw away your future on some . . . whim." She had almost said "obsession," but recalled that he had used that word to describe his father's feelings toward her mother, and she had no desire to verbalize the analogy that she was certain must have occurred to him.

"Whim?" He stared at her in disbelief. "Is that what you think you are to me? A whim?"

It was then, in that moment when she saw the challenge and the fierceness in his eyes, that Jennifer knew. He actually believed that they had a future together. It wasn't just a refusal to accept reality. Michael had created his own reality in his mind—and he believed it. Shock transformed her features, widening her eyes and deepening their color. Her lips parted, but nothing came out for a few moments as she strove for control.

When she did speak there was a brusqueness in her tone, a need to deny his version of reality. "Michael, don't be ridiculous. You know there's no future for us. We've both known that from the beginning."

His jaw jutted out combatively. "I'm not going to let you go, Jennie. I can't. I love you with a love I know I could never find again. It's a miracle I found it in the first place."

He meant it, every word. A tremor ran through her that was part exultation, part fear. She couldn't have said which was uppermost, but still she had to protest.

"What about your career and your family?" Did he really need to be reminded about these things?

"If I have to give up politics, I will. But I don't think it will come to that. And as for my family, they'll just have to accept you. It's time the past was laid to rest."

Jennifer shivered. Michael fully intended to sacrifice his future and his strong family ties for her. She realized quickly that what could be flattering in theory was often horrifying in reality. Then she was engulfed in a sea of self-doubt. What did she have to offer him? She wasn't at all certain that she was capable of the degree of love that *his* love demanded.

Michael was watching the play of emotions across her face, and he reached for her, wanting her to understand the depth of his love, wanting to reassure her. But she shrank from him and leapt quickly from the bed.

"No!" She shouted the word at him as she stood naked in the middle of the room. "I won't let you destroy yourself for me. I want you to leave, Michael. Now." And in that moment, she meant it, as though his leaving could erase everything they had known together from her mind and heart.

When he threw back the covers and started to get out of bed she ran from the room. But under the circumstances there was no place for her to go, and he caught up with her quickly as she stopped in the living room, shaking and trying her best not to cry.

Michael slid his long arms about her and drew her back against him. "I love you, Jennie, and I'm not leaving." His breath fanned warmly against her neck as he lowered his head to kiss her softly.

Nothing more than a strangled sound that was partly

an admission of her love and partly a protest came from her as she sank back against him. How easy it would be to believe in Michael's optimism. But it would be a mistake.

"Michael," she said finally, using his very name as a protest against his view of the future.

"No. I won't listen to anything you have to say right now, Jennie." He turned her around in his arms, bringing her face to face with him.

"I want to make love to you. I want to feel the way you tremble when I touch you. I want to make you a part of me—the most important part of my life. Don't try to deny me that, Jennie. You love me. Why else would you have let me have you?"

The force of his love and his unshakable faith in their future stifled her protest, but a gnawing fear remained, a fear of the price they would both have to pay. Only she seemed to recognize that.

Michael bent to her, curved himself around her, made her feel both his strength and his desire. Held like that, cherished within the warmth of his love, Jennifer could believe in their shared future—because the alternative simply didn't bear thinking about.

He stroked her, letting his love flow through the fingertips that slid over her body, dispelling the chill of reality. She felt herself slipping into that realm where anything is possible, even a doomed love.

When he knew that he had soothed away her fear, he lifted her onto a low footstool that brought her face to a level with his.

"I'm not rebelling, Jennie, except against your idea that love isn't possible for us. You've become so precious to me that there are no words to describe it."

Then he knelt at her feet and kissed them, moving upwards slowly with his lips, taking his time. With each movement, each light caress, she felt the flames of desire leaping higher, burning away rationality. By the time he reached her upper thighs her capacity for thought had been consumed and a passion that obliterated all else had taken its place.

He took her there, supporting her slender weight as she wrapped herself about him. She ceased to exist except as a part of him as their bodies gave and received with a sweet fierceness and wild abandon. Michael reached deep within her in far more than the physical sense. She had opened her whole being to him, let him into a part of her that could never deny him again. This time they did not make love—they *were* love. They were all the songs, all the poems, all the words that had ever striven incompletely to describe that perfect union between man and woman.

He continued to hold her until she could feel the muscles in his arms tremble with the effort, and she slid regretfully down him to touch the floor, staying close to him. They were both shaken from the power of their joining and sank onto the sofa together, replete with fulfillment but still wanting to cling to its incomparable beauty.

Jennifer gave up. She knew it was useless to try to make Michael see the impossibility of their situation, and it was so tempting to let him carry her along in his dream. She watched him bemusedly, marveling at his almost boyish good looks, his quiet gentleness, his easygoing charm, and found it difficult to believe his strength of will.

She decided that Michael was a very deceptive man. While there was no suggestion of weakness in him, neither had she really suspected before the very great depths of strength he possessed. And now that she saw that fathomless reservoir she knew that he had every intention of marrying her—and damn the consequences. She could almost believe that he could carry them both beyond those consequences.

As for her own feelings, she no longer doubted her ability to love him as he loved her. His love had drawn from her all the feelings that had been hidden deep inside over the years. They poured forth now, suffusing her with a glow that only added to her beauty. Michael's eyes never left her, and they both feasted endlessly on the banquet they had created. It nourished them both against the future that would have to be faced.

Chapter Six

$\mathcal{I}$ thought we'd have dinner tonight at the Lygon Arms," Michael said casually as they returned from a late afternoon stroll.

"No," she protested immediately. "We can't go there. American tourists love that place; it'll be filled with them. There are other places we can go that are less . . . public."

She glanced up at him as they entered the cottage and saw that his jaw muscles were set rigidly. After two days of living in their ephemeral world, reality was reasserting itself. She wanted to push it away for just a little longer.

"We're going to the Lygon Arms, Jennie. I'm not going to sneak around like you're someone I should be ashamed of. We have to face this sometime, and this is a good way to start. I went along with you the last time you didn't want to go there, but I shouldn't have, even then. Now we're going."

Then his expression softened, and he gave her a smile. "Besides, I really think you exaggerate your newsworthiness at this point. Even if you are recognized, what makes you think anyone would care? You know as well as I do that there's nothing duller than yesterday's news."

Jennifer sank down into a chair, wanting to believe him, but remembering the time she herself had fallen into that trap.

"A little over two years ago I flew back to New York to renew my passport. I'd been thinking just what you said, and I didn't even try to disguise myself.

"But I was spotted as I was leaving JFK, and some reporter followed me to my hotel. I refused to talk to him, but he just waited with a photographer in the lobby. Finally I checked out and went to stay with an old friend of Mother's."

She exhaled with a soft sigh. "You're right—I am yesterday's news. But there are these *paparazzi* types who chase around after anyone who was ever news in any way, and if I were seen with you . . ." She paused and made a beseeching gesture. "Michael, maybe they wouldn't pay much attention to me alone, but the two of us together . . . ? Don't you see what could happen?"

"No, I don't see what could happen. It was so long ago that the only people who remember it are us, and only because we were involved. You've exaggerated this thing in your mind, love, because it was so bad for you at the time."

"That isn't it at all," she said hopelessly, knowing that he was deliberately refusing to see the situation clearly.

"What about your family, Michael?"

"Both my brother and I agree that it's time that whole

matter was aired, then finally laid to rest. Everyone has been tiptoeing around it for too long.''

She gave him a startled look. ''You've told your brother about me?''

He nodded. ''Jim and I have always been close, and I needed to talk to someone.'' He made an amused sound. ''I suppose that sounds juvenile, but after talking to Sandra and then to Mother and Dad, and having them all look at me as though I'd suddenly grown another head, I just wanted to talk with someone I could be honest with.''

''And what does Jim think your relationship with me will do to your political career?''

Michael shrugged. ''Jim has no real knowledge of or interest in politics. But he agreed with me that something that happened—or, in your case, didn't happen—twelve years ago couldn't possibly have any effect on me now. And he's right.''

Jennifer looked at him sadly. She was convinced that Michael was living in an ivory tower, totally out of touch with reality. But in a sense, it made her love him more. He was so optimistic, so trusting and had such faith in others being as good as he was. By contrast she felt cynical, and very old.

He refused to reconsider their dinner plans, and Jennifer gave in after offering a silent prayer that they wouldn't attract too much attention. She deliberately chose a plain, almost severe dress in a dull beige shade, one of the dresses that had occasioned the unfavorable comments from her grandmother.

She dressed quickly while Michael was in the shower. Then she twisted her long hair into a knot at the nape of her neck and carefully pinned back any tendrils that struggled to escape the unattractive confinement.

When he entered the room, bringing with him the masculine scent of his after-shave, she was peering at herself in the mirror, trying hard to see herself as others would.

He came up behind her and frowned when their eyes met in the mirror. But then, before she could say anything, the frown was replaced by a smile.

"It won't work, you know. You couldn't hide your beauty if you wore a flour sack and pigtails. Remember, I spotted you in a crowd that first day, even in those baggy pants and shapeless sweater." He turned her around to face him. "And I'm not going to dinner with my maiden aunt. I'm going to dinner with the very beautiful woman I love. So send Aunt Tillie back to the closet where she belongs and bring back my Jennie."

She had to laugh at his characterizations, but she protested that she had nothing else to wear.

"Then wear the dress you wore the first night we went out to dinner. And we'll do something about your wardrobe if I have to take you shopping myself. I've never shopped for a woman in my life, but if you don't, I will."

By the time they left the cottage Jennifer had changed into the silk paisley dress and brushed out her long hair into an inky cloud about her shoulders.

All through what seemed to her to be an interminable dinner Jennifer was very conscious of the others in the crowded dining room. She had breathed a sigh of relief when they had been shown to a quiet corner table, but that was quickly drawn in again as she overheard numerous American accents around them.

She would have ignored the excellent meal if Michael hadn't given her a pointed look, then threatened to spoon-feed her.

"If you really want to draw attention, that should do it," he said warningly.

He was obviously at ease and talked casually, while she sat silently for the most part, actually growing irritated at his disregard for her discomfort. But she knew he was aware of it when he reached out to cover her hand.

"I know this is difficult for you, Jennie love. But it'll get easier, you'll see. It's only because it's the first step."

She nodded, but she wasn't sure she believed him. She felt that there was a spotlight on her, and imagined that everyone in the room was speculating about where he had seen her before. But each time she risked a glance at the other diners they were completely oblivious to her.

She and Michael did receive some attention, of course, but in all honesty she had to admit that their looks alone would have guaranteed that. They made a striking couple.

After a while she allowed Michael to draw her out. She began to relax almost visibly, feeling the tension leave her body. Michael saw it, too, and gave her a broad wink of approval.

Still, she was glad they finally rose to leave. The tension returned briefly as she imagined that sudden lulls in conversations as they passed were brought about by minds that were struggling to retrieve a memory. Michael's hand slid to her waist, and she knew he could feel her unease.

They had almost reached the front door when a voice hailed Michael, freezing them both in place.

Michael turned to greet the gray-haired man approaching them, but his arm stayed firmly about Jennifer's waist, even though she tried instinctively to pull away from him. The distinguished looking man was trailed by a much younger blond who peered at Jennifer with interest.

"Dr. Howell, it's been quite a while." Michael extended a hand, appearing relaxed and even pleased.

"It certainly has. You've met Virginia, I believe?" The older man indicated the woman, who took her eyes off Jennifer reluctantly.

"Several times," Michael acknowledged with a smile as he drew Jennifer even more closely to him. "Jennie, this is Dr. Richard Howell, an old friend of Dad's, and Mrs. Howell." Then he shifted his attention to the other couple.

"I'd like you to meet Jennifer Wellesley."

The color drained from her face. They hadn't discussed it, but she had assumed that he would introduce her as Jennifer Bromleigh. Had it been a slip of the tongue? She had no time to consider it as she saw the puzzlement, then surprise, on both their faces.

"Oh," said the woman after a silent moment. "Now I know why you looked so familiar to me. You do look like your mother."

There was no condescension or distaste in her tone, but Jennifer looked up at her husband to see that he still hadn't recovered from his shock. He shot Michael a quick, questioning look, opened his mouth briefly, then snapped it shut again as he turned to Jennifer with an attempt at a smile.

"Yes, there's a strong resemblance," he acknowledged, picking up on his wife's remark.

Virginia Howell was more curious than surprised, however. "But you never made any other films, did you? Surely I would have heard . . . ?"

Jennifer managed a tight little smile, realizing that she

was subconsciously moving even closer to Michael, drawing upon his strength.

"No, I'm a writer now."

That only whetted the woman's appetite for more details, and Jennifer was soon explaining what she wrote and learning that Virginia Howell had read her novels and liked them.

Finally they separated, the Howells off to the dining room, and Michael and Jennifer out into the cool evening air.

"Michael," she said with a frown as soon as they were alone, "why did you introduce me by my real name? You know that's not what I'm using now."

"There's no point carrying on the charade any longer, Jennie. When they found out later who you are, or if they remembered, they would have wondered why we were hiding it. I told you that I'm not going to sneak around, and I meant it."

"But your father . . . That man's his friend . . . he'll tell him."

"That isn't likely for at least a month. You heard their itinerary. They're going on to Scotland, and then to Ireland. And by that time it won't matter."

"What do you mean?" She felt as though she were waiting for the proverbial other shoe to drop.

"The family usually spends most of the month of August at our summer home on the Delaware shore. And you're going to be there." Michael's manner was very casual as he helped her into the car.

"You can't be serious," she said in amazement, even though she could tell that he was.

"I'm very serious," he continued patiently. "Mother and Dad are in California for a few weeks, visiting friends. When they return I'm going to tell them about us. Then you're coming over to spend at least part of the month with us—and then we're getting married.''

She wanted to laugh, and then she wanted to cry. What finally came out was a mixture of both emotions. ''Michael, you're so . . . believing. You really think this will all work out, don't you?''

''I do,'' he replied firmly. ''And it will. So you'd better start thinking about some American settings for your novels, because you're going home.''

Home. The word touched something inside her. She had never really had a home. Michael had meant home to America, of course, but that country, although she was its citizen, had never seemed home to her. Nothing had, not in all her life. She supposed that her little cottage was the closest thing to a home she had known.

For a few moments she allowed herself the luxury of dreaming about the home she and Michael could have.

Michael seemed to have picked up on her thoughts. ''We'll look for a house outside Washington, maybe in Virginia. I like the area around McLean. It's rural, but still not too far to commute.''

He began to question her about the types of houses she liked, and she answered the questions, very much aware that it was an attempt on his part to divert them both from the real issue. It reminded her sadly of a game of make believe.

Even later, as she lay in the warm circle of his arms, the feeling persisted. She was playing a role, pretending to be as excited and happy as he was. It continued to amaze her that Michael could be so optimistic, as though by sheer will power he could sweep all obstacles from their path.

Michael had already succumbed to a love-drugged sleep, but Jennifer lay awake, wondering what he would do when he was finally forced to confront reality. That moment would come very quickly once he made his announcement to his family. She considered it very likely that he would be forced to choose between her and them, and she suspected that he would choose her without hesitation.

But if that happened, she knew that at some point he would find his love for her tainted by his estrangement from his family. She knew how much they meant to him. She shuddered at the thought of being responsible for destroying all that.

And even if, by some miracle, they did accept her, she was sure she could never fit into their constricted, tradition-bound world.

She finally fell asleep, still caught in the web of reality, while trying desperately to cling to the dream.

"Michael, just what does a senator's wife do?" Jennifer asked as they went out for a walk the next day. She had decided to try a different tactic. Perhaps if he saw that she just couldn't fit into his life, he might reconsider his proposal of marriage.

Michael cocked a brow in amusement. "So you've got me elected already, have you?"

"Just thinking ahead," she responded, realizing that she hadn't even considered the possibility that he might lose. How could anyone not vote for him?

"Well, apart from attending a steady round of parties, there really isn't anything for you to do. Unfortunately most of the nation's business isn't conducted within the walls of the Capitol. Instead everything is settled one way or another in Georgetown dining rooms or on Embassy Row. I'm afraid there's no getting out of it. You can expect more invitations than we can handle, especially because of who we are."

Jennifer frowned uncomprehendingly at the last remark, and he bent to kiss her.

"Look in the mirror, love. We make a striking couple. Washington hostesses like glamour as much as anybody, maybe more so, because there isn't a lot of it available."

Jennifer was thinking that this wasn't getting her anywhere. "I don't like parties," she said rather desperately.

"Neither do I, so we'll just go to the ones we have to, and give them ourselves only when absolutely necessary."

"But there must be other things for senators' wives to do," she persisted, unwilling to let the issue go.

"Oh, sure. Some of them get involved in various charities, and these days some of them have careers of their own."

Jennifer shifted the topic slightly to ask, "Do you really think you'll win?" She was beginning to think hopefully that they could make a quiet life for themselves if he lost. What a terrible thought, she chastised herself. Michael wanted to be a senator. But if he were forced to return to private life . . . ? She let the thought go, not wanting to be disloyal, and not wanting to be drawn into his dream.

Michael laughed. "Now you sound doubtful. Yes, I think I'll win. I suspect the race may be close, but I think I'll win."

"And if you don't?"

Once again he laughed. "Such confidence. If I lose, then it's back to Philadelphia, either to practice law or to work with Jim, managing the family's interests. I'd probably choose law, and go in with the firm that handles our business."

Jennifer could just picture the type of firm he meant.

She discarded her earlier half-formed thought that they might have a future if Michael were out of politics.

"I doubt very much that they'd offer you a partnership if I were your wife," she said matter-of-factly.

He stopped and swung to face her. "Jennie, you know what your problem is? You've been beating yourself over the head with that scandal for so long that you don't see yourself as you really are. So let me tell you what you really are: a very beautiful, intelligent woman, with the kind of grace and manners that would stand you in good stead with any group—including a stuffy old Philadelphia law firm." He punctuated his sentence by kissing the tip of her nose. "And that, my love, is the truth, even though I don't expect you to see it."

She didn't see it. But she refrained from mentioning the fact that he could hardly be counted upon for an objective appraisal of her. Oh, he was right in a sense. If her name were Susie Smith, everyone would agree with him. But her name was Jennifer Wellesley, and when people heard that name, they began to dwell on the film, the scandal and whether or not she resembled her mother in more than the physical sense.

For the remainder of their brief time together they played out their dream, holding reality at bay as they talked and laughed and loved. During their silences Michael planned for their future, while Jennifer moved between wondering how she would survive the loss of him to being carried away by his belief that she wouldn't have to.

Chapter Seven

$\mathcal{D}$ad, there's something I have to talk to you about."
Michael slipped his putter back into the leather bag.
Both men were standing on the eighteenth green. "How
about a drink in the bar?"

As they walked toward the clubhouse Michael wondered if the bar might be too public for the discussion
they were about to have. The course hadn't been
crowded, though, so presumably the bar wouldn't be,
either. But he just couldn't be sure of his father's
reaction. He had let Jennifer believe it would be easy,
but he knew it wouldn't.

"I still think you should be campaigning more this
summer," J.T. said as they found a quiet corner table
and the waiter brought their drinks.

"That isn't what I wanted to talk to you about,"
Michael said, still amused at his father's reawakened
interest in politics. Ever since he himself had left the
Senate, J.T. had shown the subject no interest whatever,

but when Michael had announced his own interest, his father had come to life once more, living vicariously through Michael. Michael took a deep breath, resisting the urge to just blurt out his intentions.

"When I was in England after the conference in May I met Jennifer Wellesley. The meeting was purely an accident—but it was the luckiest one of my life." Michael watched shock, then pain and finally a strange gentleness cross his father's face, and he doubted that the older man had even heard his final words.

"Jennifer?" J.T. spoke the name almost wistfully. "Little Jennie? How many times I've wondered what happened to her."

"She lives in the Cotswolds. That's where I met her. She's writing historical romances."

"That kid had a tough life. And then that damned story . . ." J.T. scowled, a murderous gleam in his eyes. Michael was about to speak once more when J.T. continued.

"Those bastards took an innocent scene and put a filthy interpretation on it. She was just a kid, for God's sake, and she was going through a bad time. I was probably the closest thing she had to a father."

Michael nodded. "That's exactly what she said." He realized now that it had never entered his father's mind that any of his family might believe that "filthy interpretation." Michael felt ashamed, even though he had always had doubts about the truth of the story.

But it seemed that J.T. was considering the possibility now. The hatred left his face as quickly as it had come, and was replaced by a look that was as close to pleading as Michael had ever seen on the man.

"You do believe me, don't you?"

Michael nodded, then hesitated for a fraction of a second, choosing his words carefully. He knew that it was very important to his father that he be believed. "Yes, Dad, I believe you. I have what I guess could be called incontrovertible proof that you never had an affair with her."

J.T. frowned uncomprehendingly for a moment, then began to nod slowly. Michael could almost hear the wheels turning in his father's mind.

"I love her, Dad, and I intend to marry her." Michael dropped his bombshell as quietly as he could, then held his breath, waiting for his father's response.

To his surprise, his father chuckled softly. "Who was it who said that the past is always with us?"

"Dad, I want your blessing—and Mother's. But I'll marry her even without it."

J.T. heard the unmistakable commitment in his son's voice. "Even if it means the end of your political career? You have thought about that, haven't you?"

"Yes, to both questions. But I don't think it'll come to that. Twelve years is a long time."

J.T. snorted derisively. "The so-called gentlemen of the press have long memories. Don't ever underestimate them. And don't make the mistake of thinking that this is going to be easy, son."

"Mother is my main concern, Dad." Michael could sense that despite his father's misgivings, he would give his blessing.

J.T. leaned back with a deep sigh. "Ah, yes, your mother. She's never really been willing to let it rest. Not that I blame her, really. What I did was wrong, and it would have been bad enough without the press rubbing her nose in it."

He paused, resignation stealing over his face. "But I think it's probably way past time that she and I talked about it. We never really did, you know." He threw Michael a sad smile. "We both just ignored it. I don't know, maybe she believes I had an affair with Jennie, too. But I'd like to think she knows me well enough to know that that wouldn't have happened."

"I'm sorry to be dumping this on you, Dad. But you must know that I wouldn't be doing this if I didn't really love her. Hell, I don't even think I knew what the word meant before I met Jennie." Michael shook his head in wonder. How he needed and wanted her.

J.T. nodded, and Michael had a sudden sense of certainty that his father had understood his words in a very personal sense. He began to reevaluate his feelings about his father's affair.

"I'll talk to your mother."

"Something feels so wrong, Michael." Jennifer cradled the phone against her ear, wishing that he were there. It was the second time he had called her since his return to the U.S., but the calls that should have warmed her seemed only to emphasize the distance between them.

"What's wrong, Jennie, is that we're thousands of miles apart. If we'd had more time together it wouldn't feel this way. We'd have a whole storehouse of memories to draw upon, instead of just a few days here and there. That's why I want you to come to Bellemar. We'll have a couple of weeks together then." He hesitated, then went on. "If you still have doubts after that, I'll listen to you. It won't change the way I feel, but I'll listen."

After their conversation had ended Jennifer acknowledged that he was undoubtedly right. But knowing it and feeling it were two entirely different things, and at the moment she was at the mercy of her feelings.

She was, however, very happy about one thing. Michael had told her about his conversation with his father. Jennifer looked forward to seeing J.T. again; she knew that he would welcome her, but there was just no way that his wife would do the same. In all honesty Jennifer couldn't blame her. She shuddered at the thought of what she would have to face.

She thought briefly of suggesting to Michael that they go somewhere alone, but then she dismissed the notion. It would do them no good at all to pretend that their problems didn't exist. If they had a future at all, she knew that they couldn't live in a vacuum, away from his family and the rest of his life. Their problems had to be faced. She thought of Michael's strength and knew that he could face them—but could she?

June drifted into July, and Jennifer received a note from Michael's mother. Michael had already told her that she could expect it, so she wasn't surprised when her mailbox yielded the expensive, monogrammed envelope.

It was a very brief note, inviting her to spend the month of August at Bellemar and saying that the family was looking forward to meeting Jennifer. Jennifer stared at the lovely handwriting and guessed just how difficult it must have been for Mrs. Bradford to write that note. She also wondered just what, if anything, Michael's mother might do to discourage their relationship. Perhaps it was unfair of her to harbor such suspicions, but she knew that she had to be prepared.

Michael had said very little about his mother's reaction to the news, and Jennifer had no idea whether he was deliberately withholding the information because he knew it would upset her or if he actually didn't know. From Michael's descriptions of his mother, Jennifer had formed an impression of a rather aloof woman who tended to keep her emotions firmly in check, at least since the time of the scandal.

She put the note into the box that held Michael's letters. In addition to the regular telephone calls, they had begun to correspond.

She smiled now at the sizeable pile of letters in the box. He wrote very well and was able to put into writing things that eluded them in their phone conversations. She read the letters again and again, especially when she became depressed about their future, in an effort to keep the dream alive.

Finally, with less than two weeks remaining before her trip, Jennifer realized that she was in dire need of a new wardrobe. She recalled Michael's threat to take her shopping himself and decided that she had better spare him that task. Besides, it was time to visit her grandmother. There were questions to be asked. She called her and made her plans.

Jennifer arrived in Kensington to be greeted warmly by the only real family she had. "Gram," as Jennifer had always called her, was a very regal, almost austere looking woman whose outward appearance hid a very affectionate and open nature.

Gram had always played a pivotal role in Jennifer's life. Every time one of her mother's marriages or affairs had gone sour, Jennifer had been sent off to spend some time with her grandmother.

It wasn't long before Jennifer opened up and told her grandmother about Michael. Her fears about the upcoming trip and all it entailed were too strong for her to suppress them.

"Well, well, child, you do seem to have climbed out of that pit into which you so willingly cast yourself." The old woman's blue eyes sparkled.

"Something like 'out of the frying pan and into the fire,' don't you think?" Jennifer smiled ruefully.

"Perhaps, perhaps," was the thoughtful response. "But if Michael is even half of what you say he is, he'll save you both from that fire."

"I love him, Gram, and I want to marry him. But I'm so afraid. If the press drags out the whole story again it could destroy Michael's career and hurt his whole family. It would be history repeating itself."

"Yes, well, that story is a perfect example of just how sordid the public's taste can be. Even coming as it did when the film was first released, people should have known better." Gram's indignation over that episode hadn't lessened over the years. Jennifer would be eternally grateful to her for her unquestioning belief that the story had been false.

"At least, child, you've had considerable experience at dealing with recalcitrant relatives. I really do believe that you've made some headway with that stuffy family of mine. Edgar actually asks about you now, and that's a definite improvement. He even ventured the opinion over lunch last week that living in England has been very beneficial for you." She smiled.

Jennifer was astounded. Her Uncle Edgar, the present Earl, had always been the most disapproving of them all.

This bit of news buoyed Jennifer's spirits for more than one reason. First of all, she was very happy to learn that after all these years her father's family might be ready to forgive her for her mother, and to see her as her own person.

But the more immediate reason for her happiness was that she was beginning to see some hope where Michael's family was concerned.

Gram was right. She *did* have a wealth of experience

in dealing with the dislike of relatives. Perhaps all those hated trips to Essex had paid off, after all. They had certainly taught her patience and forbearance, if nothing else.

Jennifer was so buoyed by this positive aspect to what had always been a painful situation that she had to call Michael to tell him.

"Well, all I can say is that my already-high opinion of your grandmother has just grown even higher. In fact, I think I'll send her some flowers. She deserves something for putting that smile into your voice."

He asked Jennifer what kind of flowers her grandmother preferred, and the very next day a huge bouquet of pink roses appeared, to Gram's delight.

"Now I know you've made the right choice. There just can't be anything wrong with a young man who would send flowers to his fiancée's grandmother." She bent to sniff appreciatively at the pink cloud.

Jennifer had received her own, smaller bouquet—of violets. She smiled as she remembered how Michael had once stared into her eyes in the midst of their lovemaking and told her that he had never before seen eyes that could shift so dramatically from cornflower blue to violet.

She was feeling so much better that she even enjoyed her shopping excursions to nearby Knightsbridge far more than she had expected. She selected her wardrobe very carefully, buying clothes that were conservative, but not overly so. She suspected that if she showed up dressed like a schoolmarm Michael's mother would think she was deliberately trying to project such an image. In truth, her tastes simply didn't run to the flamboyant, so she had no trouble finding things she liked that were appropriate.

Even the swimsuits she purchased were a far cry from

the brief bikini that had figured in that infamous photograph. She concentrated on more discreet maillots, buying only one bikini that might raise eyebrows in very staid quarters.

On her last day in London she was leaving Harrod's with the last of her purchases when she was confronted by a tall, slim man whose American origins were obvious when he hailed her.

"Jennifer Wellesley. It is you, isn't it?"

Jennifer's heart skipped several beats, and she glanced quickly about, relieved to see that no one seemed to be paying them any undue attention. She thought about denying it and hurrying on, but she knew that she might well have to face much more of this soon, so she acknowledged that she was indeed Jennifer Wellesley.

"I don't believe it. I hadn't heard your name mentioned in years until recently, when an old friend asked me what had become of you. Are you living here now? And what are you doing? My name's Greg Jones, by the way."

Jennifer tilted her head to one side, rather amused at his very American behavior. "Are you a reporter, Mr. Jones? You seem to be very full of questions."

He gave her a slightly sheepish grin. "Am I that obvious? Yes, I'm a reporter, but not a show business reporter. I cover the political scene."

"I see. But someone asked you about me?" She was beginning to think that twelve years hadn't been so long a time after all.

"Yes." He frowned, then scratched his head in thought. "You know, he was here in England at the time—in the Cotswolds, as I recall. And he said that he'd seen someone who reminded him of you. Is that where you live?"

Something clicked suddenly in her mind. Hadn't Michael mentioned a reporter friend he had planned to see in London before he met her and changed his plans?

"Who is your friend?"

"Michael Bradford. He's a congressman." Then, after a pause, he added, "J.T. Bradford's son."

Relief washed over her in great cooling waves. So it had been Michael, after all. She hesitated, then decided to be honest. "Yes, I thought it might have been Michael. I met him, probably just after he talked to you."

She saw the light dawning slowly in his eyes. "So that was why he called to cancel our plans to get together. Can't say I blame him. Are you and he . . . ? Uh, that is. . . ." He stumbled, suddenly losing his bravado.

Once again she hesitated. She was torn between the knowledge that he was Michael's friend and the fact that he was a reporter. But he had said that gossip wasn't his field. "Yes, I'm going to be visiting him in the U.S."

Greg emitted a low whistle. "Oh boy!" He shook his head. "Talk about dragging skeletons out of the closet." Then he threw her an apologetic look. He seemed about to turn the look into words when she saved him from his embarassment.

"Do . . . do you think anyone will remember?" She could dismiss the fact that he remembered because he was a friend of Michael's, after all. But for the first time she was asking the question of someone who might be in a position to know the answer.

He ran a hand distractedly through his sandy hair. "Most people have probably forgotten, but there are always those who enjoy jogging the public memory. Have you two thought about that? I know Michael's in the middle of a campaign."

Jennifer nodded sadly. "Yes, but Michael doesn't believe it will happen, or that, if it does, it will have any effect on his career."

"Hmmph," he responded. "Can I assume that you two are pretty serious, then?"

Again she nodded. "We're planning to be married."

"Well, I'll be damned. I bet that's gone over well with his family." He chuckled.

"Do you know Michael's family?"

Greg nodded. "I spent some time with them, but that was years ago, when we were in college. A very impressive group."

"That story about J.T. and me wasn't true. There was never anything between us." Jennifer had vowed that she wasn't going to waste her time denying the affair to anyone, but the words slipped out, nonetheless.

"I never did quite believe that one. I'd spent enough time around J.T. to find it hard to believe that he'd get involved with a teenaged kid. It's things like that that make me ashamed of my profession sometimes." He shook his head in disgust, then turned back to her. "How does J.T. feel about all this?"

"Michael says that he's given us his blessing. It's Mrs. Bradford who worries me. I don't blame her for any bad feelings she has."

Jennifer suddenly changed the subject. "Greg, you aren't going to do a story on this, are you?"

He shook his head firmly. "No way. Gossip isn't my bag, and Michael's a friend. Whatever gets out won't come from me. I'm leaving for South Africa tomorrow, in any event. So don't worry."

But she did worry. Not about Greg, she believed him. However, their conversation had brought back all her fears about the press and about Michael's mother.

If only she didn't look so much like her mother, she

mused. Perhaps Mrs. Bradford didn't believe the story about J.T. and Jennifer, but the woman was still going to be faced with a constant reminder of her husband's affair. Worse still, Jennifer knew that the specter of unwanted publicity that haunted her would be ever-present in Mrs. Bradford's mind, too.

Chapter Eight

Jennifer unbuckled her seat belt and glanced around. The reality of her situation was now staring her in the face. The time for worrying and running various scenarios through her mind was almost over. In a few all-too-short hours she would have to face Michael's mother. Even the thought of seeing J.T. again gave her very little pleasure at this point.

She had been hoping that she and Michael might have a day or so alone together before they joined his family, but he had insisted that they go to Bellemar right away. With an absence of his usual sensitivity he had declared that it was a perfect place for her to relax and sleep away jet lag. He had said that both Philadelphia and Washington were so hot that she wouldn't be able to stand them after the almost perpetual coolness of the British climate.

But Jennifer knew that heat of a very different sort lay

waiting for her along the Delaware shore. And as for relaxation, that was plainly out of the question. She was still thousands of miles away, and already tension was building within her at an alarming rate.

She was actually holding her breath when she disembarked in Philadelphia, her eyes darting about for her only anchor in the imminent storm. By the time she glimpsed his tall form, he had already seen her. Drawn by that powerful chemistry between them, they moved through the crowd that separated them, a crowd that blurred to an indistinct blend of color and sound as they found each other and threw themselves into each other's arms.

The strength of their feelings for each other had never been more apparent to them. Sexual need was there, of course, but what each of them felt in that moment was a completeness, even though they hadn't been aware of its opposite.

When they finally moved apart, smiling in embarrassment as they realized the scene they were creating, that sense of union lingered, binding them together.

After they picked up her baggage Michael guided her to a silver-gray Cadillac, parked ostentatiously in a "No Parking" zone. Jennifer raised a brow at that, and he declared blithely that being a congressman did have some perks, after all.

Then she was staring in awe at the impressive array of dashboard instruments and the spacious interior. Michael caught her look and smiled.

"Given my choice, I'd still have my Porsche. But one of the first lessons I learned when I went into politics was that image is important. Pennsylvania is a major steelmaking center. That industry's been very badly hurt in recent years, and one of the chief reasons is the slump in domestic car sales. So I said a tearful farewell to my Porsche and bought this.''

His explanation bothered her. The idea of sacrificing personal preferences in order to project the proper image was unpleasant to her. She wondered if this presaged the type of life they would lead, being forced to submerge their own feelings for the sake of image. She thought, too, that it seemed out of character for Michael. But she said nothing and let the thought slip into the back of her mind.

Michael noticed her silence, however, and asked if she were tired from her trip.

''I'm too nervous to be tired,'' she said honestly.

He reached over to cover her hands with one of his. ''It's going to be all right, Jennie. You'll see.''

''Michael, your mother will never welcome me into the family.'' There was no rancor in her tone, only a quiet resignation.

''If she wants to continue to have two sons, she'll accept you.'' Michael's voice had grown very cold.

Jennifer twisted in her seat to stare at his profile. She had the distinct impression that something unpleasant had already passed between mother and son, but she knew better than to ask. Michael would never tell her. With a sudden chill she wondered just how much he was prepared to sacrifice for her. There were limits, even to a love like theirs.

By the time they drove up the long driveway to Bellemar Jennifer had settled into a fatalistic attitude that had the perverse effect of calming her nerves. How familiar that feeling was to her. How many times during her itinerant childhood had she been forced to accept new and strange situations: a new stepfather, yet another temporary home, a different tutor? After a while she had learned to accept them all with an equanimity that hid the fears buried deep inside.

The car rolled to a stop before a rambling white frame house. The smell of the ocean filled her nostrils as soon as she escaped from the air-conditioned confines of the car.

Michael wrapped a long arm about her shoulders and dropped a light kiss on the top of her head. "Everyone is probably out back on the terrace for drinks by now, so we should be able to get the introductions over all at once."

"Everyone?" she echoed, having thought that only Michael's parents would be there.

"Mother and Dad, my brother and his wife, and Max Haver, an old family friend and what you could call my political mentor. Max is a politician's politician. I think you'll like him once you get to know him."

The big house was silent when they entered, although there was a distant murmur of voices, barely audible over the sounds of the ocean. Jennifer's overall impression of the house was positive. It was light and airy, with casual, sturdy furniture that could withstand sand and salt water. Her previous acquaintance with seaside homes had been limited to elegant Mediterranean villas, and she was unprepared for the far more informal atmosphere here.

Michael led her up the stairs and down a long hallway to the room that had been assigned to her. Like the rest of the house it was bright and sunny, with bare wood floors covered in places with small bright rugs and rattan furniture.

"It's very nice." She smiled at Michael as he set down her bags.

"Your bathroom's over there." He pointed to a door

that opened off the room. "And the room's main advantage is off this way."

He pulled her after him as he walked to the other side of the room and opened a door to a connecting bedroom. "Would you like to guess who has that room?"

"How very clever of you," she murmured wryly as she began to picture the two of them on that bed.

He winked. "It took a bit of maneuvering, I'll have you know. Your room is usually used by my brother and his wife, and my room was a sort of nursery for my niece. But I convinced Jim and Kathy that since Leslie is now six years old, she didn't need to be so close by."

Jennifer had to laugh at his machinations. "Somehow I suspect that your mother might have guessed you had ulterior motives."

Michael grinned at her. "Maybe, but Kathy had Leslie well coached to tell Grandma that she wanted a room where she could hear the ocean, and I generously volunteered to give her mine."

They continued to smile in silence at each other for a few seconds, then moved at the same time to close the small space between them.

Lips met and clung, and bodies reacted to the anticipated lovemaking. Michael pressed her against his length, fitting her into the cradle of his thighs. Their erotic movements against each other tormented them both, but they were powerless to stop. Jennifer felt the insistent pressure of his desire and her own throbbing answer. As if to compensate for that which they must for now deny themselves, they deepened the kiss, giving free rein to tongues that explored, advanced, retreated.

With an anguished groan Michael ended the kiss. "No one will be surprised if you decide to make an early night of it, you know. And I've had a busy day myself."

She grasped his meaning immediately and nodded solemnly. "Yes, I think I'll find myself stifling yawns quite early."

She freshened up quickly and allowed Michael to lead her back downstairs and out to the terrace. Their few moments together lingered like a warm afterglow and kept the nervousness at bay.

She was smiling as they stepped onto the terrace, and the first person she saw was J.T. He had aged considerably in the twelve years since she had seen him last, but she saw immediately that the years hadn't changed the man inside.

"Jennie." He came to her quickly, holding out his arms.

As he embraced her she remembered that he was the one person she had allowed to call her that, just as his son now did.

"J.T., it's so good to see you." She smiled up at him; there was a tiny catch in her voice and a definite wetness in her eyes.

He held her at arm's length and peered at her. "You still look like a seventeen-year-old kid. How is it that you haven't aged and I have?"

"J.T.," she said with a smile, "you haven't aged, you've just grown more distinguished."

He chuckled delightedly. "Sounds to me like you must have been hiding in Ireland, instead of England, but it gladdens an old man's heart to hear the blarney, anyway."

Then, keeping one arm securely around her shoulders, he drew her to the others. Jennifer had been totally unaware of them, but now she saw four pairs of eyes riveted on her.

"Jennie, honey, this is my wife, Caroline."

The slim, elegant woman to whom she was being presented smiled graciously. But the smile remained firmly on her lips and didn't venture up to her eyes.

"Welcome to Bellemar, Jennifer. We're all so glad you could join us."

Jennifer knew a well-rehearsed speech when she heard it and responded with one of her own. "Thank you, Mrs. Bradford. It was kind of you to invite me."

In short order she was introduced to the others, and then J.T. had pressed a drink into her hand. Each time their eyes met she felt gratitude toward the older man for his unreserved welcome and obvious joy at seeing her again. It certainly helped to dispel the formal chilliness of his wife's greeting.

As conversation resumed around her and Michael slipped quietly to her side once more, she noticed that Caroline Bradford wasn't the only one who hadn't truly welcomed her. Max Haver had been polite, but Jennifer would have been a fool not to have noticed his lack of warmth. She wondered why.

Jim and Kathy proved to be very friendly toward her, and she already had the feeling that she could count on them. After all, they had demonstrated their feelings by conspiring with Michael over the room assignment.

She continued to wonder about Max Haver's attitude, but she had little opportunity for serious thought since J.T. monopolized her time, wanting to hear all the details of her life since he had last seen her.

At one point, when he and Jennifer were standing slightly apart from the others, she tried to explain to him the doubts that plagued her. "J.T., when I met Michael, I tried to make him understand that it could never work between us, but he wouldn't listen."

J.T. gave her a sad smile. "I'm sure you did, honey,

but there's a lot of my own stubbornness in Michael."
He took both her hands in his. "There's something I
want you to know, Jennie. A long time ago I thought of
you as the daughter I never had, and I'm going to be very
happy to have you as a daughter-in-law, no matter what
happens. Remember that."

Love for this man surged within her; she wanted never
to hurt him. She was about to tell him so when Michael
joined them with a mock remonstrance to his father
about keeping Jennifer all to himself.

J.T. laughed. "Just remember, son, I knew Jennie
long before you did." He paused, then added with an
ironic grin, "Although not as well as some people
thought."

At first stunned by his remark, Jennifer quickly
recovered and saw that it had served a purpose. All three
of them laughed, and that laughter seemed to finally lay
to rest an ugly part of the past. Then she caught
Michael's mother watching them, and she knew that not
all of the past would be laid to rest so easily.

Dinner was an informal affair, held in the glass-walled
dining room that looked out to the beach. Here, too, the
casual ambience of the house was maintained, with
wrought iron cushioned chairs and a glass-topped table.
Several huge staghorn ferns adorned the walls, and
Jennifer admired them aloud.

Her comment, made to no one in particular, drew the
first informal words from Caroline Bradford, who was
very proud of her success with them and surprised that
Jennifer could identify them. For a few moments as the
group arranged themselves around the table the two
women carried on a spirited conversation about plants.

But the conversation quickly died, and Jennifer recognized it sadly for what it had been. She, too, had been

schooled to seek common interests even in people she would rather not talk to at all. They were two well-bred women who had been forced together and were making the best of it.

Dinner was accompanied by sporadic discussions about anything and everything, and Jennifer joined in easily, but not once could she forget the presence of the woman at the end of the table who smiled with her mouth, but not with her eyes. Jennifer watched the others for signs that they were aware of the tension, but she saw nothing. For a moment she wondered if Caroline Bradford was always so aloof and concluded that it was entirely possible, even likely. Perhaps she shouldn't be taking the woman's behavior so personally.

But then, as she laughed at some remark of Michael's and turned briefly, tossing her head to send her hair swinging back over her shoulder, her eyes met Caroline's and she knew that her first instinct had been wrong. It wasn't hatred she saw there, it was pain, deep, terrible pain.

Hatred, however terrible, might have been easier for her to handle than this. How could she face a lifetime of polite, meaningless conversation with a woman who suffered every time she laid eyes on her?

She had been staring at her plate as she thought, and when she looked up once more it was to find Max Haver's pale blue eyes on her. There was no hatred there, either, but there *was* something. She was trying to identify it when J.T. drew her attention with the remark that Kathy had brought him one of her books, and he intended to read it during his vacation.

She laughed. "Please don't expect another F. Scott Fitzgerald," she said, remembering how much he admired the author.

He seemed pleased that she remembered. "As an actress you were superb, Jennie, and I'm sure you're just as good as a writer."

Coffee and brandy were served on the terrace, where a delightful sea breeze had dispelled the heat of the day. Once more Jennifer found herself in a conversation with Caroline Bradford, this time about the south of France, where Jennifer had lived immediately after her mother's death. She felt that Michael's mother really was making a valiant effort, but she knew that it was almost a reflexive action for a woman who had spent a lifetime as hostess. It certainly wasn't the effort of a mother to get to know the woman her son intended to marry.

Before long Jennifer really did begin to grow tired, as much from the effort required to keep up the conversation as from jet lag, so she excused herself, saying that it was nearly four o'clock in the morning her time.

She had just drifted off into a troubled sleep when she was awakened by movement in the bed. Michael had come in and sat down next to her. She opened her eyes to the dim light spilling in from his adjoining room and saw him, bared to the waist, watching her intently.

"You really are tired, aren't you?" he murmured as he bent to kiss her.

"Mmmhmm," she responded sleepily as she reached for him and drew him down to her.

"I like my women to be awake and responsive," he teased as he slid a hand beneath the cover to caress her intimately.

"Michael, I think I'd be responsive to you even if I were truly dead." She clasped her hands about his neck and pulled his face down to receive her kiss.

"I'm not sure I like being thought of as a sex object," he protested as he continued to explore her body.

"You'll get used to it," she replied, wriggling sensuously at his touch. It seemed that their words were being slowly drowned out by the language of their bodies.

Long moments passed as they tormented each other by kissing deeply while withholding the total intimacy they both craved. It was a sweet agony, a sensual aching and yearning. Then Michael stood and stripped off his remaining clothes.

"Are you sure you're not too tired? Maybe I should just leave." His tone was teasing as he faked a turn toward his room.

She sat up in the bed and let her covers slip away. "Michael . . . ?"

He chuckled and came back to her quickly.

Emboldened by her need and his teasing, she began to rain small kisses across his hard chest and flat stomach. Then she paused, her breath fanning softly against him.

Michael groaned and wrapped a hand around the back of her head, drawing her to him. Her intimate caresses tormented her as much as they did him. Greedy flames were lapping around the edges of her consciousness, blurring her vision, dulling her hearing and leaving only Michael at the very center of her world.

Using her name as a plea, Michael pulled her on top of him and she took him into herself with a strangled cry. Wildfire raced through them, welding them together with its heat until they were in the vortex of the fire, blinded by its brightness and powerless against its force.

Finally they slept, drugged into unconsciousness by the power of love, still existing as one being.

Their union had been so complete that Jennifer awoke the next morning to an immediate sense of loss. Michael was gone, and even though she recognized the need for discretion, she was irritated by it. If only they had been able to go away somewhere alone.

Still, she felt better. Perhaps the worst was over. J.T.'s affection, and Jim and Kathy's acceptance, helped offset the behavior of Caroline Bradford and Max Haver. Since she had already imagined the worst possible scenario, the reality was a definite improvement.

She showered and donned a light batik printed shift to cover her swimsuit, then went downstairs, hoping to find Michael alone. But when she found him out on the terrace both his mother and Max Haver were with him. Although the three of them were seated together at one of the tables, it seemed to Jennifer that Caroline Bradford was maintaining an aloof distance from the conversation between Michael and the other man.

Max was facing her, and when he saw her, she thought she detected a certain guilt in his expression. The feeling persisted when he got to his feet quickly and greeted her a bit too heartily.

Michael had a frown on his face that vanished as soon as he saw her. Only his mother's expression remained unchanged, although she greeted Jennifer politely.

Already somewhat uneasy from her impressions, Jennifer was embarrassed when Michael kissed her lingeringly, and she barely responded, drawing another frown from him.

As if to goad her into the response he sought, he continued to touch her at every opportunity, kissing the bare curve of her neck when he brought her breakfast and playing erotic games with her bare toes beneath the table.

By the time they excused themselves and ran down to the beach hand in hand Jennifer had forgotten all about her initial reactions; indeed, she had forgotten that anyone else existed but Michael.

Bellemar was one of a small enclave of summer homes that shared a long stretch of private beach, and they had their particular part all to themselves at the moment. They waded into the warm surf, then paused when the water was up to her waist.

Jennifer was about to dive headfirst into the gentle waves when Michael caught her about the waist and swung her high out of the water before drawing her to him. His hands slid beneath the low back of her suit to caress the soft flesh of her bottom as he lowered his head and began to tease her with small kisses.

"Michael," she said breathily as she pushed against his chest, "this may be a private beach, but there are people around. Behave yourself."

"I am behaving," he protested. "If I weren't, we'd both be naked and I'd be making love to you in the surf."

The images he conjured up shivered through her, and she let him have his way until a taunting male voice floated out to them.

"Maybe it's the latest thing in morning exercises, Kathy."

They turned reluctantly to find Jim and Kathy, clad in tee shirts and running shorts, watching them from the beach.

Michael laughed as they returned to the beach. "It's a hell of a lot more fun than running. You should try it sometime."

But Jennifer's gaze was on the terrace, where she saw that Caroline Bradford had turned so that she had her back toward them. Max Haver, however, had swiveled his chair so that he faced them, and although she couldn't make out his expression from this distance, she continued to feel his disapproval.

She swung her attention back to the group just in time to learn that Jim and Kathy's daughter would be joining them later in the day, along with a playmate who would visit for a few days.

Then Jim proposed a tennis match of mixed doubles on the court at the far side of the house, saying that they should take advantage of the still comfortable morning temperature. Jennifer agreed readily after warning them that she hadn't played in years.

In her teens Jennifer had been a strong and aggressive player, and had frequently played against serious competition. It took surprisingly little time for her to regain her skills, and she knew that Michael was shocked at her strong showing.

Michael himself was a power player, and they soon took a set, after which they all collapsed. Then, laughing, they all trooped back to the terrace for some refreshment. Jennifer found herself liking Jim and Kathy more and more. Jim and Michael were very much alike, even in looks, although Jim was slightly taller and Michael definitely more muscular.

Kathy was sweet and genuinely friendly, something Jennifer appreciated, since she had never been able to make many women friends. Kathy had honey blond hair and the quiet, well-bred good looks generally associated with the Junior League and country clubs. Jennifer thought that no doubt Caroline Bradford would have been delighted if Michael had chosen to marry someone like Kathy.

That thought prompted her to glance over at the older woman, and she was met with a faintly disapproving look, even though Caroline's half-smile remained firmly in place. Jennifer was beginning to wonder if it was no more than a natural curve of the woman's lips, since it was always there—even when the rest of her was sending very different signals.

Late that afternoon, when she and Michael were strolling slowly along in the surf, Jennifer once again raised the subject that continued to plague her.

"Michael, will you be able to live with the fact that your mother and I will never be friends?"

"Yes," he said quietly. "I'm not as unrealistic as you sometimes think I am, Jennie. I know that Mother will never be as close to you as she is to Kathy. But in a way your closeness to Dad compensates for that. I've never seen Dad show that much affection toward Kathy—or even toward Leslie. I know that part of it may be the way he felt about your mother, but that doesn't explain everything."

"There were times when I used to wish so hard that he was my father. I never felt that way with . . . the others, and of course, I never knew my own father."

Michael squeezed her hand affectionately. "Damned good thing you didn't get your wish. Incest is frowned upon in polite society, you know. And I sure couldn't see myself feeling very brotherly toward you."

Jennifer laughed, but Michael's mother was still on her mind. "Do you think your mother actually believes that J.T. and I had an affair?"

Michael shook his head emphatically. "No, that's one thing she and Dad have straightened out. He told me that she said she never believed it, and I don't think she did. She knows him too well to believe such a thing of him. It's just that you remind her so much of your mother."

They walked on in silence for a while, and Jennifer turned the conversation to something else that bothered her. "Max Haver doesn't like me, either."

Michael gave her a sidelong glance. "I told you that Max is a politician. He has nothing against you personally; it's just that he's thinking about the possible damage to my career—something he cares about more than I do.''

"Michael, if he's worried, then it must be with good reason."

"Maybe so, but like I said, it bothers him more than it does me. I love politics, Jennie—but I love you more. It's as simple as that."

She wondered if it truly were as simple as that. If Michael were forced to give up his career because of her, wouldn't the day come when he would resent her for it? He might pretend that it didn't matter, but she thought differently. She had heard Michael talk about what he had already done, and what he hoped to do if he became a senator, and she knew that he wasn't being honest with her about the subject. Perhaps he wasn't even being honest with himself.

She determined to get Max Haver alone at some point and find out just what he thought. From all she had heard, and from her own observations, he should not only be the best one to provide an answer to the question, but he also wasn't likely to spare her feelings.

Jennifer felt that they had passed one hurdle. They were both willing to accept Caroline's coldness toward Jennifer. But ahead of them loomed the other and possibly bigger hurdle: her acceptance by Michael's constituency.

Even if they somehow cleared that one, could she really be the kind of wife Michael needed? There could be a vast difference between what one wanted and what one ought to have, and Jennifer was increasingly certain that for Michael she fell into the former category.

Chapter Nine

Jennifer awoke alone in her bed, as usual. But memories of Michael's lovemaking lingered. She smiled as she recalled Kathy's having told her that the relationship between her and Michael had occasioned some pointed questions from Leslie. When the child had been told that Michael and Jennifer planned to be married, she had stated rather emphatically that she hoped it would be soon, so that the two of them could share a bedroom and she could return to her old room. Then she had approached Jennifer shyly and asked if she could be a flower girl at their wedding.

Jennifer had been touched, but had carefully explained to the child that sometimes people didn't have large weddings, but instead just went away somewhere and got married, without bridesmaids and flower girls. Leslie had given her a doubting look that said quite clearly that she wasn't at all certain that such things were proper.

After the child had departed Jennifer had sat on her beach chair and watched Leslie and her friend for a long time. She thought how little she knew about children. Later she admitted candidly to Kathy that she had never even held a baby in her arms, let alone changed a diaper or given a bottle. While Kathy had laughingly proclaimed how lucky she was, Jennifer had added this revelation to the list of problems she foresaw in her marriage to Michael.

She had been surprised at Michael's ease with children. It was obvious that Leslie adored him, and equally apparent that he truly liked children. She was sure that he assumed that they would have several of their own. She, on the other hand, wasn't at all sure how she felt. She was inclined to regard them as strange little creatures, a mystery that had been revealed to the rest of the world, but not to her. In fact, the thought of being responsible for one of them terrified her. She wondered if there were something lacking in her nature, or merely in her experience.

Jennifer sat cross-legged in her bed and stared at the depression in the pillow beside hers. There were so many things she and Michael should be discussing. Did he just assume that she wanted children and knew how to deal with them? Would he insist on a big wedding? Jennifer didn't want that, either. She had no one except for her grandmother, and she couldn't stand the thought of a lavish wedding among strangers, at least some of whom would be opposed to the marriage.

Yes, they should be talking about these things, but it seemed that every time they were alone together they were too enraptured by each other to spend any time talking about practical matters. Instead they just drifted along, oblivious to a future that Jennifer, at least, still regarded as questionable. The more these problems loomed large in her mind, the further away Michael, with his eternal optimism, seemed.

However, she had to admit that the first few days of her visit had passed peacefully enough. J.T. remained openly delighted at having her there, leading Michael to grumble good naturedly that it was bad enough having his father constantly involved in his career without having to find him taking over his future wife, too. Caroline continued to be polite enough, and so too did Max Haver, even though she had as yet to find a way to speak privately with him. Jim and Kathy were friendly and open, and Jennifer was beginning to think that she might have found a true friend in Kathy.

Jennifer didn't make friends easily in the first place, and her self-imposed isolation in a country known more for its polite restraint than for open friendliness had only eroded whatever capacity she did have for forming friendships, so she was hesitant about accepting the hand of friendship being offered to her by Michael's sister-in-law. But Kathy seemed to understand that, and didn't force herself on Jennifer. Still, it was very comforting to know that the offer was being made.

Finally she got out of bed and dressed in a swimsuit with a striped cotton shift as a coverup. By the time she was ready to go downstairs her thoughts were turning with considerable trepidation to the day ahead of her. Michael, Jim and J.T. would have already left for Philadelphia for the day, to take care of some family business, and Kathy had elected to go with them, to do some shopping. Jennifer had been invited to join them, but had declined when it appeared that their absence might provide her with the opportunity to talk privately with Max Haver. As far as she could determine without actually coming out and asking, he was remaining at Bellemar.

But the reason she had given Kathy for declining the invitation was also a valid one. Even here at the shore the days had been almost unbearably hot for her, and she was certain that Philadelphia would be far worse.

She stepped out onto the terrace to find it empty except for a maid. It occurred to her suddenly that if she had been wrong about Max's remaining there she would be left alone for the day with Caroline. Even Leslie wouldn't be around, since she and her friend had been invited to spend the day aboard a neighboring family's boat as companions for the couple's own child.

Her stomach fluttered nervously and she took only tea and one of the marvelous croissants that were always set out on the breakfast table. As she seated herself she thought that she really should eat more now, before the heat of the day destroyed her appetite completely.

She was trying without success to convince herself that she wanted some of the scrambled eggs, sausages and hash browns that were kept in warming trays when Caroline appeared on the terrace.

The two women exchanged greetings and commiserated over the weather. Then Jennifer found an opportunity to inquire after Max, only to learn to her dismay that he had made a last-minute decision to join the others on the trip to Philadelphia.

Although another opportunity to speak to Max had been lost, Jennifer was relieved to learn that Caroline was expecting company for the day—an old friend and her daughter. She couldn't help wondering if the visit might have been arranged at the last minute, since it hadn't been mentioned at dinner the previous evening, when the day's plans had been discussed.

By the time Jennifer finished her breakfast she could feel the heat of the day becoming oppressive, so she went down to the beach to seek the coolness of the surf. Caroline's company arrived while she was in the water, and she met them a little while later when she returned to the terrace.

Lillian Weston was very much like Caroline herself, and Jennifer couldn't help thinking that Sandra, her daughter, was almost a carbon copy of Kathy, with the same well-bred good looks that bespoke a privileged background. Also, like Kathy, she was outgoing and friendly with Jennifer, who quickly put aside her shock at the name. Sandra had been the name of Michael's fiancée, and he had mentioned that the families were friends. But it wasn't an uncommon name, after all, so Jennifer dismissed the thought in the face of Sandra's obvious warmth.

Later Sandra changed into a swimsuit and she and Jennifer strolled down to the beach.

After splashing about for a while they settled themselves companionably in beach chairs. Sandra's friendliness continued, and Jennifer could sense that it was genuine. The other woman asked Jennifer about her life, and they discovered a mutual love for the Cotswolds. Then they talked about Jennifer's writing, and that led Jennifer to ask Sandra what she did.

Sandra wrinkled her straight nose. "Nothing, I'm afraid, unless you count charity work. There have been some changes in my life recently, and now I have to begin to think seriously about a career." She turned away from Jennifer for a moment, but not before Jennifer saw the pain in her eyes. After a pause she asked, "Have you and Michael . . . set a date yet?"

Jennifer heard the slight hesitation in Sandra's voice,

but she ascribed it to the fact that Sandra might have thought she was asking too many personal questions.

"Michael wants to be married at the end of this month," she replied honestly.

Sandra raised a brow in surprise. "Isn't that what you want, too?"

It was Jennifer's turn to hesitate, but she finally answered honestly. "I love Michael, and I do want to marry him, but I'm worried about the . . . consequences."

This time there was a lengthy pause before Sandra spoke again. "Yes, I can understand that. Michael loves politics, and being forced to give it up would be very difficult for him. But I'm sure he's given that a lot of thought."

"I wish I could be that sure." Jennifer smiled ruefully. "Sometimes I think Michael lives in a dream world where we're concerned."

"Oh, I shouldn't think so. I've known Michael for years—ever since childhood, actually—and he's very level-headed." She paused briefly, and Jennifer thought there was a strange catch in her voice. But then Sandra went on, and Jennifer decided she must have imagined it.

"Besides, even if he isn't thinking too clearly, I'm sure that J.T. and Max have brought him back to earth."

Jennifer nodded. "I'm sure they've tried, at least. I've been trying to catch Max alone to talk with him about it, but I just haven't found an opportunity yet."

"What will you do if Max tells you that marrying Michael may destroy his career?"

"I don't know," Jennifer answered simply.

Sandra gave her a sympathetic look, then asked how she was getting along with Caroline.

"About as well as we ever will, I think." Jennifer

shook her head as she bent over and began to trace patterns in the sand with one slim finger. "I just wish there were some way to tell her that I understand her feelings. If I were in her place I'd feel just as she does, I'm sure. And the whole thing is just made worse by the fact that there's such a strong resemblance between my mother and me."

"Yes, I was thinking that. You look more like her now than you did when you made the film." She sighed heavily. "Caroline has changed a lot since . . . that all happened. Did Michael tell you that she tried to kill herself?"

Jennifer nodded. "Yes. I don't think I'd really ever given that much thought to the reaction of J.T.'s family until I met Michael. I guess I was too busy feeling sorry for myself."

"But it must have been terrible for you, too. I mean, now that I've met you and can see how different you are from your mother . . . That is, from what I'd read about your mother . . ." Sandra stopped, obviously embarrassed. "I'm sorry," she said softly. "That was rude of me."

"Don't apologize," Jennifer said, touching the other woman's arm briefly. "I have no illusions about my mother. She was what she was. Believe it or not, though, she was a good mother in many ways. I've just learned to think about that, and try to forget . . . the rest."

"You know, when I was growing up, I would have given everything I had to have looked like her. Every girl I knew felt the same way. There was something so . . . electrifying about her." Sandra gave Jennifer a sheepish look. "I shouldn't be saying this, but when I found out about J.T. and her, I was actually thrilled that I knew someone who actually knew her. I guess it just shows you that we never quite get over star worship. Of course, I felt very sorry for Caroline, and for Michael and Jim, too, but still . . .''

Jennifer smiled. ''Mother really loved that kind of thing, having people react to her that way. I guess it was understandable, when you consider her background.''

Sandra's mouth dropped open in shock. ''You mean that's really true . . . that her mother was a prostitute? I always thought that was just publicity.''

''It's true,'' Jennifer affirmed. ''When you realize the effect of a background like that, you can understand her constant need for the public's adulation—and even her marriages and affairs. She needed all that to make her feel loved. And the men she usually chose were dominating types, as though she were looking for a father figure. Except for J.T., that is,'' Jennifer added.

''You're very fond of J.T., aren't you?'' Sandra asked.

Jennifer nodded. ''My own father died when I was just a baby, and there'd never really been anyone else. He was so good to me. Michael's very much like him.''

Sandra nodded. Then she touched Jennifer's hand briefly with her own. ''I really do wish you two all the best. I'm sure things will work out.''

Jennifer was touched by the woman's warmth and her candor, and they drifted on to other subjects. Later the other women joined them, and the conversation became more general. By mid-afternoon the heat was bothering Jennifer even at the beach, and she excused herself to go lie down in her air-conditioned room. By the time she awoke from her nap the two women had departed, and shortly after that the rest of the family returned.

Michael dropped a kiss on her mouth, telling her that she had been wise to remain at Bellemar. Kathy said that she had confined her shopping to one large air-conditioned suburban mall.

Michael lost no time in getting out of his business suit and into his swim trunks, and the others did the same. J.T. declared that he intended to eat his dinner in his swimsuit, and might just want it served in the water, so it was decided that they would eat on the terrace, and at a later hour than usual.

Jennifer donned a brightly printed loose-fitting sundress and sat on the beach while the others rejuvenated themselves in the water. Then she and Michael went for a short stroll along the sand, enjoying the pleasant breeze that now blew in off the water.

"How did you and Mother manage for the day?" he asked as he clasped her hand tightly.

"Very well. She had company, and that helped."

"Oh? Who was here?" Michael seemed surprised, confirming that it had indeed been a last-minute decision on his mother's part.

"Lillian and Sandra Weston. Sandra and I spent most of the day together. I like her." Jennifer had turned to him, and when she saw the shock on his face she knew that her initial suspicion had been correct. She was stunned. "She *is* the Sandra you were going to marry, isn't she?"

Michael's expression became grim. "Yes, and I don't see how Mother could do something like that."

"Michael, they *are* family friends, and besides, I doubt very much that Caroline realizes that I know about Sandra. And Sandra must have known I would be here." Jennifer defended his mother almost absently, still in a state of shock over what she had learned.

Michael kicked at the sand for a moment, then admitted grudgingly that she was probably right. "But it can't have been easy for Sandra."

"She's still in love with you, then?" Jennifer remembered small pauses, tiny inflections, the one time when she thought she had seen pain on Sandra's face.

Michael shrugged. "I suppose so."

"She was very friendly, genuinely so. I just can't believe it."

"Sandra is a very nice, very honest person. I care for her very much, as I told you once. Until I met you, I thought that was all there was to it." He drew her hand to his lips briefly.

"I just don't see how she could have been so nice to me. I'm not at all certain that I could have been so pleasant to a woman who had taken my man from me."

Michael stopped and drew her into his arms. "That's not something you'll ever have to face, love. No one's going to take me away from you."

Jennifer nestled against him happily, but one thought persisted in her mind: No woman would ever take Michael away from her—but something else might.

Over the next few days Jennifer became obsessed with finding Max Haver alone. Her quest took on all the aspects of a third-rate thriller in her mind. During her few moments away from Michael, she would sneak about the big house, hoping she could appear casual if she found her quarry. But she was thwarted at every turn. When Michael left her side, it was usually to spend time conferring with his father and Max and the other members of his campaign staff who showed up at Bellemar regularly.

Michael always introduced her to these people as his fiancée, and invariably their shock was transmitted to her. Then they would turn questioningly to Max, whose craggy face remained placid at all times. Although Michael never discussed with her the content of these meetings, except in a general way, she was very sure that he was forced each time to soothe jangled nerves. She wondered if he were successful.

From Michael and J.T. she learned that thus far Michael had made campaign appearances only in the far reaches of the state, where he was less well known. Michael had explained to her that Pennsylvania's population was centered mostly in the two opposite ends of the large state: Pittsburgh and Philadelphia. He and his counselors both believed that he would carry the Philadelphia vote with no difficulty, since he was both well known and popular in his home town. But Pittsburgh was another matter altogether. Then there were the smaller cities and the vast rural areas of the state. At present, J.T. told her, they were concentrating on a strategy for Pittsburgh, where the polls showed Michael's opponent to have a fairly substantial lead.

One afternoon, after several days of fruitless attempts to corner Max Haver, Jennifer came down slightly earlier than usual for pre-dinner cocktails. As she stepped out onto the terrace she saw success within her grasp. Max stood alone on the terrace, glass in hand as he stared out over the gray-green sea.

But just as Jennifer began to move forward Michael appeared behind her, kissing the bare nape of her neck playfully. Annoyance flashed through her, and she responded to his caress with difficulty. She was forced to spend the next half hour in conversation with Michael and Max, all the while wishing that Michael would be called away, then chastising herself for her thoughts.

She listened to the two men talking politics as usual and interjected only a few brief comments and a question or two. She did notice that Max seemed moderately impressed with her knowledge of the issues of the day.

Wherever she had lived, Jennifer had always kept up with happenings in her native country.

It did occur to her writer's mind that she was being presented with a perfect opportunity to garner information for a novel. She was now privy to all kinds of behind-the-scenes maneuverings and strategies.

"I think we're boring Jennie," Michael commented, catching her faraway look.

"Not at all." She smiled. "In fact, I was just thinking about how all of this would make an interesting book." Then she saw a slightly worried look on Max's face and hastened to reassure him. "Don't worry, Max. It was just a stray thought."

Michael, however, seemed to take the idea more seriously. "It's not a bad idea, honey. After all, political novels are always popular. Maybe you should think of switching to something contemporary."

After a dinner at which campaign strategy was the chief topic of conversation, despite Caroline's best efforts to the contrary, Michael and Jennifer went for a stroll along the nearly deserted beach. Jennifer's mind was still on the dinnertime discussion.

"Michael, I know that candidates' wives are generally expected to campaign with them, so don't you think we should consider postponing our marriage until after the election? After all, I can scarcely be of any help to you. In fact, we both know that I could be just the opposite."

But he brushed aside the idea firmly. "I need you with me, Jennie. I'll see to it that you have to do very little actual campaigning, no more than a few dinners. But I want you with me. You have no idea how much I hate campaigning—all that ridiculous gladhanding and talking in platitudes. Having you there as much as possible will be the only thing that can make it bearable. Besides, if I try to hide you and we marry afterwards, it will look as though I were ashamed of you. If they plan to make an issue of you, then it's going to be now, not after the election.''

"I don't know. The voters may forgive you for having an affair with someone like me, but I'm not so sure they'll feel that way if I'm your wife. People seem to set different standards for affairs and marriages.''

Michael chuckled and squeezed her hand affectionately. "By the time this is all over, you're going to be replacing Max as my political advisor. Just stop worrying, Jennie. It'll be over soon enough, and then we won't have to go through it for another six years.''

"Unless you decide to run for something else, like the Vice-Presidency, for example.'' She was thinking of something J.T. had mentioned over dinner.

They had stopped near the water's edge, and Michael laughed as he hugged her to him. "Just what I need—someone else planning my political future for me.'' Then he turned serious. "No, I don't think I'd go for the Vice-Presidency, despite what Dad said. Given the right exposure, the Senate can be just as good a springboard as the Vice-Presidency for a shot at the top job.''

A tremulous thrill ran through her as she stood quietly within the circle of his arms. Awestruck, she thought for the first time beyond these discussions. For days now she had been listening to all this talk without considering just where it might ultimately lead. She recalled Michael's words about no one ever going into politics without seeking the ultimate prize.

Would he be President one day? The thought struck her with all the subtlety of an earthquake. She moved back a bit and stared up into his face. For just a moment he was a stranger to her. She had a sense of power, of a force far greater than she had ever imagined. Although she was certainly no stranger to fame, she could feel the difference. Fame was an elusive, often transitory thing. In fact, she was praying that such was the case with her. But power? Michael already had power of sorts as a member of an enormously wealthy and distinguished family. But what she saw now for the first time transcended all that.

"It is scary, isn't it?" Michael studied her expressive face. His voice was strangely hushed. "Sometimes you can get so caught up in the game that you forget the ultimate goal."

"Do you want that, Michael?" Her voice was almost quavery.

He reached out to run a finger along the side of her face in a soft caress. "I told you, Jennie, it's the Grand Prize. Everyone wants it. I'm no different in that respect."

But I am, she cried to herself. I've seen what it's like to live under the public's scrutiny. And then she thought about the servile position of First Ladies. So very few of them had ever been people in their own right. It was an irony of sorts that as she felt herself grow stronger because of Michael's love, she also felt an increasing need to carve out a niche for herself, something that was hers and not just a reflection of Michael.

"Jennie, love," he said, running a gentle hand along her spine, "it doesn't happen all at once, you know. There'll be plenty of time along the way to get used to the idea—for both of us."

"But I could never be happy cutting ribbons to open hospitals and accepting bouquets from children at day care centers. I need something for myself."

Michael laughed. "Jennie, sometimes you're too traditional. The times are changing. In a country where more than half of all married women work, it's past time that we had a First Lady with a life of her own. It might cause a stir at first, but I think the country's ready to accept that. Despite what's happening elsewhere politics, particularly at the top level, has remained a veritable bastion of male chauvinism. The nation elects a man to be President, then just assumes they've got his wife, too. I'd really like to be the one to change that.''

Michael's words impressed Jennifer. His sense of fairness never failed to make her proud of him. But she knew as well as anyone that fairness often fared better as an ideal than a reality. However she soothed herself with the thought that after all this was far into the future. Besides, there must be hundreds of men who were dreaming Michael's dreams. Still, the possibility continued to fill her with both wonder and terror.

A few days later, just when she had all but given up hope of catching the elusive Max Haver alone, the opportunity presented itself without any assistance from her. She was down at the beach alone and hadn't even known that the men had returned from a nearby golf course.

Max appeared suddenly, greeted her, then went for a quick swim in the ocean. A short while later he settled his considerable bulk into a beach chair next to her.

''How did the golf game go?'' she inquired politely, excited and fearful all at the same time.

Max grunted. ''I find it very unpleasant to be reminded of my age by a couple of kids who insist on walking the entire course. I think that in spite of his health problems even J.T.'s in better shape than I am.

''Michael said he'd be down later, by the way. They're discussing some family business. Seems a tender offer's being made for one of their stocks.''

Jennifer nodded. This was the perfect opportunity, then, since the other men would be occupied for a while, and both Caroline and Kathy had gone into Philadelphia for a committee meeting.

Deciding not to waste precious time, she began. "Max, I've been hoping to find a time to talk with you privately." And that, she thought, is an understatement if I ever heard one.

Max gave her a sharp look, and she was sure that he knew just what she wanted to discuss with him.

"I've been very worried about the effect I could have on Michael's political career, and you seem to me to be the best person to ask about that."

Max gave her a slightly wary look. "But surely you and Michael have talked about it?"

She nodded with a smile. "Yes, of course. But Michael doesn't always think too objectively when I'm involved."

Max gave a loud, rather mirthless laugh. "That's putting it mildly." He paused to pull a cigar out of a small box he had carried with him, then occupied himself for a few moments with lighting it. Then he began to speak again.

"Understand, first of all, that anything I say isn't to be taken personally. To my surprise I think I like you." He gave her a somewhat sheepish grin. "But there'll be trouble. I feel it in my old political bones. I'm not worried about it coming from Michael's opponent. He's an honorable guy. But the damned press . . . I'd be willing to bet that the vast majority of the public has forgotten all about J.T.'s affair and the ugly mess about you and him. But some reporter's going to drag it out again, and even if it doesn't play for long, Michael will still get some bad publicity out of it. He doesn't need that in a race that's tight enough as it is."

Jennifer stared sadly out at the almost colorless sea. "I could cost him the race." She was thinking about

Michael's dream. How could she let him be stopped at the first hurdle?

Max nodded soberly through a cloud of cigar smoke. "It all depends on how quickly it blows over. Something like this in a California election, or maybe in New York, would cause a stir and then cease being an issue. But Pennsylvania's Middle America. Even in the big cities you don't have the same level of tolerance for that sort of thing that you have elsewhere. It's going to be ugly, Jennifer, for you and Michael—and for J.T. and Caroline as well." He shifted to face her. "Michael tells me that you want to stay out of the campaign as much as possible."

Jennifer nodded. "I'm sure you can understand, Max, that I've had my fill of publicity. Besides, I thought that staying out would be best under the circumstances. Michael thinks differently."

"Michael's right. We talked about it. If the press blasts away on this, your staying out will only give them more ammunition."

She shook her head sadly. "It's a no-win situation, isn't it? If I get involved the press can have a field day baiting me, and if I stay out of it they'll be speculating in print about the reasons."

Max nodded solemnly. "That's about it. But on the whole I'd say it's better if you do get involved. That is, if you can take the heat. And I'm not talking about the temperature."

Jennifer released a long sigh. "I don't really have much choice, do I?"

Chapter Ten

$\mathcal{A}$ perfect day for sailing," Michael exulted, tipping back his golden head to look up at the deep blue sky, where cottony clouds glided along sedately.

Jennifer watched as the breeze caught the burnished gold wave that fell across his brow. His hair had gotten lighter from days in the sun, even as his skin had become more bronzed. He was wearing a white knit shirt and old faded jeans, and both molded themselves perfectly to his lean, fit body. She had smiled at the attention Michael had gotten from women who saw him as they made their way along the docks at the marina where Michael kept his boat. Those looks would get him a lot of votes. She disliked that thought, but since she knew that he deserved their votes, she didn't let it trouble her.

"There she is," he said, pointing to a sleek fifty-foot craft near the end of the dock.

"Odyssey," Jennifer laughed. "How original."

Michael chuckled. "Actually, she's Odyssey II. I had just finished reading the book when I got the first one as a gift from Mother and Dad."

"I pictured you as a sailor from the beginning." She grinned, remembering her first impression of him.

"I've been sailing all my life. In fact, when I was at Princeton I crewed on a boat that competed in the America's Cup challenge. We came in second in the trials, although not for lack of effort."

Jennifer knew very little about sailing, since her experience with boats was limited to the palatial yachts on which she and her mother had been frequent guests. But she told Michael that she wanted to learn, and he began to instruct her enthusiastically.

Before long they were gliding smoothly across the wide expanse of Delaware Bay, heading for open water. Jennifer even took a turn at the helm, with Michael hovering behind her, issuing instructions.

They were both happy to have a day to themselves. Michael had been spending an increasing amount of time with members of his campaign staff, who put in almost daily appearances, sometimes even spending the night at Bellemar. Judging by the group that had already gathered in the Bellemar library when they left, Jennifer guessed that Michael's decision to spend the day sailing with her must have been made with difficulty.

"Were they angry that you're playing hooky today?" she asked, leaning back against him and brushing a kiss across his throat, where the open neck of the shirt revealed an expanse of bronzed skin.

His arms tightened about her. "It's their problem if they were. I wasn't going to spend another day in a smoke-filled room thinking about you, or watching you down at the beach." He chuckled. "Poor Max must be convinced by now that I've gone round the bend.

Yesterday he had to repeat himself three times, or so he said. I wouldn't know, since I was standing at the window, watching you play in the water.

"Anyway, with me gone and Max in Washington, it will give them a chance to make some decisions on their own. That is, if Dad stays out of it."

"But if they're making decisions that affect you . . . ?"

"They have to learn to do that sometime, especially those who will be coming on my staff if I win. In a job as complex as a senator's some responsibilities have to be delegated. There's just no way I can personally keep on top of everything, especially since I intend to spend as much time as possible with my family."

"Your family?" she echoed, thinking that he meant his parents and brother.

"You and the children we'll have," he answered, bending to kiss her bare shoulder.

Jennifer stiffened at the mention of children, and he noticed it immediately.

"You're worried about that, aren't you, Jennie? Having children, I mean."

Had she been that transparent? She nodded. "I've never been exposed to children, Michael. I don't understand them."

"I could see that you've been a little uneasy around Leslie and her friends. There's nothing to be afraid of, love. It's just a matter of common sense. And we don't need to rush things, in any event. I'd rather have you all to myself for a few years."

"What if I don't feel any differently by then?" she asked in a strangled tone.

"Jennie, honey," he said, wrapping his arms about her tightly, "I'd be willing to bet that in a few years you'll want children as much as I do. You just need time to get used to all these changes in your life. And if you don't want them then, we won't have them. My feelings wouldn't change if you couldn't or wouldn't have children. Nothing is as important to me as you are. You know that, or you should by now."

Jennifer wasn't at all sure that her feelings about children would change with the passage of time. Was this yet another sacrifice he would make for her?

She moved away from him, feeling tears sting her eyes. When he let her go she stumbled to the stern of the boat, wanting to stay out of his sight.

But she didn't realize that Michael could set the wheel and join her. She was staring unseeingly out to sea when he came up behind her and pulled her once more into his arms.

"Michael," she said in an agonized tone, "you're making so many sacrifices for me. It isn't fair. I have no right . . ."

He cut her off with a lingering kiss, then withdrew slowly. "Jennie, I'm not the only one making sacrifices. Do you think I don't know how hard it is for you to give up your quiet, secure life to come back into the world?"

"That's different," she protested.

"No it isn't. We're both making sacrifices. And it isn't really a sacrifice when you gain more than you give up. I'd say we've both gotten the better of the deal." He gave her his boyish grin.

She laughed, more than willing to cast off her bleak mood. "So you think you're worth my giving up my peaceful rural life, do you?"

"Definitely," he said, drawing her down onto a padded mat that was fastened to the wooden deck. "It's time you began to appreciate what you've got, woman. Didn't you notice all those come-hither looks I was getting when we arrived at the marina?"

She sat up and arched a dark brow. "Aha! The truth finally comes out. You're a closet Don Juan."

He threw back his head and laughed, then let his dark eyes travel slowly over her bikini-clad form. "Right now I feel more like Ulysses being tempted by Circe."

"I'm not sure I like that analogy. She was an evil woman. But you're in no danger. I don't even like pigs."

"Ah, but you're a temptress, all the same." He kissed her bare foot, then began to work his way slowly up along the inside of one leg. "When I met you at your cottage that first day I remember thinking how delicate and fragile you seemed. I hadn't expected that. But I was wrong, Jennie. You're one of the strongest people I've ever known. It takes a lot of strength to have gone through all that you did and still be willing to risk it again."

She stared down at his golden head as he continued to caress her leg, by now having worked his way up to her knee. She wasn't feeling very strong at the moment. She was, in fact, feeling very trembly deep inside.

His lips and tongue flicked against the sensitive skin of her inner thigh, and she made a move to withdraw. But he sprawled forward, grasping her hips with both hands and holding her immobile.

Her bikini bottom was cut very high at the sides, and he was now teasing the satin smooth skin at the very top of her thighs. She leaned forward and grasped his head.

"Michael, stop that. If you don't, I won't be able to."

"Good," he replied, his breath fanning warmly against her. "I want to taste you, Jennie. I love the way you taste and feel when you're aroused."

"We can't. Not here." She struggled, but felt herself growing warm and soft inside, a wonderful liquid feeling. Desire was dissolving more than her will power.

He propped himself up on one elbow and looked around. "Why not? It looks private enough to me."

"But someone might come along." .

"Do you see anyone?" he asked as he resumed his struggle with the bikini.

"No, but . . ."

"Good. Then let me know if you do. In the meantime . . ." He let the sentence trail off as he pulled the minuscule bottom down over her legs, pausing to kiss them enroute.

One last meaningless protest died in her throat as he began to caress her, murmuring his approval as she gave up and opened herself to him. It was heaven, pure heaven, to lie back and let the salt-scented breeze wash over her and the sun's warmth blanket her skin while Michael worked his special magic upon her. She luxuriated in the growing heat she felt, a heat that obliterated everything else from her mind.

She felt the approaching whirlwind, the leading edge of the storm. It swirled through her, leaving in its wake tiny shocks that soon joined into one continuous grid of electricity.

With a small startled cry she was invaded by the lightning. Wind roared in her ears, and Michael remained the one constant in a madly careening world.

When he finally released her and stretched out at her side, she opened her eyes and was startled to see once more the calm blue of the sky and feel again the gentle warmth of the sun. It was as though she had been propelled to some other place, some far distant plane.

Michael saw her reaction and chuckled as he stroked her still fevered skin. "I guess you didn't see that Navy destroyer that pulled alongside for a while. I thought you were going to keep a lookout for company."

For just a second she didn't grasp the fact that he was joking. She was still trying to return to the real world. She sat up abruptly and turned her head, seeing only empty water.

Michael laughed delightedly, enjoying her momentary loss of reason. Finally his laughter brought her back to reality.

She gave him a mock frown. "So you think I'm funny, do you?"

He nodded, his dark eyes glimmering with tears of laughter.

"Then let's see how you react." She grabbed at the waistband of his swim trunks and began to pull them off.

When she had flung them away she turned back to find him watching her with a look of eager anticipation, so she covered him with herself, then began to slide down his hard, muscular body, pausing to torment him with tiny kisses as she went.

She felt him tense beneath her and knew that he was struggling to maintain control of himself. That knowledge only goaded her to greater torments as she began to return his intimate caress. But even as she was sending him into the same storm she had just left behind, she could feel his desire pulling her along with him.

Michael was almost rough as he lifted her from him and lowered her to the mat, then plunged into her even as his body covered hers. Once more the storm surrounded them, then tossed them up, up to a blinding light. Lost in each other and in the beauty of their creation, they protested together as the storm slowly began to die away, dropping them softly back to the reality of the gently rolling deck.

"Did they come back for a second look?" Michael asked as he sat up and looked about them.

Once again he almost caught her, but she recovered and laughed. "Yes, and this time they brought friends."

"Must be the Atlantic fleet, out on maneuvers. I can see tomorrow's headlines: 'Senate candidate caught in shipboard debauchery.'"

"I always wanted to entertain the troops." She grinned, caught up in his playful mood.

It was a very special day for them both, a perfect counterpoint to a life that was growing increasingly hectic for Michael and more frightening for Jennifer. Bathed by the warm afterglow of their lovemaking, they sailed along Maryland's Eastern Shore, docked and had a marvelous seafood dinner at a restaurant that had its own marina. They were so deeply into their special world that they didn't even see the attention they were receiving. Some of the other patrons recognized Michael, and a few recognized Jennifer, although they couldn't believe their eyes and speculated endlessly to each other.

On the return voyage Michael remained at the helm, taking full advantage of the freshening breeze to get them home just as the crimson sun dropped below the dark fringe of land.

They returned to Bellemar, joining the others on the terrace, where dinner had just been completed. Two of Michael's staff were staying the night, and Max had just returned from his trip to Washington.

Michael and Jennifer were the focal point of all eyes. A nimbus of soft light seemed to surround them, and they never left each other's sides. Even crusty old Max Haver's fears were laid aside for the moment as he watched them and thought that nothing could ever come between them. Their love for each other touched everyone there. Caroline Bradford almost forgot just who Jennifer was, and J.T. Bradford was remembering another time, long ago—and a woman who had made him feel special.

"You remind me so much of your mother when you wear that color." J.T. smiled as Jennifer came up to him. It was the beginning of the cocktail hour, and they were confined to the large living room by a threatening storm. Jennifer was wearing a brilliant red sundress, high-necked in the front, but with an almost nonexistent back.

"Yes, it was one of her favorite colors," she murmured, thinking that she had been insensitive to his feelings by wearing it.

"She'd be very proud of you if she could see the woman you've become." J.T. smiled fondly at her. "And I think she would have approved of Michael, too."

"I'm not so sure that she'd be all that proud of me," Jennifer countered. "She was always taunting me about what she called my 'upper crust' ways." Jennifer heard the bitterness in her own voice and felt ashamed. In the past she had always been able to balance her feelings about her mother, but lately it seemed to her that Diana's liabilities outweighed her assets. The problems she and Michael faced, and the pain in Caroline's eyes, had shifted the balance.

"You're being unfair to her, Jennie. I won't let you do that. If you have to blame anyone for the difficulties that you and Michael face, then blame me. I was the one who pursued your mother—not vice versa."

Jennifer remained unconvinced. "I doubt that, J.T. No one could escape once she had set her sights on them."

"Honey, you're giving your mother more credit than you should. Of course I was dazzled by her beauty; any man who met her felt that way. But I knew exactly what I was doing. I'm not proud of it, but I can't get out of it by saying that she was responsible. In fact, she tried to prevent it."

Jennifer stared at him speechlessly for a moment, then finally said, "She did?" in an incredulous tone.

J.T. nodded. "She knew I was married, and she knew what the consequences could be to my career, and how much I loved that career. But the only thing she could prevent was my marrying her." He stopped, lost in dark ruminations for a while. Then he spoke in a wistful tone. "And a part of me will always regret that I listened to her."

Jennifer's world was spinning. This was all news to her. She had been with her mother for only part of that time, and Diana had spoken very little about her relationship with J.T. Now that Jennifer thought about that, it was strange. Diana had usually gone on endlessly about the men in her life.

J.T. watched the parade of expressions cross her face. "She never told you that I asked her to marry me, did she?"

When she shook her head slowly he went on. "I did, and I would have. But she refused, saying that she wouldn't be responsible for destroying my career." He sighed heavily. "As it turned out, it happened anyway although it wasn't anyone's fault but my own. I might have been able to get myself reelected, but that would have kept the scandal in the public's eye, so I took the coward's way out and didn't stand for reelection."

Jennifer was thinking about her mother's life after the affair with J.T. For a brief time there had been a steady stream of new men, and then there had been none. Had she been trying to forget J.T., then just given up? Jennifer had never thought about that before.

But still she couldn't see the two of them married. In fact, she'd never been able to see the two of them together at all.

"Why, J.T.? I mean, why did you fall in love with her? You weren't at all like the others."

He shrugged. "It's a hard thing to put into words, Jennie. Your mother had those contrasting qualities of strength and vulnerability that I see in you. I think Michael sees them in you, too. And she had a vitality, almost a rage for living, that called out to something in me. I don't see that in you, and that's for the best, since it can often be destructive, as it was in her. But it was something that was missing, and always had been, in my own life, and I loved her for it."

Jennifer was silent, still absorbing these revelations, and at the same time wondering how J.T. could continue his marriage. Now she felt sorry for him as well as for Caroline.

"You're wondering how I can continue to stay with Caroline, aren't you?" he queried gently.

When she nodded, he continued. "Just think of it this way: For a brief time I was as happy as it's possible to be. Now I'm content. I don't love Caroline any less for having loved your mother more. I think she understands that now."

"Michael and I have that kind of happiness, too, and it frightens me." She frowned, feeling tears welling up. "I wish I had my mother's courage. If I did, I would leave before Michael's career is destroyed."

"No, Jennie. If you have your mother's courage you'll do just the opposite. You'll stay at Michael's side and weather the storm. Politics meant more to me than it does to Michael now. And the reason it meant more was that there wasn't that kind of love in my life—before I met your mother, that is.

"Michael has you, and everything else is secondary. That's the way it should be. If he has to give up politics—and I don't think he'll have to make that choice—he'll still have you. But if he's forced to give *you* up, he'll have nothing. One day he'll be an old man like me, living in his memories and just existing in the present. I don't want that for him . . . for either of you."

"But it will be bad for you, too, and for Caroline. How can you want that?"

"I don't want that, Jennie. But it's not too high a price to pay for your happiness—yours and Michael's. I think that deep down inside Caroline agrees with me. Of course it will be worse for her, but in a strange way maybe that's not so bad." He paused, groping for the right words. "In a sense, maybe it's better to be touched, even by something unpleasant, than to remain forever apart. It's the difference I mentioned earlier between living and just existing. Perhaps I'm not putting it too well, but I hope you understand what I mean."

Jennifer thought about their conversation all through dinner, and her thoughts kept her out of the steady stream of conversation. Several times she looked at Caroline Bradford, cool and aloof as ever, and thought that she did understand what J.T. had meant.

And then she realized with shattering clarity that she herself had been headed in that direction. Before she met Michael she had been simply existing—apart, just as J.T. had said. Fortunately for her, what touched her life was beauty, the beauty of their love.

Later that evening, when the storm had passed, leaving in its wake a cool, refreshing breeze, Michael suggested that they walk on the beach.

"You've been awfully quiet, honey. Are you angry with me for being tied up all day?"

"No," she said, squeezing his hand to show that she meant it. She hesitated for a moment, then told Michael of her conversation with his father, leaving nothing out.

"I'll be damned," Michael said wonderingly. He was recalling the day his father had learned of Jennifer's mother's death. "I guess I should have known. That's why he kept saying he was sorry." Michael told her about his father's reaction to the news and his drunken ravings. "At the time I thought of it as an obsession. Love that powerful hadn't come into my life then—and never would have if I hadn't met you." He stopped and drew her to him.

Jennifer felt that moment keenly, pressed it into her very soul. But still she feared the tests that were to come.

Chapter Eleven

Jennifer stared at her reflection in the full-length mirror. She certainly couldn't say that she was happy about *anything* at that moment, but she was satisfied with her appearance. Her long dress was pale mauve silk, with a modest leg slit and an interestingly asymmetrical neckline. The closure was topped with a delicate diamond pin, a gift from Michael.

She had piled her shining raven hair atop her head. Dark wings framed her face and set off the diamond stud earrings that had been a Christmas gift from her mother on their last Christmas together. The effect was coolly sophisticated and she hoped it would carry her through what promised to be a very trying evening.

They had all come to Philadelphia the previous day to attend a country club reception and fund raiser for Michael's campaign. Michael hadn't told her about it until the day before their departure from Bellemar, saying that he didn't want her to worry unnecessarily.

Unfortunately, the result was that she had gone straight to panic.

Michael had attempted to soothe her by saying that those in attendance would be mostly old family friends and acquaintances, implying that she would encounter no hostility. But she knew better. Those were the people who would be least likely to accept her, even though they might be genteel about it. Jennifer thought privately that she would rather encounter open hostility than the icy politeness she was certain she would face that night, but she kept silent about her fears, knowing that Michael would not agree with her. These people were important potential contributors to his campaign, after all, and she knew that she had to carry the evening off somehow. It would be her first taste of the life of a politician's wife, and she knew that she would be facing a severe personal test.

Back here, in the stately mansion set amidst acres of carefully tended lawns and gardens, she felt herself to be more of an outsider than she had in the relaxed atmosphere of Bellemar. The atmosphere here reeked of power, wealth and tradition: the house itself, the family portraits, the priceless heirlooms. Certainly it was no more elegant than her father's family home, but she had always been an outsider there, too.

Contributing still further to her unease was the knowledge that Michael was upset with her for refusing to allow him to announce their impending marriage that evening. Her glance strayed to her hand, where a beautiful emerald cut diamond flashed with reflected light.

An unctuous representative from Philadelphia's oldest jeweler had arrived late the previous afternoon with a selection of rings for her approval. Once again Michael hadn't told her about it until the last minute. Despite the man's ill-disguised attempts to persuade her otherwise, she had chosen one of the smaller stones. She had small hands and felt that the large diamonds the man tried to press upon her looked out of place. Michael hadn't taken sides, saying only that the decision was hers. Then they had jointly selected simple platinum wedding bands.

Looking at the ring now, Jennifer had a sense of being trapped, set upon a path that could lead only to heartbreak and devastation. And yet she felt powerless to change any of it.

She began to slip the ring from her finger, then hesitated. For a moment she was tempted to wear it and allow Michael to make the announcement. His love for her had never been more evident. That he should choose such a critical juncture in his career to make such an announcement was no accident. He wanted her—and the whole world—to know how he felt, and damn the consequences, as he himself had said.

But she was more cautious. In fact, she had every intention of insisting that they delay their marriage until after the election. She planned to suggest that she return to England until then, even though the thought of being separated from him for more than two months was excruciatingly painful. The problem was that she doubted very seriously that she could get him to agree with her plan. Perhaps if things went badly tonight, if he saw that people wouldn't accept her . . . She put the thought aside.

Finally she slid the ring from her finger and put it in her small white kid evening bag before going downstairs, where she knew the others would be waiting for her.

The sound of voices drew her to the paneled library which served as a gathering place for the family, rather than the elegant but somehow cold living room. She paused briefly in the open doorway, seeing that they were all gathered there: Michael, J.T. and Caroline, Jim and Kathy. All heads turned toward her.

Michael immediately set down his drink and came to her, his dark eyes dancing with appreciation for her beauty. He took both her hands, and she saw a frown of disappointment cross his face briefly as he glanced down at her left hand. Once more she almost gave in. But the moment passed as he led her over to the others.

She accepted the drink Jim offered her and handed her ring to Michael, to be put into the concealed wall safe. Kathy exclaimed appreciatively over her dress, and Jim noted drily that no one was likely to notice the candidate that evening.

Jennifer was reminded of Jim's statement a short time later as she entered the large ballroom of the club on Michael's arm. Instinct told her that the excited buzz of conversation that greeted their entrance was due at least in part to her presence. Already she felt countless pairs of eyes on her; she could almost feel memories being searched and confirmations being sought from others.

Never had she been so grateful for her acting skills as she was now. Feeling as though an invisible spotlight were following her progress, she held her head high and smiled graciously at each introduction, though her stomach was churning all the while.

At first Michael stayed by her side, and she knew that she was leaning on his quiet strength. She soon noticed that either J.T. or Jim materialized quickly if she were separated from Michael. Surely this was no coincidence. Michael must have arranged this beforehand with his father and brother. She was simultaneously touched by his thoughtfulness and more than a little shamed by her fears.

For a while she found herself straining her hearing to

catch any references to the ugly past. She did hear her mother's name mentioned in quiet murmurs, but that was all.

She marveled at J.T.'s strength and self-control as he propelled her through the crowds, introduced her to any and all, and kept her hand tucked into the crook of his arm. Once when she turned to see his expression she found him looking at her, and he gave her a broad wink.

I think he's actually enjoying himself, she thought in astonishment. And yet he knows the images of the past that he's raising. But a few minutes later she realized that by almost flaunting his fondness for her, he was trying to dispel those images.

When both Kathy and even Caroline took their turns introducing Jennifer around, Jennifer decided that this had all been very carefully orchestrated to show these people that she was accepted into the Bradford family. She had to admire their unity and sense of commitment to Michael's candidacy. The evening was opening her eyes, as nothing had done before, to the strength and security of family.

Michael had warned her that there would be reporters and photographers present, but Jennifer wasn't approached by any of them until she finally succumbed to a hunger that overwhelmed her nervousness.

She made her way to the extravagant buffet set up along one wall of the ballroom. A waiter stood by huge platters of prime ribs, and there were cold lobsters, split in half to be served with an herb mayonnaise. Hundreds of jumbo shrimp were piled high, creating delectable pyramids.

Jennifer was trying to decide between the prime ribs and the lobster, and at the same time scanning the rest of the offerings with interest, when she heard her name being called. She selected some lobster, then turned to face a rather heavily made up middle-aged woman who was smiling at her expectantly. She had no recollection of having met the woman earlier, but wasn't surprised to find that she herself was recognized. By now everyone in the place knew who she was.

"I'm Trish Hailey, a reporter for the *Herald*. Would you mind, for the sake of my readers, telling me who designed your gown?" The woman smiled at her.

Relieved at such an innocuous question, Jennifer responded easily. But Trish Hailey's next question banished that relief.

"Are you planning to marry Michael Bradford?"

Jennifer chose her words very carefully. "Michael and I haven't known each other very long. His family invited me to join them at their summer home, and that's why I'm here."

"Where did Michael meet you? I understand that you've been living abroad."

"I met Michael in England," Jennifer responded, not really answering the question about where she was living. She began to turn her attention back to the buffet table, hoping that the woman would take the hint and leave.

The reporter persisted. "You said that Michael's family invited you?"

"Yes, Caroline Bradford invited me." Jennifer saw the look of surprise that the woman made no effort to conceal. No wonder, she thought as she spooned some salmon mousse onto her plate. It didn't sound altogether believable that Caroline would invite into her home a woman widely believed to have had an affair with her husband.

To Jennifer's very great relief Kathy joined them at

that moment, greeting the reporter familiarly and bubbling with bright enthusiasm over the lavish buffet. Jennifer shot Kathy a look of gratitude, which was acknowledged by a wink as she succeeded in turning the reporter's attention to the food.

Michael found her just as she and Kathy had seated themselves at one of the tables on the fringes of the room. He carried two plates heaped with food and proceeded to attack them with relish.

When Kathy kidded him about it, he said between bites that he "had to be sure he was getting his money's worth." He seemed quite relaxed and happy, Jennifer noted. Had she been wrong once more? Perhaps they really did have nothing to fear.

After Michael had eaten he moved his seat closer to hers and curved one arm along the high back of her chair.

"How's it going, love? Have you had any problems?" He reached out to smooth back a stray wisp of ebony hair from her face, then let his fingertips remain against her cheek in a caress.

She shook her head. "Not with all the 'protection' I've had this evening."

Michael grinned. "Pretty efficient, aren't we? Kathy almost missed her cue when that society reporter had you cornered."

Kathy laughed as she rose to leave them. "Give me a break, Michael. I was all the way on the other side of the room at the time."

Jennifer laughed with them, but her earlier suspicions had been confirmed. When they were alone she gave Michael a serious look.

"I feel like a helpless invalid, the way you've all hovered around me tonight."

Michael took her hand and carried it to his lips. "Not an invalid, Jennie, love. Just a very beautiful and very vulnerable woman. I knew that I couldn't be at your side all evening, much as I wanted to, so we arranged it all ahead of time."

They stared at each other, allowing the noisy crowd to vanish for a moment. Before she could stop him, Michael bent his head and kissed her softly.

Breathless from his unexpected kiss, she protested huskily. "Michael, there are people watching us."

He had his back to the room and didn't bother to turn. "Let them. Why shouldn't they know how we feel about each other?"

She laughed. "Well, for one thing, I just told that reporter that I didn't know you very well."

"You did?" He raised a brow. "In that case maybe I should tear off the gown and make love to you right now."

"You know, I believe you would." She picked up her wineglass as a warm flush began to creep over her.

"You're tempting me," he murmured. But he contented himself with making love to her with his dark eyes, smiling victoriously when she began to squirm uncomfortably.

His hand stole beneath the long tablecloth to caress her bare leg where the slit in her dress had fallen open. His fingers traveled slowly up to her knee, and he stopped only when she squeezed her legs together primly, all the while glaring at him.

"Stop it," she ordered, ending with a small gasp as he forced his way between her knees and continued his ascent.

Just then Max and J.T. came up to their table, but despite their presence Michael withdrew his hand slowly, with obvious reluctance. His eyes never left her as he talked with the men, and she saw the wicked gleam in his dark gaze.

The eroticism of the moment stayed with her long after they had left the table to join the crowd once more. Michael's hand against the back of her waist sent tremors through her. It was never still, tracing tiny, sensual circles through the thin fabric of her dress. He held her close to him with that tormenting hand, and the hard pressure of his thigh against hers brought an almost painful desire into full bloom deep inside her.

Then the evening was finally over, and Jennifer felt herself beginning to relax as they prepared to leave the club, only to be confronted by a group of photographers and reporters. The whole family had gathered together by this time, with Max also in attendance, but Michael still kept her securely at his side as he fielded questions. The questions were political in nature, and Jennifer paid them little attention. But she couldn't ignore the incessant flash of the cameras aimed at them. Her smile remained firmly in place, even as she trembled inwardly. Michael must have sensed her fear, because without missing a beat in his answer to a reporter he drew her even closer to him.

Finally the questions came to an end, and they escaped. Once she was in Michael's car Jennifer sighed deeply and leaned back against the leather upholstery.

Michael bent over and kissed her lingeringly. "It's over, love. It wasn't too bad for you, was it?"

How did one define "too bad," she wondered. Well, she had survived, if that was what he meant. She saw the worried look on his face and shook her head.

Michael continued to trail soft kisses across her creamy throat, and rubbed a thumb against the silken covering over her breasts. She shivered with anticipation at his sensual touch.

"I can hardly wait to get you home. I wonder what my supporters would think if they knew that all I had on my mind all evening was getting you into bed."

Jennifer laughed, a low, throaty sound. "I thought you sounded very impressive on the subject of welfare reform."

"Rote, pure rote. Just ask the question and out pops the answer. Not that I didn't mean what I said, of course. But welfare reform wasn't exactly the uppermost thing in my mind at the time." He gave her one final kiss and started the car.

Jennifer looked up just in time to see the society reporter passing their car on her way to the parking lot. Immediately she wondered just how much the woman had seen. She groaned when the woman was out of sight.

"She must be thinking that I'm one of the world's great liars."

Michael laughed. "Serves you right. If you didn't want to admit that we're getting married, you might at least have said that we're 'very good friends.' That's the term that's generally used these days."

As Michael pulled out into traffic Jennifer wondered why she had been so vague about their relationship. Was it only her natural antipathy toward talking to reporters? Or was she still attempting to put some distance between them—in the public's eye, at least?

A short while later they were winding their way up the long driveway to the Bradford home, where they had decided to stay. The others had arrived before them, including Jim and Kathy, who stayed for coffee and a recap of the evening's events. Max was there, too, along with the local party chairman.

Jennifer surprised herself—and pleased Michael—by entering into the discussions. Perhaps it's contagious, she thought, noting that all the others, even Caroline, were very much involved, too.

She had to admit, although reluctantly, that she found it all quite fascinating. And it seemed even to her that the evening had gone rather well. Of course she had to admit also that Michael's scheme to protect her had undoubtedly helped quite a lot.

But still she felt quite good, a feeling that lingered as she went upstairs after everyone had departed. Michael came quietly into her room just after she had gotten into bed. From the moment he appeared she could feel the desire emanating from him in waves that quickly triggered an answering response in her. He did no more than shrug quickly out of his jacket and rip off his tie before he fell onto the bed to cover her with himself.

"Don't you think that you should at least get undressed?" she teased as he sought the fragrant warmth of her skin. "After all, you have me at a disadvantage."

"How would you like to play personal valet, so I can save my strength for other things?"

Laughing, she slid out of bed and knelt naked beside him. She fumbled impatiently with buttons and zipper while he lay passively, watching her. Desire threaded its way through them, binding them, hurrying her. Fingers encountered flesh that cried out to be touched. Electricity leapt between them, crossing and re-crossing a path laden with anticipation.

Finally she had stripped off all his clothes, and she got out of bed to hang them in the closet. But he reached out suddenly to wrap a hand around one thigh.

"Michael," she protested, "at least let me hang up your clothes."

But he ignored her, sliding his hand up along the inside of her thigh until he had reached the goal he sought.

"Leave them and get back here where you belong." He toppled her back into the bed with him, and before she could protest his cavalier treatment he had covered her mouth with his own.

By the time Jennifer joined the others the next morning she could see that the morning papers had arrived and been read by the family. Everyone seemed cheerful, but she still picked them up with trepidation. On the front page of one was a picture of Michael and her, with J.T. and Max hovering in the background. She scanned the accompanying article quickly, her nervousness betrayed by an unconscious gnawing at her lower lip.

The article described the elegant, black-tie affair, mentioning various prominent people who had attended to demonstrate their support for Michael's candidacy. The thrust of his campaign was described as an increased emphasis on government's responsibilities in the area of human services, while endeavoring to trim the excess from defense spending. Several quotes were mentioned, answers to the questions posed by the reporters. The candidate's charisma was also noted.

Finally it was mentioned that he was accompanied by Jennifer Wellesley, daughter of the late film superstar, Diana Lansing.

Jennifer released her pent-up breath and glanced up to find Michael smiling at her with an I-told-you-so look. She returned his smile, then searched for the society page, still not wholly convinced that the past hadn't been resurrected.

There was a picture there, too—this time of the whole

family, plus Jennifer, of course. Michael's arm was plainly visible around her waist, and his rapt attention to her was equally obvious.

"The undisputed star of the soiree—other than the candidate himself, of course—was the breathtakingly beautiful Jennifer Wellesley, absolutely stunning in a mauve silk gown. The super smashing brunette is the daughter of the late Diana Lansing, and starred with her mother in the unforgettable *Two Loves* when she was just sixteen. Jennifer has since turned her talents to writing and lives in England, where she met Michael Bradford. No one present could deny that the couple appears to be very much in love. Are Michael's carefree bachelor days over at last?"

Once again Jennifer sighed in relief. She wished that the film hadn't been mentioned, but on the whole the article was far better than she had expected. She had to smile at the reference to them as being "very much in love." Michael had certainly seen to that.

Michael leaned over her shoulder to see what she had been reading. "I guess she didn't believe you, did she?" His tone was one of smug self-satisfaction.

"Thanks to the performance you put on," she returned with mock sarcasm.

"Wrong. Thanks to the performance we both put on. Or are you going to pretend that you were indifferent to me?"

She laughed. "I've never been able to be indifferent to you—not even at the beginning."

"Hmm," he whispered thoughtfully. "We just might have to stop at a motel en route to Bellemar."

An hour later they were in Michael's car and on their way back to the shore. Each time they passed a motel Michael expressed an interest in stopping and Jennifer found something wrong with the place. It became a teasing game that had them both laughing.

He suddenly became serious. "You're not going to worry anymore, are you, Jennie?"

She shook her head, smiling happily. How good it felt to have her worst fears proved groundless.

Michael reached over and grasped her left hand, where the diamond sparkled brightly once more. After carrying it to his lips, he flicked a brief glance at her.

"Good, because we're flying down to the Virgin Islands at the end of next week. I've made reservations for us at Caneel Bay on St. John, and I've already checked to be sure that we can be married there."

"Michael," she protested, "there you go again, springing things on me. But at least you gave me a week's notice this time."

Jennifer was secretly pleased at the thought that they would be leaving Bellemar sooner than she had expected. She had enjoyed herself more than she had thought she would, but she still wanted time alone with him.

The idea that she would be Michael's wife in a week's time bothered her not at all—an amazing change in such a short time. She now accepted that Michael had been right all along; the past had remained buried. She felt as though a terrible weight had been lifted from her, leaving her giddily free to love without reservation.

Jennifer spent that day and most of the next in a blissful state, with Michael almost constantly at her side. They went sailing again, but the choppier waters they encountered kept Michael at the helm, to their mutual regret. Still, as she stood beside him while he wrapped one long arm securely about her, she knew that she had never been happier. Visions of their beautiful future together came easily and brightly now. They spent the hours at sea talking about the kind of house they hoped to find and the life they would lead. Then they talked about the upcoming campaign, particularly her role in it.

Now that he could see that she had abandoned her fears Michael was pushing her to take a more active role. Jennifer still balked at the thought of making numerous appearances, but she did agree to make at least some. She also promised to study up on the issues, saying that she didn't want to sound like an idiot if she were asked questions.

When Michael approved of that she said with a wicked grin, "But what if I decide that I don't agree with you on some things?"

"It isn't likely that you'll be asked many political questions. Reporters seem to take it for granted that candidates' wives agree with their husbands. It's a pretty ridiculous attitude when you consider that most of *them* have wives who probably disagree with them on some things. It's just another example of the double standard imposed upon those who serve the public.

"On the one hand the public is always condemning politicians for being greedy and self-serving, and on the other they insist on a standard of behavior that they themselves seldom live up to. If one of their acquaintances is divorced, or has an affair, they accept it, but if a politician does the same, it's a big scandal. They condemn us for being devils, then demand that we be saints. It doesn't make any sense."

Jennifer listened, then smiled when he had finished. "Somehow, in the midst of that oration, you failed to answer my question. Should I express my own views?"

Michael frowned at her, then threw back his head in laughter. "See what a good politician I am? Evading questions is a time-honored practice. Yes, you should express your views. If they can't accept that, that's their problem. Remember, honey, we have to accept some compromises for me to be in public life, but only those that are absolutely necessary.''

They returned to Bellemar late in the afternoon, still immersed in their visions of the future. Possibly for that reason, Jennifer failed at first to take note of a change in the atmosphere. Max Haver had returned, even though Jennifer had thought he was staying in Philadelphia for the week. He and J.T. were on the terrace, as were Kathy and Jim. Jennifer assumed that Caroline was not yet up from her customary nap, or that she had gone to see to dinner preparations.

Jennifer didn't stay long with the others, since she wanted to go upstairs and shower away the effects of a day at sea, and dress for dinner. Her first sense that something was wrong came when Michael started to follow her, only to be called back by his father. Jennifer turned, too, and caught a grave expression on J.T.'s face that vanished as soon as he saw her looking at him.

She left them on the terrace and proceeded upstairs alone, wondering if she had imagined J.T.'s expression. Suddenly the brief conversation with the others began to seem too bright and cheerful. But her happiness quickly overcame that momentary concern as she started down the hallway to her room.

On her way she passed the closed door to the bedroom shared by J.T. and Caroline. Suddenly she stopped. In the silence of the big house she could hear muffled sobs coming from behind the door.

A chill banished the warmth of her happiness in an instant. Something was indeed wrong, and whatever it was, she was deliberately being shielded from it. After hesitating for only a moment, she flew back down the stairs. It was possible, of course, that it didn't concern her at all, but her instincts told her that it did.

Only Kathy saw her pause in the doorway to the terrace, since the others had their backs to her.

"Damn those filthy . . ." Michael left the statement unfinished as he flung a newspaper across the terrace.

Jennifer gasped. It took only a few seconds for her to guess the reason for Michael's anger. As they all became aware of her presence at the same time, she ran quickly to retrieve the scattered sheets of the tabloid-style paper.

A sound was torn from within her, the cry of an animal in pain. She stared at the article on the front page then closed her eyes briefly before forcing herself to open them again.

The paper had run two photos side by side. The first was the infamous shot of J.T. and her on the beach, and the other had been taken at the country club affair. It showed Michael with an arm securely about her waist, and their faces were turned toward each other.

Worst of all was the caption, done in the tabloid's usual bold style: "Jennifer Wellesley—a Father and Son Affair?" In one of those strange, random thoughts that can occur under such circumstances, she wondered if anyone would even see that question mark at the end.

J.T. was the first to reach her. The older man wrapped his arms about her in an unconscious imitation of the gesture in the photograph of the two of them.

"I'm sorry, honey. We didn't want you to see it." He patted her back soothingly as she shuddered with pain.

Michael's enraged voice caused them both to turn. "I'm going to sue those bastards. They won't get away with this."

Jennifer saw the tears in his eyes and flew from J.T.'s

comforting arms into Michael's. He crushed her to him almost painfully.

"That's not the way, Michael." J.T.'s voice was old and tired.

"It won't do you any good," Max Haver said bitterly. "They know by now exactly what they can say and what they can't. It's all innuendoes; that's how they work." He made a disgusted sound. "Anyway, how could you prove that nothing ever happened between J.T. and Jennie? Have you thought about that?"

"I can prove it," said Michael with certainty, his voice growing calmer, if no less belligerent.

Jennifer, near hysteria now as she saw her beautiful world grow cold and ugly, spoke up without thinking. "What proof do you have, Michael? Do you really think anyone's going to believe you when you tell them that I was a . . ." She stopped, suddenly recalling the presence of the others. "You have no proof that you can use," she mumbled, calming down somewhat in her embarrassment.

There was silence for a moment. Both Max and Kathy looked rather startled, but she received nods of understanding from J.T. and Jim.

Michael folded her into his arms more gently now. His blind rage had passed for the moment, and the only thing on his mind was how best to protect her. He could feel all her old fears and doubts returning. It occurred to him that she might attempt to run away, and he tightened his hold.

"We're getting married, Jennie. Right away. If I can change the reservations for Caneel we'll get married there. If not we'll get married here."

Jennifer felt the implied declaration of love and sensed his overwhelming need to protect her. But the old feelings had taken hold once more. The walls were slowly going up again.

Max came over with drinks for them, and the group sat down. Jennifer was the first to break the silence.

"Caroline is upstairs crying. That's when I knew that something must have happened. I feel so badly for her. She's been hurt enough as it is." She avoided J.T.'s gaze, but saw a look of respect on Max Haver's face.

"Surely this will all blow over quickly, won't it, Max?" Kathy asked.

Max heaved a rumbling sigh as he stared morosely at his drink. "I don't know. I hope so. Usually rags like that move on to something else pretty quickly."

But Jennifer noted sadly that he didn't really sound convinced. The paper had an enormous circulation, which certainly included large numbers of Michael's potential constituents. With the race already a close one, that article could be the deciding factor.

"Well, we know that Garrity won't try to capitalize on it," Jim offered, referring to Michael's opponent.

Michael nodded mutely, his expression still murderous. How it hurt Jennifer to see him like that. Sunny Michael, always in a good humour, unfailingly gentle and optimistic. She had destroyed all that. An indescribable anguish began deep within her, spreading its ugly tentacles outward until she felt it with every fibre of her being.

At that moment J.T. got up heavily, saying that he was going up to see his wife. But before he did, he went over to where Jennifer sat beside Michael. "We'll get through this, honey. Never doubt it." He squeezed her shoulder, then left.

Jennifer watched him go, her eyes once more misting over with tears as she saw him shamble off like a man suddenly grown old. The past echoed about her.

At that moment the housekeeper appeared in the terrace doorway and announced that there was a call for Michael. It was Thomas Garrity, Michael's opponent.

Michael and Max exchanged glances, then got up. Michael went to the phone on the terrace, and Max disappeared inside to another extension.

Jennifer was unable to judge the brief conversation, since Michael had his back to her as he spoke. In a few moments he returned to her side. Then Max reappeared, and the two of them exchanged satisfied glances. Jim asked the question that was on everyone's minds, and Michael answered it.

"He just wanted to assure me that he has no intention of using this. He's as disgusted by it as we are."

Everyone looked pleased by the news, but Jennifer's smile came more from the desire to please Michael than from genuine pleasure. While she appreciated Garrity's sense of personal integrity, she knew full well that he didn't represent the general public. That question mark would be totally ignored by most of them, as the editors of the tabloid had very well known.

Jennifer forced herself to read the brief article that accompanied the photographs, even though Michael tried to dissuade her from doing so. It was, as Max had said, full of vague innuendoes calculated to titillate the readers. Her mother's affair with the then Senator Bradford was brought up, of course, and the film was mentioned. The article even referred to Michael's broken engagement to a "daughter of a Main Line family," just months before he was first seen with the "seductive Jennifer Wellesley."

She wondered if Sandra had read the article, and what she was thinking. Jennifer was grateful for the fact that Sandra's name, at least, had not been mentioned. Too many others had already been dragged through the mud because of her, and it was a relief of sorts to know that no one else had been added to the list.

Dinner that evening was a subdued affair. Caroline Bradford appeared on her husband's arm, pale, red-eyed, but composed. Jennifer watched as Michael went to his mother and hugged her briefly. She wanted to express her own regret in some way, but fear of rejection kept her immobile. The two women did exchange glances, but Jennifer could read nothing in that haunted expression.

As soon as dinner was over Michael and Jennifer left the others to their various pursuits and went down to the beach. Both were silent as they kicked off their shoes and wandered onto the soft white sand.

Michael flung an arm across her shoulders as they began to walk aimlessly along the beach. "We both knew that something like this could happen, Jennie. It'll blow over quickly, especially once we're married."

She took a deep breath, then tried to make her voice as forceful as possible. "Michael, we're not getting married—at least, not now." As she added the last she heard an inner voice say "not ever."

He stopped in his tracks and cupped hands around her shoulders. "We *are* getting married, and as soon as possible. It's the only way to show those . . . people how wrong they are."

She shook her head. "It wouldn't prove anything, Michael, except that I'm an accomplished seductress and you're a willing fool. Can't you see that?"

"Damn it, Jennie," he exploded, gripping her shoulders tightly, "I'm not going to let you talk like this. Just this afternoon I was thinking about how you'd finally let go of the past and started to think about the future—our future. I wouldn't force marriage on you if I didn't know that you love me. But you do, and nothing else is important. Can't you see that?''

"Right now nothing else may be as important to you," she admitted. "But years from now you're going to regret this. I couldn't bear to see you turn against me, Michael. I love you too much to be able to take that.'' She drew a ragged breath. "Don't you understand? You're the one person I couldn't stand to have reject me. I don't care about all the others. Let them think what they want. But if you rejected me, it would destroy me. You said once that you thought I was very strong, and I am in many ways. But loving you has made me vulnerable in a way that I never was before. I'm afraid of that vulnerability.''

She had finished in a voice that was no more than a whisper, and then she turned away from him. He kept his grip on her, however, and she could do no more than avert her face.

"What you're really saying is that you doubt my love for you. That's what this is all about.'' He ignored her look of protest. "If you were sure of that love you would know that I could never turn against you. Not now, and not years from now. You'd know that I would love you even more then, Jennie, for having shared my life with you. And the only way I can prove my love to you is to marry you now.''

"I don't doubt your love for me now," she murmured. "But when you're forced to choose between two things you want badly, the one you do choose rarely manages to be everything you want it to. By choosing me over your career you're setting impossibly high standards for me. I could never live up to those expectations, and sooner or later you'd come to hate me for not doing so.''

"Damn it, Jennie, stop this." He gripped her shoulders so tightly that she cried out in pain, and he immediately let her go.

He turned away from her for a moment to stare broodingly at the darkened sea. "How can I get through to you? You won't accept my love—or at least the permanence of it. You won't marry me. And you're convinced that I'll be forced to choose between you and my career. You're completely wrong about all three, but even if you were right about the last one, I should be allowed to make that choice myself and not have it forced upon me by you. I won't let you sacrifice our love for the sake of my career. How can I make you understand that?"

"I'm afraid, Michael. How can *I* make *you* understand that?" Her voice was a mere whisper, barely carrying above the sounds of the ocean.

He faced her once more, his eyes filled with pain. "We're talking *at* each other, Jennie, not with each other. And I do understand your fears. I've always understood them. That's why I want to marry you now. It's the only way I know to calm those fears. If there's another way, tell me."

She shook her head slowly. "I don't know of one. But marriage won't calm them, either. I want to wait until after the election."

He made a deprecatory sound. "Don't you see what that would do? It would make everyone think that I hid you away until I could get elected. I don't give a damn what they think of me, but I won't have anyone thinking that you're something that has to be kept secret."

She shrugged. "Let them think what they want. I stopped caring about that long ago. If you win you'll have six years to prove yourself, and by that time they'll be ready to re-elect you on that basis alone. I won't matter.''

He gave her an exasperated look. "It would be a hollow victory to be elected by concealing the one thing that truly matters in my life.''

"How we feel about each other isn't any of their business. I know how you feel, and that's all that matters.''

Hearing the finality in her voice, he came back to her and took her into his arms. "We're both too upset to be making decisions like this now, Jennie. Let's go to bed and forget about it for a while.''

She tipped back her head and stretched up to kiss him softly. She knew that what he was really saying was that he believed he could convince her to marry him if he took her to bed and made love to her. She knew he was wrong, but even so she wanted him now, needed the reassurance of his tender lovemaking. They could have tonight. Tomorrow could wait.

Chapter Twelve

$\mathcal{J}$ennifer ran from the water, followed closely by Michael. They both stumbled through the surf and he caught up to her at the edge of the beach, wrapping his long arms about her from behind. He buried his face in the wet hair that clung heavily to her neck.

"How I love you, Jennie."

She turned within the circle of his arms and reached up to smooth back the tangled blond hair that stood up at odd angles in its wetness.

"And I love you." It was a simple, unadorned statement, but the force behind it was clear. Even though she felt with all her being that she should be pulling away from Michael after the ugly news of yesterday, she knew that they had grown even closer. The fervor of their lovemaking had increased tenfold, something she would not have believed possible. Every casual touch produced a reaction out of all proportion to the action itself. Every exchanged glance held a fierceness, a hunger, that shivered through them and strengthened their need for each other.

Michael gathered her more tightly to him until she could feel his rising passion. They kissed wantonly, exploring each other's mouths greedily.

"Let's go inside," he breathed urgently against her neck.

She was about to protest such blatant behavior before the others when she felt him grow suddenly stiff and wary. After looking up at him questioningly she followed his gaze to the long rock jetty that thrust out from the far end of their beach.

A man was standing there with something in his hand. It took Jennifer a few seconds to recognize that object as a camera, with a long telescopic lens, and in those seconds Michael had left her and begun running in long strides toward the jetty.

"Michael, no!" Her cry followed him, only to be drowned out by the ocean. She turned frantically toward the house, but the terrace was empty.

For another moment she stood where she was, fighting the leaden feeling in her feet. Then she began to run toward the jetty.

Michael had already reached it and stood waiting for the man, who was now beginning to scramble down the rocks. As she ran toward Michael she could see the anger evident in his wide-legged stance.

Jennifer was only a few yards away when the man finally finished his descent. A cry tore from her as she saw Michael raise his arm. The camera, which the man had been holding by its strap, suddenly went flying in a wide arc out over the water. Jennifer was close enough now to hear the sound of it smashing against the rocks of the jetty.

Both men had turned to watch it, and Jennifer stepped

up to Michael just in time to grab the arm that was once more being raised.

"Michael, no!" She held tightly to his arm, feeling the muscles tense.

The photographer, whose expression had been somewhat dazed, appeared to recover at the sound of her voice. Backing off a few steps, he gave them a smug look.

"You won't get away with this."

"Get out of here while you still can." Michael's voice was quiet, but all the more threatening for its icy control. Even Jennifer winced slightly at the unfamiliar sound.

The photographer heard it, too, and continued to back away until he apparently decided that he was safe. Then he turned and stalked off angrily through the coarse beach grass that separated Bellemar from its nearest neighbor.

Jennifer's hand still lay on Michael's arm when he turned to her after the man was out of sight. He covered it quickly with his other hand, and they both stared down at the trickle of blood across his knuckles.

"I scraped it on the camera," he said in a strange tone, as though he were finding it difficult to believe what had just transpired.

Jennifer looked up at him and went cold at his haunted expression. He was shocked at his own violence. *What have I done to him, to have brought him to this?* The question echoed through her mind.

"What happened?"

Jim came running up to them, followed at some distance by J.T. Neither Jennifer nor Michael had seen the two men approaching.

As soon as his father had drawn close enough, Michael told them what had happened.

J.T. shook his head in a satisfied gesture and clapped a hand to Michael's shoulder. "Good for you. We'll probably have to pay for his camera, but it'll be worth every penny."

Jim laughed. "I have to admire your restraint. I would have been tempted to take a swing at more than the camera."

"I probably would have if Jennie hadn't stopped me," Michael admitted rather sheepishly.

"I'm going to see about getting some guards posted." J.T. glared at the now empty expanse of sand.

A few hours later uniformed guards were patrolling the beach and the rest of the property. Jennifer stood alone on the terrace, watching them. Michael was inside somewhere, closeted with J.T. and Max.

After the incident with the photographer they had returned to the house and gone up to their rooms. By that time Jennifer had been feeling dazed and sick. She hadn't doubted Michael's words to his brother. He might very well have hit the photographer. Michael, gentle, easygoing Michael. She shuddered even now, thinking about it.

Jennifer had wanted only to be left alone, to try to deal with the heartsickness that was gripping her. But Michael had followed her into the room, then quickly taken her in his arms. She wasn't sure if it had originally been intended only as a protective gesture, but if so, the contact between their scantily clad bodies had soon turned it into something else entirely.

For the first time in their lovemaking, though, Jennifer hadn't given all of herself to Michael. Her body had responded, just as it always did, but something in her stayed at a distance.

And that sense of distance was still with her as she

stood watching the guards patrolling the stretch of sand. If not for her, they wouldn't be there. If not for her, Michael would never have had to face an ugly side of himself. If not for her, Caroline wouldn't be trying so hard to keep up a front of being calm and in control while her eyes betrayed her.

Michael had once chided Jennifer for having taken onto her shoulders a very heavy load of misplaced guilt. Intellectually she knew he was right, but in that place where the emotions rule she could not rid herself of that feeling she was in fact responsible for so much unhappiness. While it was true that she was innocent of all the charges that could be made against her, she was still the center around which all the destruction occurred.

She had to leave. She thought about her mother's courage in sending J.T. away. Jennifer had never really thought of her mother as being courageous, and yet she knew that it had taken something strong to have risen from such an inauspicious beginning to the pinnacle of success. Did she have her mother's courage?

Would Diana have advised her to get out or to stay? It was a strange thought, since she had never been in the habit of using her mother as a guide to her own behavior. In fact, quite the opposite was true. She had spent most of her life doing things exactly as her mother would not have done them.

She suspected that her mother would have told her to stay and simply ignore all the lies and ugliness. Perhaps she could have done that if not for her concern for Michael. It startled her to realize that she was trying to protect him from all the degradation, all the ugliness she had endured.

And most of all she wanted to prevent the day when

his love for her would turn to hate, or at least to resentment.

"I want to leave, Michael. I have to leave."

"No."

She heard the finality in his voice, but pressed on nevertheless. "It's the only way. I'll come back when the campaign is over."

"We've been through this before, Jennie, and the answer is still the same. I won't let them drive you away, and I won't have people thinking there's any truth to those stories."

"I won't marry you now." She had adopted his tone.

"I can't force you to marry me, as you very well know. But I want you to—and now." He paused, then bent down to pick up a starfish that lay struggling in the receding tide and fling it back into the sea.

They faced each other. She saw the determination written on his face, a tautness in the muscles along his jaw and a glint of steeliness in his dark eyes. He saw in her that strength he had seen before, summoned up from somewhere to rearrange her normally soft features in a subtle fashion.

Michael sighed. "All right. Maybe it's time for a compromise. Max and Dad think I should step up my campaign now to combat the effects of the story. I agree with them in principle, but I told them that we were going to get married and take at least a brief honeymoon. If you won't marry me now, then maybe we should start campaigning."

"We?" she asked in surprise. She had been thrown off-balance by this shift in the conversation and his willingness to compromise.

He nodded. "I told you that I wanted you with me as much as possible. You won't have to do any actual campaigning, of course, but I want you there. It's the only way to fight that story. And you'll soon see that people didn't believe it anyway.''

She couldn't look at him, so she turned her face to the sea. She knew that he believed what he was saying, but she was convinced that he was wrong. Many good and decent people who never read such trashy tabloids would still hear about it, and in a campaign where there was so little difference between the candidates, it could create one.

''All right. I'll come with you. But you must promise me that if you see that I'm harming your campaign, you'll let me go.'' She saw his mouth open in protest and hurried on. ''Promise me that, Michael. I won't do it if I don't have your promise.''

''All right, I promise. But you're wrong.''

Jennifer peered at herself critically in the mirror, then gave a mental shrug. Did it really matter how she dressed? Probably not. Those among the audience who believed the stories would go on believing them even if she dressed like Alice in Wonderland.

She took one last look, satisfied that she had done the best she could. Her long hair was pulled back in a neat chignon, with soft shining waves brushing her cheeks. Her makeup was minimal, as always. And her carefully selected dress conveyed the appropriate image— elegance and good taste. It was silk organza, black as her hair, with a modest vee neckline and short, ruffled sleeves. The ruffles were repeated at the full hem that hovered just above strappy black kid sandals.

Jennifer rarely wore black, since it tended to maximize the paleness of her skin. But with the tan she had acquired the effect was stunning. Her skin gleamed with golden warmth.

The others awaited her in the sitting room of their Pittsburgh hotel suite. Max and several of his campaign aides were with Michael, who turned to her with a smile as she entered.

How handsome he is, she thought proudly. The weeks at the beach had enhanced his tan and lightened his hair. He cut a striking figure in the formal evening clothes he wore so well. Michael was one of those rare men who looked equally at ease in black tie and in faded jeans. To carry that off required a personal style that owed nothing at all to clothing, and he certainly had that. The smile that lit up his face when he saw her turned a boyishly handsome man into a devastating one. He had made joking references to his "candidate's smile," but she knew it was genuine. Smiling came naturally to him, and it showed.

The affair they were to attend that evening in Pittsburgh was a $100-a-plate fund-raising affair. His advisors had wanted to go for a more expensive evening, but Michael had refused, saying that the steel city was a depressed area and he would feel that it was inappropriate to press for more money there, even though many of those who would be in attendance could easily afford to spend whatever they wanted.

Michael had already addressed a breakfast gathering of union officials that morning, but Jennifer had been excused from that appearance. This evening would be her first test since they had reached their compromise.

Jennifer was far too sensitive not to have noticed the unspoken disapproval of some of Michael's campaign aides. She sensed it most strongly among the female members of his staff, but had to admit that some of them might have disapproved of any woman associated with Michael.

Surprisingly, though, she no longer felt that Max

disapproved of her. In fact, the veteran politician seemed almost contrarily proud of her. While she didn't quite understand the reason behind this change, she was enormously grateful for it. ·

The dinner was being held in the hotel, so they took the elevator down to the mezzanine level, where the doors opened on a noisy crowd scene. Michael crooked his arm, then covered the hand she placed on it as he gave her an encouraging wink.

Even so, she tensed as she heard the tenor of conversation change when they were spotted. She forced herself to scan the faces that were turned toward them, never lingering very long on any one of them. Then, satisfied that she had seen no outright hostility, she turned her attention to the introductions that were being made.

A short while later they were progressing through the crowd to the head table. Jennifer kept her hand on Michael's arm and her smile firmly in place, but her ears were once again attuned to the sounds from the crowd.

". . . so much like her mother."

"You'd never guess that she . . ."

". . . read her books and . . ."

The snatches she overheard indicated keen interest, rather than condemnation. She wondered if anyone were paying attention to Michael, then decided that at least some people were when she saw the looks on the faces of several of the women. The men seemed to be interested enough in shaking his hand, but they kept their eyes on her. She cringed inwardly at some of the looks she received, but had to admit that they were no worse than what she had grown accustomed to long ago.

Finally they were seated at their table on the raised dais. Jennifer sat calmly through remarks by various local politicians. She felt better now, reassured by the absence of overt hostility and by the small but important distance between her and the large crowd. Michael clasped her hand briefly beneath the tablecloth, then gave her a scrutinizing look. For the first time that evening she smiled naturally, and he seemed satisfied. She was touched that even in the midst of such an important affair he was thinking of her welfare, but her pleasure was mitigated by the knowledge that his ever present concern for her could cause him problems at some point.

Then the speeches were over and dinner began. Michael was scheduled to speak afterwards. "Fill them full of booze and good food, then send me on," he had joked to her. Jennifer was seated between Michael and Max, an arrangement that she was certain had been carefully planned.

Max leaned toward her when Michael's attention was claimed by the man on his other side. "So far so good. I haven't seen anyone who looks ready to paint any scarlet letters on you."

Jennifer returned his conspiratorial smile, certain now that he was on her side. "Thanks, Max." Her tone and her eyes conveyed a great deal, and she knew that he understood what she was saying.

After dinner she listened carefully to Michael's speech, part of which she had already heard during a brief rehearsal. Once more she scanned the crowd and saw that for the first time they were paying more attention to Michael than to her. She breathed a quiet sigh of relief.

As Michael spoke he was interrupted several times by spontaneous applause. Of course, she reminded herself, this had to be a friendly crowd, since no one opposed to his candidacy would be likely to spend a hundred dollars to hear him speak. Max and Michael had told her that it was this type of event for which her presence would be required. She knew that they were thinking that she would be far less likely to encounter hostility in such settings, and yet her presence would be duly reported by the press. It was all so carefully orchestrated that she would have found it amusing if she hadn't been so nervous.

Michael received a standing ovation, after which photographs were taken. Then they left the table and entered the crowd once more. Everyone was milling about informally as the waiters began to clear the tables. Michael kept her at his side, taking every opportunity to show the assemblage that she wasn't just another member of his entourage. He's tempting the devil, she thought, but she knew that she couldn't have remained in the background in any event.

When it became obvious that they would be there for a while Jennifer slipped away from Michael to find the ladies' room. It was empty when she entered, but she had no sooner gone into a stall than the door opened and conversation floated in to her.

". . . cost him a lot of votes. But he doesn't seem to care, the way he flaunts her."

"Isn't it amazing how innocent she looks? You'd swear that butter wouldn't melt in her mouth."

"Hmmph. Her mother could pull that off, too. They're both actresses, after all."

More women entered then, and the voices she had heard were lost in the general babble. Jennifer took a deep breath and returned to the lounge. Conversation stopped as soon as the women saw her.

She walked over to the mirrored dressing table and took a seat, uncomfortably aware of being the center of attention. Although the attention itself bothered her, she was far more concerned about what was going on in their minds than she was about their stares. These women, after all, were voters. Then she was struck by the irony of that thought. Michael had certainly succeeded in turning her into a politician of sorts.

As the evening wore on several women approached her and identified themselves as readers of her novels. One had even brought a copy for Jennifer to autograph. Since she had been writing pseudonymously this was the first time Jennifer had encountered her fans. The experience was far more gratifying than she would have thought possible. It made her realize how little she had thought of herself as a writer. She was proud of her work, but until this evening it had been no more than a comfortably quiet way of supporting herself.

She told Michael about it later, and he grinned at her. "See? I'll help you sell your books, and you'll help me become a senator. A nice even exchange."

She laughed. It had been very nice to be known for something that didn't smack of scandal. She held that thought close.

"Michael, please. I'm all right." Jennifer had repeated those words so many times in the past fifteen minutes that she thought she had begun to sound like a recording.

She stared down once more at the ugly red stains on her pale blue dress. The odor of rotten tomatoes assailed her nostrils. She had already washed her face and rinsed the mess out of her hair, but she hadn't taken off the dress. Someone had been sent for her luggage, and she was waiting for it to arrive before changing.

"She was one crazy woman out of a whole crowd.

You have to understand that.'' Michael was repeating himself, too, and she stifled a retort to that effect only because she could see how distraught he was.

"I know that," she said soothingly, then suggested that he go down to see if the luggage had been found yet.

He left after giving her one last worried look.

The smell was beginning to nauseate her, so she slipped out of the dress. She knew that she should attend to the stain immediately, but instead she just let it fall in a heap on the floor.

Of course the woman had been crazy. There was no doubt in Jennifer's mind of that. The air of strangeness about her had been the only reason that Jennifer had taken note of her at all in the crowded park.

They had left Pittsburgh early that morning to drive back to Philadelphia, via Allentown, where they had scheduled a brief stop for a rally in a downtown park. Driving rather than flying had been Michael's idea because it provided an opportunity for Jennifer to see his home state.

Jennifer had been impressed by its vast farmlands and forests, and the small towns that dotted the countryside. But by the time they reached Allentown she had grown tired of sitting in a car, so she had decided to accompany Michael to the rally. A hotel room had been arranged for them, to allow Michael to shower and change. She could have stayed there, but the beautiful weather drew her to the park with him.

As she had stood on the platform with Michael and some local politicians she had surveyed the crowd, just as she had done in Pittsburgh. Once again she could see that she was receiving as much attention as Michael himself was.

Michael had been about halfway through his short

speech when Jennifer had first spotted the woman working her way along the fringes of the crowd, moving slowly to the front. She was a small, dark-haired woman of indeterminate age, and she carried a brightly colored plastic shopping bag.

Jennifer had continued to watch her, sensing something not quite right about her. She seemed very agitated and given to brief, jerky movements. The people she passed had given her looks that corroborated Jennifer's impressions. Finally the woman had come to a halt at the side of the platform about ten feet from Jennifer. Jennifer noticed that she seemed to be paying little attention to Michael's speech.

Then, just as Michael finished to an enthusiastic round of applause, the woman had taken a few steps forward and begun to shout in a shrill voice that carried even over the applause. "You're evil. Evil! Go away!" With that she had reached into her shopping bag and withdrawn the tomatoes.

Jennifer's first thought was that the woman meant Michael, and she turned to him in alarm. Only then did she realize that she herself was the target.

Before the woman was subdued by nearby police officers she had succeeded in pelting Jennifer with two tomatoes, one that struck the side of her face and one that hit the center of her dress, just between her breasts. A third tomato had splattered harmlessly on the platform beside her. They were overripe and had burst open to cover her with juice and seeds.

The crowd was stunned into momentary silence. Michael was at her side in an instant, but Jennifer pushed him away to avoid covering him with the mess. Then as the shock had begun to wear off she looked down at herself and laughed. It had been a reflexive action at the time, but as she thought about it now, she knew it had been the right thing to do.

The formerly silent crowd had erupted into murmurings and even a small amount of applause. Even at the time she knew they had been applauding her ability to laugh it off and not signaling their approval of the woman's action. Several women had even stepped forward to offer remedies for the ugly stain.

All in all, despite the shock of the attack Jennifer wasn't really upset—except that she knew it would be reported in the media and draw still more attention to her and to her past.

She also worried about Michael's reaction. It seemed to her that she had taken it far more calmly than he had. Instead of being flattered by his concern for her, she worried that she was burdening him at a time when he had other, more pressing concerns.

An impatient rapping at the door drew her out of her reverie, and she opened it a crack to see Michael standing there with her luggage.

She hadn't let him near her while she was still covered with the tomatoes, but now that she had removed the dress she didn't try to stop him when he drew her into his arms.

"Jennie, are you sure you're all right?"

"For the last time, yes. Tomatoes aren't exactly lethal weapons, you know. No damage was done, and the stain will probably come out of the dress."

"Do you want to stay here tonight? We could wait to drive to Philly tomorrow."

She shook her head. She knew that it wasn't fair to blame this city for what had happened to her, but she wanted to get away from it.

"No. Just let me change my clothes, and then we can be on our way."

Michael sat down on the bed to watch as she sorted through her bag for something to wear.

"The police want to know if you want to press charges."

Jennifer gave him an uncertain look. "I wouldn't want to see the woman go to jail, Michael. But she does need help."

Michael nodded. "The chief said that they've taken her to a hospital, where she'll be examined by psychiatrists, and he has no doubt that she'll be committed. He thinks she's probably been institutionalized before. One of his men said that he remembered her from another incident."

"Well, in that case I think we should let it go, don't you?"

He nodded again, then reached over to pull her onto his lap. "Are you sure you want to go on? I wouldn't mind staying here."

He was already fumbling with the clasp of her bra. Desire mixed with a slight irritation, pulling her in two directions at once. Her first reaction was that this was Michael's way of making her forget the incident. But she dismissed the thought. His protective instincts had been aroused, and it seemed that any time that happened, desire followed very quickly.

"I think you should let me get dressed, so we can leave," she said in a voice that was growing husky.

He slid the bra straps off her shoulders, then bent to tease the creamy skin he had exposed. She shifted slightly on his lap, and the movement made her aware of the strength of his desire.

A soft, small cry of surrender escaped her. It was so easy to forget, to slip with him into their special world. She began to unbutton his shirt as he tugged at the waistband of her lacy panties. Nothing existed except the two of them. It was as though everything else had been cast into shadow, while they themselves were bathed in a hot, white light.

Finally they gave in and their bodies joined in a moment that seemed an eternity, but ended all too soon.

Michael slid reluctantly from her, then fitted her against him, still caressing her. For Jennifer these moments after their lovemaking always proved his love to its fullest extent. Even with his desire slaked, he stayed with her and loved her still more. She began to drift slowly into sleep, and Philadelphia seemed entirely too far away.

"I'm going to hire a bodyguard for her." J.T.'s voice was angry and determined.

"I'm not sure she'll go for that, Dad." Michael was afraid that she'd see it as one more indication of her notoriety, but he agreed reluctantly. If anything did happen, and he had failed to take precautions, he would never forgive himself. He'd convince her somehow.

"Are you sure she's all right?" J.T. was still worried.

Michael smiled into the receiver. "She's fine. Right now she's sleeping, so we'll stay here tonight."

He hung up the phone, frowning. She really was all right. The incident seemed to have bothered him far more than it had her. Did that mean that she had expected something like this, or was she really accepting it for what it had been—a crazed attack?

It seemed to him that she had been making progress, finally ridding herself of the burden of undeserved guilt she had carried around for so long. He could almost feel her growing in confidence and independence, and he found that he liked that, even though it meant that she depended less on him.

Suddenly he wanted to be near her again. He opened

the door into the bedroom, then stood at the side of the bed, looking down at her. Her beautiful face was relaxed in sleep, the full lips slightly parted, the sooty lashes resting against the flawless skin.

He thought about his first reaction to that perfect face and how much more he saw in her now. From a guilty fantasy she had grown into a wondrous reality, and he had belatedly learned the true meaning of love.

Chapter Thirteen

The days hurried along. Nick, the big, blunt-spoken bodyguard Jennifer had accepted very reluctantly, followed her around like a love-stricken St. Bernard. Michael joked that he fully expected to find the man sleeping at the foot of her bed some night.

They made a trip to Erie, then to the Wilkes-Barre–Scranton area and there were no further incidents. People stared, and they were definitely curious about her, but other than an occasional leer from a man or a look of hostility from a woman, she encountered no problems.

Back in Philadelphia, Michael had purchased a townhouse and had his furniture moved in. Although in fact Jennifer stayed there with him, she continued to make the Bradford family home her "official" residence. Both of them knew that they dared not flaunt their relationship.

The quiet, peaceful times at his townhouse were their

only respite from the hectic campaign, and they cherished those moments that served to remind them of the pleasure they could find in just being with each other, something that tended to get lost when they were surrounded by Michael's campaign staff and the public.

Near the end of September, Michael commissioned a poll to determine his areas of strength and weakness. They awaited the results on a rare weekend in Philadelphia; a Sunday rally in nearby Reading was their only scheduled event.

It was a gray, rainy Saturday afternoon when Max arrived at the townhouse with the pollster, a thin, nervous young man. Jennifer and Michael had been discussing the poll, and Michael had as usual been optimistic. But when Jennifer saw the grim set of Max's features she knew that her concerns had been warranted.

The news was not good. As expected, Michael held a substantial lead in his hometown and the surrounding districts. In Pittsburgh, which lay near his opponent's home district, it seemed that Michael's efforts had been in vain. His opponent still led by a fairly substantial margin. The other urban areas of the state appeared to be almost evenly divided, as they had been at the time of the previous poll.

But in the vast rural stretches of the state the situation had changed for the worse. Michael was losing.

Jennifer sat quietly beside Michael and listened to the pollster. She was no expert, but she could still guess at the reason for his poor showing with the farmers and small town residents of the state.

More sophisticated urban dwellers might have disregarded his notorious companion, but to those in the smaller communities she was a destructive force. It seemed to her that whatever advantage she brought Michael as a drawing card at fund raisers and rallies was far outweighed by the harm she was causing with the more conservative voters.

With Pittsburgh almost certain to go to Michael's opponent, and the other cities evenly divided, winning a large chunk of the rural vote was essential to Michael's campaign. Even she could see that.

As soon as the pollster had finished his presentation and the discussion began, Jennifer excused herself to go make coffee for the group. She knew that her presence would prevent the man from speaking frankly about the reasons for Michael's poor showing, and she wanted to spare them the embarrassment of talking around the subject.

She hugged herself against a chill that had nothing to do with temperature. Her emotions were once more being subjected to a sickening seesaw. She had been feeling so confident, so happy, counting the days until the election, then allowing herself to dream of their life afterward.

But now came the nauseating downward ride, ending with a brutal thump. Michael could very well lose the election, and it would be because of her.

He had listened so calmly to the pollster, betraying no disappointment. But she was sure that it was an act for her benefit. No one would work so hard for something he didn't want very badly.

She was standing there, lost in her dismal thoughts, when Michael appeared suddenly in the doorway. He paused for only a few seconds, then came over to her and drew her into his arms.

"Please don't be upset by this, Jennie," he murmured as he stroked her long hair. "It has nothing to do with you. I just haven't campaigned hard enough in the rural areas. We've been avoiding them because of the time factor. It takes so much more of my time to reach so few people that way.''

"It won't do any good even if you do campaign there, Michael. It's me they're against—not you. If that man is honest with you, he'll tell you that.''

Instead of replying he crooked a finger beneath her chin and tilted it up, then covered her mouth warmly. How quickly they both forgot about everything else as their bodies fitted together and their tongues met, issuing erotic invitations.

Michael's hand slid beneath the soft velour top she was wearing to trace sensual patterns over her bare skin. He surrounded her, sheltered her, drew her against his demanding hardness, becoming the only thing in her world.

"If you don't stop, you're going to embarrass us in front of our guests,'' she finally reminded him. As she drew slightly away from him, she thought that once again he had sought to calm her fears with his lovemaking. She hadn't objected, of course, but she knew what he didn't seem to understand: It was a temporary remedy at best.

"Unfortunately you're right,'' he groaned. "I'd forgotten all about them.'' He began to draw her after him back to the living room.

"Michael, I think they'd feel freer to discuss this if I weren't there.''

"But I want you to be there,'' he said stubbornly, pulling her along after him.

She gave in and returned with him to the living room, where Max and the pollster were deep in conversation. Michael threw her a look that said that he doubted if they had been missed at all, then darted a glance toward the stairs that led up to the bedroom.

Jennifer shot him a reproving smile, though she thought that perhaps she *had* overreacted. Certainly Michael didn't seem at all concerned about the results of the poll.

"Well," said Max, when he finally noticed them, "it looks to me as though you're going to be spending a lot of time in the boondocks from here on out. I think we can find the time by eliminating the rest of the local appearances. Your lead is nice and safe here."

Michael nodded, then grinned at his mentor. "Just as long as you don't expect me to put on bib overalls."

Max chuckled. "Well, now that you mention it, maybe we could get matching pairs for you and Jennie."

Jennifer smiled at the image he conjured up, but then she quickly grew serious. "Max, surely you don't think I should go there with him?"

"I know what you're thinking, Jennie, but if you don't go, it would be too obvious. After all, you've been with him at most of his other appearances."

Giving up on Max for the moment, Jennifer turned instead to the young pollster, who had remained silent during this exchange.

"Mr. Harmon, will you tell me honestly if I'm the reason that Michael isn't doing well in the rural areas?"

At her blunt question the young man became even more nervous, shooting quick beseeching glances at both Max and Michael. Then, seeing that he would get no help from either of them, he answered slowly, obviously very uncomfortable. "Uh, we didn't really ask the reasons for people's preferences, Miss Wellesley." He looked away from her very quickly.

Jennifer gave him a skeptical look. "But isn't it important to know why people are planning to vote for the opposition? I would think that would be one of the chief reasons for taking a poll like this."

When he flushed and remained silent she went over to pick up the computer printouts that lay on the table beside him.

Harmon moved toward her as though he intended to snatch them away from her, but she was too quick for him. She saw him throw another pleading look in the direction of Michael and Max.

She carried the pages back to the sofa and sat down to spread them out on her knees. There was silence in the room as she bent over them, reading quickly. Finally, she looked over at Michael. "You've already seen them?" she asked quietly.

He nodded, taking them from her and flinging them onto the coffee table. "Those people haven't seen you yet, Jennie. Once they do—"

She cut him off abruptly. "Once they do, they won't change their minds. People see what they want to see. You can't expect them to see what you see, Michael. They're not in love with me."

The sharpness of her tone startled him, and she took full advantage of his momentary silence to press her point home. "According to what I read, the biggest reason for your lack of popularity in the rural areas is a question about your 'personal integrity,' a euphemism if I ever heard one. Don't try to pretend that you don't know what they mean."

Michael flung himself from the sofa and began to pace the room, rubbing the back of his neck in a characteristic gesture.

"I don't give a damn, Jennie. Let them think what they damned well please. If I campaign heavily there at least some of them will change their minds—and the rest can go to hell."

"You need their votes," she reminded him quietly, feeling the rage within him, though she knew it wasn't directed at her. At times like this she was fearful that he would quit the campaign altogether. A quick glance at Max confirmed that the same thought was on his mind.

"I don't need them that badly," he answered more calmly. "Besides, the poll shows my lead in Philadelphia to be even bigger than we had thought. And that's the crucial vote, because it's by far the largest. If I concentrate on Pittsburgh and the smaller cities where the poll shows I have a good chance, the rural vote won't be that important."

Jennifer turned to Max for confirmation, and the older man nodded. "It'll be more cost effective, too. Reach more voters in a shorter period of time. But we still have to get you out to the backwaters as much as possible."

As they began to discuss changes in Michael's schedule the pollster stood to leave, and after Max and Michael had thanked him, Jennifer went with him to the door. She could see that he was still somewhat nervous around her, so she smiled at him.

"I'm sorry if I put you on the spot, but Michael tries to keep things from me sometimes, and Max isn't much better."

He returned her smile. "Well, for what it's worth, he's got my vote. And don't sell yourself short. I think there's a lot of curiosity out there about you, and if people see the two of you together, well . . ." He stopped for a moment, then went on rather hesitantly. "Your feelings for each other are pretty obvious, I'd say. And you've heard the old saying that 'all the world loves a lover.' I think some of them just might change their minds."

She thanked him and stood for a moment at the door as he walked down the brick sidewalk. Behind her, Max and Michael were discussing strategy.

She wished that she could believe that the man's final words had been a professional opinion, but she suspected that they had been no more than a personal observation. By now she was sure that Max's changed attitude toward her resulted from his having seen the love between them, too. But it was impossible to convey those feelings to a large crowd, and especially to one that might already be predisposed to think of her as an evil temptress.

She closed the door on the gloomy day and wished that she could close it so easily on her gloomy thoughts.

Jennifer's reawakened interest in her writing led her to accept the offer Kathy made one day to delve into family papers stored at her mother's home. Kathy's family on both sides had been Philadelphia residents from before the Revolutionary War and had taken an active role in the formation of the United States.

While some of the papers had already been donated to museums and archives, the family had retained possession of the more personal documents, and it was these that interested Jennifer, since the private lives of those people were far more important to her research than their public experiences.

Kathy was delighted to assist Jennifer, and the two women began to spend days going through the diaries and letters.

By returning to her writing Jennifer was able to set aside her recurring doubts about her future with Michael. She continued to attend some campaign functions with him, but since Congress was once more in session he was spending most of his weekdays commuting to Washington and restricting his campaigning largely to weekends.

He had asked her numerous times to accompany him

to Washington, but she had declined, pleading a need to continue her research. She knew that he saw her refusal to go to the capital as an unwillingness to face their future, and she admitted to herself that he was probably right. But she felt that she needed a respite at this point, and the research provided just that. Once again she was using her writing as a means of shutting out the world.

One afternoon she came home to find Michael already at home and working in his study. He told her that he would be going to Washington the next day, and that she had been invited to attend a luncheon of congressional wives.

Jennifer had been asked to join the group as the guest of a woman she had met very briefly, the wife of a fellow Pennsylvania congressman. Since the woman had been no more than formally polite to her, Jennifer suspected some arm-twisting somewhere. Michael, she knew, was not above using devious maneuvers to persuade her to do what he felt she should, and that would certainly include becoming involved in Washington life.

She agreed, albeit reluctantly, since she loved him and knew it would please him. But she had a deep sense of foreboding as she boarded the Washington-bound shuttle the next morning. This would be new territory for her. It was a first step into the future beyond the election. Michael's optimism was contagious, and Jennifer was at least half-convinced that he would win the election despite the effects of her presence.

They had taken the first flight of the morning, since Michael had some early meetings, and Jennifer was left on her own to explore the nation's capital, a city she had never visited.

She toured the Washington Monument and the Lincoln Memorial, and had just begun to tackle the enormous and fascinating Smithsonian when she realized that she had just enough time to reach the Georgetown restaurant where the luncheon was being held. Playing tourist had kept her worries in check, and she hailed a cab with only minor trepidation.

But the luncheon was a disaster from beginning to end. It quickly became apparent that she had been correct in assuming that her hostess had not asked her voluntarily. Although Jennifer couldn't fault the woman's behavior in any concrete way, she was learning some sad facts about political life. Michael's position as his party's candidate for the Senate had dictated that this woman extend her courtesy to Jennifer.

As for the others present, they fell into two distinct categories. There were the older, well established women, whose husbands held important positions and had the relative security of long incumbency. They fawned over Jennifer, making it plain that they saw her as a very decorative and attention-getting addition to their endless round of parties.

The younger ones, on the other hand, made it plain that they saw Jennifer as a distinct threat to their future plans. Each of them seemed to see herself as becoming a name hostess in Washington circles, and the presence of someone like Jennifer definitely threatened those ambitions.

In the brief space of two hours she learned more than she had ever wanted to know about the hunger for power and status, and the realities of Washington life. At first she was quite simply appalled by what she saw. It reminded her of the kind of life her mother had led, where one selected one's friends and social circle almost solely on the basis of who was ''in'' and who was ''out.'' But by the time she managed to escape she was beginning to realize that she would never be able to turn her back on this unwelcome scene. Michael had already told her that as much of the nation's business was conducted in Georgetown salons and suburban estates as in the Capitol itself. He had also assured her that they would keep their social life to a bare minimum, but Jennifer now thought that would never be possible.

It had become apparent to her through various conversations at the luncheon that Michael had been very much a part of this scene. Naturally a dashing bachelor congressman from an illustrious and wealthy family would have been quite a catch for any hostess, and it seemed that Michael had allowed himself to be "caught" on a regular basis.

She didn't question his intention to stay out of the social whirl after their marriage, but she did question his ability to do so. Any plans Michael had to advance beyond the Senate would require that they lead a highly visible life—the exact opposite of her own plans.

Jennifer returned to the apartment Michael kept in the infamous Watergate complex. She felt empty and drained. The dream of a bright and happy future that had been all that had sustained her through the arduous and unpleasant task of campaigning had been shattered. How many times Michael had said to her, "When this is all over, and we're settled in Washington, things will be different."

But it wouldn't happen. Regular campaigning would simply be replaced by a more subtle but equally unpleasant form of campaigning, of being seen and known by the "right" people, of becoming a part of the power structure that determined who got what.

They had made a sad mistake. They had flaunted their love in the faces of powerful forces that would tear them apart. Slowly perhaps, but still inexorably, the man who wanted a career in politics and the woman who wanted privacy would be pulled in opposite directions until not even their love could keep them together.

"I must leave," she said aloud to the empty apartment.

Chapter Fourteen

Jennifer looked down distractedly and saw that she was gripping the armrests of the seat so tightly that her knuckles showed white against the remnants of her summer tan. She lifted her hands slowly and flexed her fingers, then noted absently that she was trembling.

She turned to the window of the plane, not really caring whether the blurred world outside was the result of clouds or of unshed tears. It didn't matter. Nothing mattered.

She still couldn't truly believe that she had actually left. Despite all the times when she had thought she should, she had never actually believed that she could. But it seemed that she had, although the details were still a bit fuzzy in her mind.

When Michael had returned to the apartment in Washington he had immediately asked her about the luncheon. She had been casually noncommittal, knowing that if she feigned enthusiasm he would immediately suspect something.

She had deftly evaded his questions by teasing him about feeling badly that she would be taking him out of circulation, and once again he had reiterated his intention to keep them both out of the social spotlight as much as possible. Once again she had believed his intentions but not his ability to carry them out. That thought, however, she had continued to keep to herself.

Then he had suggested that they drive out to Virginia, so that she could see the area where he hoped they could find a home. But she had pleaded a headache, so they had returned to Philadelphia.

She had hoped that the headache would provide an acceptable explanation for her changed behavior, and she guessed now that it must have done so, since he had apparently suspected nothing. Or had he?

She closed her eyes and thought about their parting that morning. She had stood at the window and watched him stride down the sidewalk to the garages at the far side of the collection of townhouses. When he had reached the end of the sidewalk and been about to vanish from her view, he had stopped suddenly, turned back for just a moment, hesitated again, then gone on to the garages. She had held her breath for those few moments, then released it with a sigh that she knew now had held an equal mixture of relief and disappointment.

Then she had slipped quietly away, leaving him a note that she had composed during the sleepless night. It had been a brief note, barely skimming the surface of her feelings. She had told him that she could not face the demands of his life, and that she would never be able to live with herself if she were responsible for his giving up his dreams. She had begged him not to try to contact her in any way, saying that if he did, she would be forced to move once more.

Now, as she reviewed the note in her mind, she wondered if he had understood her final sentence: "I love you, Michael, and I always will—but love isn't enough." Would he think that she had meant that she didn't love him enough, or that she believed he didn't love her enough? Like everything else now, it didn't really matter.

She landed at Heathrow in the early morning and hired a car and driver to take her home. She had originally intended to go to her grandmother's, but at the last moment she had realized that she couldn't talk to anyone now, not even her dear Gram.

When she walked into her cottage she had the immediate sense that she might never have been gone, or that she had just been out shopping. The woman she had hired to dust and care for her plants had done a good job. Only the lack of Chaucer's presence made it seem different. He was staying with her friend, Mary.

She was so exhausted from the effects of two largely sleepless nights that she could barely summon the strength to undress before she fell into bed, where she slept away the entire day.

Within a few days she had established a careful routine, deliberately calculated to keep her as busy as possible. Chaucer had returned and seemed determined to fill her in on all his activities during her absence. With the inherent egoism of his species, he paid little attention to her distraction and frequently tear-filled eyes.

She half-heartedly returned to work on the novel she had abandoned when she had gone to America. In the same fashion she began to work on an intricately crocheted sweater she had planned to finish for fall. She cleaned the cottage from top to bottom, including closets and cupboards.

Her telephone seldom rang, but when it did she lifted the receiver with a debilitating mixture of fear and hope. It was never Michael, though, and she guessed that her threat to disappear must have worked. Either that or he had understood and accepted her decision, perhaps because he agreed with it. She was unable to decide which explanation she preferred.

Late one morning, when she had been home for nearly two weeks, her seldom-used doorbell shattered the stillness of the cottage. Panic immobilized her for a moment. Michael wouldn't call for fear that she might run away—but he might very well come here. But the election was only a few weeks away, and she was sure he'd have no time to come now. She calmed herself with that thought and went to the door.

The man who stood there with a toothpaste commercial smile was definitely not Michael, and he definitely *was* a reporter.

"Miss Wellesley, I'm Bob Jamison."

"You're a reporter," she stated flatly in a voice that almost glittered with ice.

He admitted that he was, then further identified himself as working for the scandal sheet that had devastated her so recently. As he spoke he moved forward slightly, as though to block the door should she try to close it on him.

She did think briefly about doing just that, but an unusual vengefulness had crept into her, so she just stared at him for a few moments with a look of such loathing that he actually backed up a few steps.

"Our readers want to know what happened. Why are you back in England?"

"I'm here because this is my home," she said in a tone that proclaimed the utter absurdity of the question. "Surely even the illiterate thrill-seekers you call your readers can understand that a person might choose to be in her own home."

For just a moment the venom in her voice seemed to affect him, but he recovered quickly. "Are you saying that your affair with Michael Bradford is over?"

His use of the word "affair" cast such an ugly, obscene pall over the love they had shared that she actually felt nauseated by it and by him. But even so she began to see a way in which she might be able to help Michael, and she seized it.

"My relationship with Michael Bradford has ended, although I wish him well." She paused, then gave the man a cold smile. "Perhaps in twenty years or so you might want to come back and do a story on my affair with his son. Think of the headline you could have then, Mr. Jamison: 'Jennifer Wellesley—a Grandfather, Father and Son Affair.' That would certainly impress your readers."

She noted with satisfaction that the man actually had the grace to look somewhat sheepish.

"This interview has ended. Please be sure to quote me correctly. This story should certainly guarantee your paper a future readership." She closed the door, resisting the temptation to slam it in his shocked face.

Then she sank wearily onto the sofa. They wouldn't use that last part, of course. But if they quoted her about her relationship with Michael, perhaps it would change the opinions of at least some voters. They would forgive him his "fling" with her as long as they knew that he had shown the good sense to end it.

But by that evening she had begun to realize that if this

reporter had found his way to her home, others could, too. It was time to leave this place.

In a sense she had been slowly coming to that decision even before Bob Jamison had planted himself on her doorstep. The cottage was too full of Michael. The love they had found so unexpectedly seemed to linger everywhere, replaying itself endlessly in her mind.

The other factor in her decision was the possibility that Michael might come for her after the election. The more she thought about it, the more likely it seemed. She would definitely have to go.

Jennifer found a permanent home for Chaucer with Mary, put the cottage up for sale and had her furniture put into storage. Then she paid a visit to her grandmother.

"No one is to know where I am, Gram—and I mean no one. I've arranged for my mail to be forwarded to you, and you can send it on to me. Even my publisher will be contacting me through you. If any mail comes from Michael, please destroy it. It's better that way."

"Jennifer, I just don't understand you. Why are you doing this?"

"Because there's a time to fight and a time to give up. I can't fight anymore, because I know I could never win. I can never be the kind of wife Michael needs. Being in love doesn't always mean living happily ever after."

"But you do still love him?" It was more a statement than a question.

Jennifer nodded. Still and always.

Michael looked down at the street below his hotel window. Alone now, finally, he let his broad shoulders slump. The smile that had remained firmly in place all day vanished, leaving his features utterly drained of emotion.

Depression and despair—the "Double D's" as he had taken to calling them with a grim humor—had been his constant companions for weeks now. But he had managed to keep them well hidden. Of those around him, only Max knew the truth. The others had been told that Jennifer had been forced to return to England for business reasons.

All around him his staff went gleefully about the business of getting him elected. The results of a final poll, taken just a few days ago, showed Michael with a slim but growing lead. They were all optimistic, except for Michael, who felt nothing.

As a human being he had largely ceased to function weeks ago. What remained was a smoothly functioning robot that shook hands, made speeches, gave interviews to the press and smiled for the photographers. Though he was normally a man who genuinely liked people, Michael had begun to sense in himself some misanthropic tendencies. He resented both the voters and his staff for demanding so much from him when he knew that he had nothing left to give.

He rubbed the tense muscles in the back of his neck with a hand that literally ached from too many handshakes, then focused again on the street scene. For a moment he simply could not remember where he was. He stared with a frown at the steep hills surrounding the city. Oh yes, Johnstown. Next would come Altoona, then State College, then Williamsport. One final swing through the central part of the state. The election was less than a week away. Victory was within his grasp, and he didn't care.

For the thousandth time he told himself that he had to

get a grip on reality. There were so many people who had been working so hard for him, and so many voters who would be demonstrating their belief in him. But it didn't matter. He felt the guilt, but lacked the necessary impetus to translate that guilt into action.

Jennie. Until the moment when he had returned to find her note waiting for him in the empty townhouse Michael had never really known the meaning of the word despair. If only he had given in to the warning bell that had rung in his mind that morning when he had left her there. She had been so quiet, so distracted. He should have guessed the reason. But he'd never really believed that she would just disappear like that.

The despair had given way very briefly to anger. He couldn't understand at first why she couldn't have talked it out with him, given him a chance to soothe her. But then he knew. She had taken that way out because she had known that he could talk her into staying simply by appealing to their love for each other. The last line of her note had said it all, to her, at least. Love was not enough. She was wrong. Love wasn't just enough—it was everything.

The sturdy little cottage needed a coat of paint, but it still looked welcoming to a weary traveler. Jennifer smiled for the first time in days when she saw it.

"It is ready for you, Missy." The balding black man pulled up before the little house and got out of his ancient car. "You will be happy here."

His lilting Jamaican accent lingered in the tropical air after he had departed, the words somehow rearranging themselves into a command. No, she thought, I will not be happy here, but perhaps I can be at peace.

For a while she just wandered about the tiny, isolated

cottage. Her mother had bought it years ago, after using it as a hideaway for a honeymoon with one of her husbands. It was high in the hills beyond Kingston, far from the haunts favored by rich Americans and Britons. Jennifer had always loved it, although her mother had never been content to remain there for more than a few days at a time.

The last time she had been there had been with her mother, only weeks before Diana's death. They had planned to stay for two weeks, but as usual Diana had become bored in a couple of days. Still, Jennifer had nothing but happy memories of their times there. Mother and daughter had used this sanctuary to mend the often frayed edges of their relationship. Away from the necessity to be "on display" for her public, Diana could be both introspective and philosophical, though never for very long. Jennifer had once remarked to her grandmother that it was there that she saw the good side of her mother, and as the passage of time had provided her with its unique perspective, she knew that that had been true.

Jennifer's decision to hide out there had been based on two factors: The cottage was definitely isolated, and she had only pleasant memories of the place. Perhaps that was why she had never sold it, but instead had paid a local couple to maintain it for her. It might always have been in the back of her mind that she might need it someday.

That evening, as she sat on the little patio in the brief tropical twilight, she prayed that she wouldn't have to run again. Somehow she doubted that she would ever return to England to live. She would go back to visit, of course, as long as her grandmother was there. But as the velvet curtain of night descended on the beautiful island she began to hope that this might be her home.

Once it became clear that there would be no further newsworthiness attached to her name, she knew she would be safe here. No reporter was likely to stumble upon this isolated spot.

She drifted off to sleep in the lounge chair, awakening only when an unknown animal or bird cried out from the surrounding jungle. Then she took herself off to bed, where she dreamed of Michael for the first time since she had left him.

Michael, warming her chilled face with his hands; holding her to him with that lovely mixture of tenderness and ferocity; running with her through the surf at Bellemar; catching her eye at a rally; stealing quietly into her bedroom at night. The memory of Michael would be her life. In her dreams they made love endlessly, rising to that wondrous plateau of beauty where the world couldn't touch them.

October drew to a close, marked only by the end of a long period of cloudy days, occasionally interspersed with the sudden, violent storms of the tropics. Jennifer had again returned to work on her manuscript. Work was soothing, healing, and she welcomed it, slipping gratefully into the world she had created.

When she was within a day or so of completing the manuscript the generator that supplied her power broke down. While she waited for two days for a replacement to be installed she cursed herself for not having thought to bring a manual typewriter, because no matter what work she devised for herself, thoughts of Michael intruded. At night as she lay alone in her bed she didn't even try to hold those thoughts at bay. Nighttime was for those beautiful memories. But she now realized that only by working could she fend them off during the day, so she carried her water from the well, built elaborate sandcastles on a nearby beach, and tried to read by candlelight in the evenings.

Then, the novel at last completed, she immediately began to formulate plans for the next, not allowing herself the usual respite between efforts. It was unfortunate that her research with Kathy had not progressed far enough to allow her to work on that one, but she quickly found a replacement. Through the couple she had employed to care for her cottage she met a neighbor, a retired native schoolteacher whose knowledge of the island's history was truly encyclopedic. They spent long hours together, and Jennifer didn't know what enchanted her more: the woman's soft accent or her colorful tales.

On one occasion when Jennifer was visiting the old woman, her grandson dropped by. At first put off by the rather wild, unkempt look created by the myriad braids known as dreadlocks, Jennifer quickly discovered that Cedric was decidedly less ferocious than his appearance indicated. He worked occasionally with a reggae group that performed in Kingston, and otherwise supported himself by working as a handyman.

While they chatted it occurred to Jennifer that she could utilize his services. The first project on her mind was getting the cottage painted. Cedric was happy to take on the job, and the deal was made.

He began work the following day, bringing along a large battery-operated cassette recorder. He and his music were such a happy presence in her home that she didn't have the heart to ask him to turn the volume down, so the little house reverberated with the happy sounds of island music all day long. After a while Jennifer swore that she was typing in rhythm with the heavy beat.

When he wasn't painting and listening to his music

Cedric was telling her more of the island's history. One day he brought along his girlfriend, and the three of them made plans to visit some of the sites that he and his grandmother had mentioned.

None of them seemed to know anything at all about her, although they did know who her mother was, and the grandmother had seen several of Diana's films, which fortunately did not include *Two Loves*. Jennifer felt blessedly anonymous.

When she finally remembered to turn her calendar to November she saw the red circle she had drawn around the 7th. Election Day in the U.S. It was only two days away. She questioned Cedric, who told her that several U.S. papers were available in Kingston. He said he would be going there in three or four days, and she asked him to pick up a paper for her.

She spent Election Day itself in an agitated state, unable to accomplish any work at all. She knew that she wouldn't have been more nervous if she had been in Philadelphia with Michael.

Jennifer was shocked at the strength of her feelings. She had come to Jamaica hoping that the tranquillity of the place would allow her to put Michael into her past, but her present state of mind certainly seemed to deny that possibility. She alternated between telling herself that she couldn't hurry time, that greatest of all healers, and admitting that she couldn't imagine a future without him.

To punish herself for such imaginings she deliberately conjured up a future for him where he would win the election, eventually marry Sandra, or someone like her and go on to become a very great President. But even as she conjured up the images she knew that there was something very wrong with the picture.

What was wrong was that she could no more imagine Michael with anyone other than her than she could imagine herself with anyone other than him.

So what was she to do? She could wait and hope that time would dull the pain and ease him into the safe realm of memory, or . . . She left the thought unfinished.

Unfortunately her state of mind didn't improve once Election Day had passed, since she still didn't know the results. It was frustrating, to say the least. The election had been decided, and she was still in the dark.

On the day that Cedric went into Kingston Jennifer paced the deserted beach, her mood a strange mixture of elation and fear. She could have gone with Cedric, but she had decided against it, since she didn't yet want to come out of her self-imposed seclusion.

Suddenly nothing in her life seemed as important as knowing the results of the election. Why, she asked herself as she listlessly sifted sand through her fingers. The answer came at last, the answer she had been suppressing for the past few days: Because whatever his future is, that's your future, too.

A brief feeling of euphoria turned quickly into numbing cold. Could she? Why was she so afraid? By now the election was won or lost; she could have no further effect upon it.

Her fear of destroying Michael's career had been a real one. There was no denying that. But what was done was done. If he had won the election she could do him no further damage.

Sadly she admitted that she had been deluding herself. It wasn't really Michael's future that had frightened her; rather, it was her own. She had been afraid of their closeness, even as she delighted in it. She'd been afraid because the only other person to whom she had ever been that close had been her mother, and her mother had so often encouraged it, only to push her aside. With Michael she had erected barriers against that rejection, and she feared letting them down, feared linking her future inextricably with his.

For a long time she sat there, thinking nothing at all as tears streamed unheeded down her face. Finally a terrifying thought came to her. "Michael," she whispered, "have I lost you?"

One of her last memories of her mother returned to haunt her. Diana had been trying to draw her out on the subject of her life in France, and Jennifer had been reluctant to divulge any but the most mundane details. Her reluctance had stemmed from her fear that her mother would poke fun at her seriousness about her studies, since Diana had never quite stopped haranguing her about her decision to give up acting.

"You don't want me in your life at all, do you?" She could hear her mother's voice asking the question, half mocking, but half serious.

At Diana's funeral, only weeks later, Jennifer had thought about that conversation, but she had put it from her mind after that. Until now. Did Michael feel the same way her mother had felt?

Cedric didn't return from Kingston until quite late. Jennifer was sitting on her patio, where she had been for hours. Fear had almost dispelled her eagerness to learn the election results. Had Michael failed to contact her because he knew that no matter how much he might love her, he could never breach those barriers she had erected so long ago? Had he perhaps even breathed a sigh of relief when she had left him? Those questions terrified her.

But the sound, faint at first, of a Jeep struggling up the steep hill toward her cottage reawakened her interest in knowing what had happened. By the time Cedric pulled up she was waiting eagerly for him. Donna, his girl-friend, was with him, so he didn't linger, as he might otherwise have done. She thanked him, said good night to them both and ran into the house, clutching the precious newspaper.

There was, as she had expected, an entire section devoted to the election returns. But before she could begin to scan the small print listings a headline on the facing page caught her eye.

"Bradford Elected in Pennsylvania."

A shiver of delight ran through her, accompanied by a sound that was somewhere between laughter and a sigh of relief. The article was very brief, one among many.

Michael Bradford, a congressman from Phila-delphia, was elected to the U.S. Senate by a comfortable margin. The thirty-six-year-old Sena-tor follows in the footsteps of his millionnaire father, J.T. Bradford, who served two terms before retiring. Bradford, who is unmarried, has earned a reputation in the House as an articulate man who votes his conscience and is generally perceived to be a liberal on social issues but a conservative on budgetary and defense matters.

Tears of joy ran down her cheeks, ultimately blurring the newsprint. "Michael, I'm so happy for you. If only I could tell you that," she whispered aloud into the silence.

Then, knowing that it was a silly gesture, she careful-ly cut out the article and carried it with her into her bedroom, where she placed it on the table next to her bed. She fell asleep, staring at it in the semi-darkness. He came to her quickly in her dreams.

She awoke the next morning to a strong urge to call

him, but there was as yet no phone in her cottage. She had ordered one, but such matters proceeded at a snail's pace in this rural paradise. However, Cedric's grandmother had a phone which Jennifer knew she could use.

But after she had dressed she hesitated. What if her fears of the previous day were true? What if Michael had relegated her to his past? Her doubts immobilized her for a moment. Rationally, she didn't believe that that could happen. But emotionally she was terrified that it had.

Finally she decided to call her grandmother. If Michael had indeed tried to reach her, it would have been through Gram. She calculated the time difference and decided that it would be a good time to call, so she set off determinedly.

It took more than half an hour for the call to be put through to London, during which time she tried to make conversation with her kind hostess. But when the phone rang she leapt up from her chair and picked it up before it could ring a second time.

"Gram, it's Jennifer. Can you hear me?"

"Yes, dear, I can hear you. Is anything wrong?" The familiar voice had a distant, hollow sound.

Jennifer assured her grandmother that she was fine, then hurried on. "Gram, Michael won.. He's a Senator."

"Yes, I know. I made it a point to find out. Are you happy about that?"

"Oh, yes," Jennifer breathed. "He wanted it so badly, and I know he'll be very good."

"Have you called to tell him that?"

"No," Jennifer answered, feeling more and more nervous. "You haven't heard from him, then?"

There was a slight hesitation. "Do you want to hear from him, dear?"

Jennifer swallowed in an unsuccessful attempt to dissolve the sudden lump in her throat. Her eyes were stinging. "I . . . I don't know, Gram. No, I guess not. It's better left as it is."

She forced herself to answer her grandmother's questions, then ended the conversation as quickly as possible. Thanking her elderly hostess, she made her exit and ran blindly back to her cottage. She had her answer. And now she knew that until now she had never really believed that it had ended. The despair that came over her left her totally numb, unable even to move.

For the remainder of the day she lay on a chaise longue on her shaded patio, getting up only to put on water for tea, then forgetting about it until a burning odor penetrated her dulled senses. The kettle had boiled dry. She turned off the burner and went back to the patio.

She had no idea how long she had lain there, suspended between wakefulness and sleep, uncaring. If she had been capable of wanting anything at that point it would have been sleep, an unending sleep.

Gradually a sound penetrated the fog that shrouded her senses. A Jeep. It must be Cedric. She roused herself at last. She just couldn't face him at this point, so she got up rather stiffly and went inside. She wouldn't answer the door, and he would assume that she had gone out. She knew that he hadn't planned to paint that day, so she hoped he would leave quickly.

A few moments later she heard the Jeep stop outside, then heard its door slam. She hid in her bedroom, waiting for the insistent knocking to subside. When it finally did she waited for the sound of the Jeep's engine, but all was silence. Had he decided to paint, after all? She listened, but could hear nothing.

Cedric had been storing the ladder and paint in a small shed at the rear of the house, so she stole quietly to the door that led to the patio. As she approached it, her eyes were already turned in the direction of the shed, so it was a few seconds before she caught a brightly colored movement at the opposite side of the patio.

He was standing with his back to her, one hand poised at the back of his blond head. He wore khaki shorts and a red knit shirt that clung to those well-rememberd muscles.

"Michael." The name was more a gasp than a word. He couldn't have heard it through the closed door. She was trembling so badly that she couldn't move, so she just stood there, staring mutely at him. Was he a figment of her imagination?

Then he turned slowly, a puzzled look on his face. He wasn't far from her, but he didn't seem to see her. A chill shot through her as she began to believe that she must be imagining him. Then, belatedly, she realized that the sun was reflecting off the glass door, blinding him. He started to turn toward the path that led around the house, and she reached in that same instant for the door handle. But her shaking fingers refused to work properly.

He heard the sound, however, and paused, then started toward her. She finally succeeded in opening the door just as he reached it.

"Jennie." It was a sigh of relief, an admission of pain and longing, an affirmation of love. Her name had never sounded so beautiful to her.

Before he could move she almost fell through the doorway and into his arms. She couldn't get close enough as she wrapped her arms about him and buried her face in his shirt.

"Jennie," he said again, in a wondrous tone this time, as though he didn't yet believe that he held her. The hand that tried to stroke her hair was trembling. Their bodies were struggling to find that closeness they craved, that oneness that had been so long denied them.

She felt his mouth against the top of her head and raised her face, seeking his kiss. The flames that engulfed them eclipsed even the brilliant Jamaican sun. Lips tried desperately to ease the longing, only to fan the flames even higher. Hands sought ways to reach yearning flesh, impatiently tore at offending clothing.

Finally Michael picked her up and carried her inside, and moments later they were naked on her bed, making love with lips, hands, words and eyes. Neither of them even attempted to postpone the moment of oneness with foreplay. Two bodies quivered in unison, melting together into a blissful union.

"I've come to marry you, Jennie." His voice was hoarse as he still lay over her, unable to leave her.

She said nothing; she was incapable of speech at that moment.

"I've found a house for us in McLean, Virginia. It has a pool and a perfect room for you to work in, a sunporch that looks out to a stretch of woods." His tone grew urgent, as though he were expecting her to refuse.

Her thoughts were whirling too fast. She tried to say something, but still nothing would come out.

"Jennie, damn it, say something." He spoke with an impatience born of desperation.

"How did you find me?" She thought that was a stupid thing to say, but it had already come out.

He propped himself above her, frowning. "Tell me you'll marry me, Jennie."

Once again her lips refused to move, but this time she nodded. It was the best she could do.

The frown disappeared, and a smile appeared in its place, becoming broader and broader until she thought it covered his whole face. It vanished only when he bent to kiss her once more, a long, slow kiss that left them both breathless. Only then did he finally move off her, sliding down beside her and drawing her to him.

"As soon as the election was over," he began, then interrupted himself. "I won, by the way. Did you know that?"

She nodded, reaching out to pick up the article that still lay on her nightstand. He smiled at it, touched by what she had done, then continued.

"Anyway, I went to England, found the cottage all closed up, then got your grandmother's address from the post office. So I went back to London and spent most of an afternoon convincing her that I was going to find you if I had to spend every cent I have on private detectives. She finally gave in and told me." He turned them both on their sides, facing each other.

"We have her blessing, by the way, and she said that she'd like at least one great-grandchild before she leaves this world. I assured her that I'd do my best to grant her wish."

"But why didn't she tell me that you had come to see her?"

Michael looked surprised. "When did you talk to her?"

"Today, only a few hours ago. I asked her if you had been in touch with her." She faltered, then realized that Gram hadn't really answered her question. She smiled at the old woman's slyness. She had avoided Jennifer's question by asking if she really wanted to hear from him.

"Had you tried to call me?" he asked hopefully.

She lowered her gaze, unable to look at him as she shook her head. "I was afraid . . . afraid that you wouldn't want to hear from me."

"What?" The word almost exploded from him as he sat up and stared down at her incredulously.

Jennifer fidgeted unhappily and continued to avoid his gaze, at least until he reached out and forced her to look at him.

"I . . . I know it doesn't make sense, but I had begun to think that maybe you didn't really want to hear from me or see me again." She stopped, truly astonished that she could have believed such a thing. "I don't know why I thought that," she said in a small, disbelieving voice.

Michael relaxed the grip he had on her face and began to stroke her cheek softly. "I understand, Jennie. There were times when I thought you no longer loved me, too. I can't begin to tell you the number of times I started to call you. But I was so afraid that either you wouldn't be there, or that you would say that you didn't love me anymore. So I just kept holding on to the dream, waiting for the election to be over." He smiled tenderly at her. "So much for that absence-makes-the-heart-grow-fonder nonsense. All it did was to create irrational fears. In our case there wasn't any room for love to grow more. All that grew were doubts."

"Do you have any doubts now, Michael?" She looked at him fearfully. "I mean doubts about our being able to make a marriage work."

He shook his head. "No doubts. Only one certainty. I couldn't live without you, Jennie."

"But you're a senator now," she protested.

"That's right. All that means is that I won't have to run for re-election for six years. By that time all the ugliness will be so far in the past that no one will think to bring it up again. And I'll keep the promise I made, Jennie. We'll stay out of the Washington social scene as much as possible."

She sighed happily. They'd never be able to do that, but suddenly it didn't seem to matter so much. She thought about all the would-be hostesses who had made that luncheon so unpleasant for her. And then she recalled something her mother had once said.

She smiled. "Oh, I don't know. I just might decide to turn into Washington's most accomplished hostess. My mother once said that the best way to deal with gossip is to brazen it out, force the gossipers to confront you as much as possible. Maybe she had a point."

Michael laughed. "Maybe she did. But I'm just selfish enough to want to keep you all to myself as much as possible."

She gave a deep sigh of mock-regret. "Oh, well, there goes a brilliant career before it even got off the ground. Maybe just an occasional small dinner party, then." She gave him an impish grin.

"Once a year or so," he agreed as he bent to her once more, making it plain that, as far as he was concerned, the time for talking had ended.

Silhouette Special Edition

MORE ROMANCE FOR
A SPECIAL WAY TO RELAX

$1.95 each

2 ☐ Hastings	21 ☐ Hastings	41 ☐ Halston	60 ☐ Thorne
3 ☐ Dixon	22 ☐ Howard	42 ☐ Drummond	61 ☐ Beckman
4 ☐ Vitek	23 ☐ Charles	43 ☐ Shaw	62 ☐ Bright
5 ☐ Converse	24 ☐ Dixon	44 ☐ Eden	63 ☐ Wallace
6 ☐ Douglass	25 ☐ Hardy	45 ☐ Charles	64 ☐ Converse
7 ☐ Stanford	26 ☐ Scott	46 ☐ Howard	65 ☐ Cates
8 ☐ Halston	27 ☐ Wisdom	47 ☐ Stephens	66 ☐ Mikels
9 ☐ Baxter	28 ☐ Ripy	48 ☐ Ferrell	67 ☐ Shaw
10 ☐ Thiels	29 ☐ Bergen	49 ☐ Hastings	68 ☐ Sinclair
11 ☐ Thornton	30 ☐ Stephens	50 ☐ Browning	69 ☐ Dalton
12 ☐ Sinclair	31 ☐ Baxter	51 ☐ Trent	70 ☐ Clare
13 ☐ Beckman	32 ☐ Douglass	52 ☐ Sinclair	71 ☐ Skillern
14 ☐ Keene	33 ☐ Palmer	53 ☐ Thomas	72 ☐ Belmont
15 ☐ James	35 ☐ James	54 ☐ Hohl	73 ☐ Taylor
16 ☐ Carr	36 ☐ Dailey	55 ☐ Stanford	74 ☐ Wisdom
17 ☐ John	37 ☐ Stanford	56 ☐ Wallace	75 ☐ John
18 ☐ Hamilton	38 ☐ John	57 ☐ Thornton	76 ☐ Ripy
19 ☐ Shaw	39 ☐ Milan	58 ☐ Douglass	77 ☐ Bergen
20 ☐ Musgrave	40 ☐ Converse	59 ☐ Roberts	78 ☐ Gladstone

$2.25 each

79 ☐ Hastings	87 ☐ Dixon	95 ☐ Doyle	103 ☐ Taylor
80 ☐ Douglass	88 ☐ Saxon	96 ☐ Baxter	104 ☐ Wallace
81 ☐ Thornton	89 ☐ Meriwether	97 ☐ Shaw	105 ☐ Sinclair
82 ☐ McKenna	90 ☐ Justin	98 ☐ Hurley	106 ☐ John
83 ☐ Major	91 ☐ Stanford	99 ☐ Dixon	107 ☐ Ross
84 ☐ Stephens	92 ☐ Hamilton	100 ☐ Roberts	108 ☐ Stephens
85 ☐ Beckman	93 ☐ Lacey	101 ☐ Bergen	109 ☐ Beckman
86 ☐ Halston	94 ☐ Barrie	102 ☐ Wallace	110 ☐ Browning

Silhouette Special Edition

$2.25 each

111 ☐ Thorne	133 ☐ Douglass	155 ☐ Lacey	177 ☐ Howard
112 ☐ Belmont	134 ☐ Ripy	156 ☐ Hastings	178 ☐ Bishop
113 ☐ Camp	135 ☐ Seger	157 ☐ Taylor	179 ☐ Meriwether
114 ☐ Ripy	136 ☐ Scott	158 ☐ Charles	180 ☐ Jackson
115 ☐ Halston	137 ☐ Parker	159 ☐ Camp	181 ☐ Browning
116 ☐ Roberts	138 ☐ Thornton	160 ☐ Wisdom	182 ☐ Thornton
117 ☐ Converse	139 ☐ Halston	161 ☐ Stanford	183 ☐ Sinclair
118 ☐ Jackson	140 ☐ Sinclair	162 ☐ Roberts	184 ☐ Daniels
119 ☐ Langan	141 ☐ Saxon	163 ☐ Halston	185 ☐ Gordon
120 ☐ Dixon	142 ☐ Bergen	164 ☐ Ripy	186 ☐ Scott
121 ☐ Shaw	143 ☐ Bright	165 ☐ Lee	187 ☐ Stanford
122 ☐ Walker	144 ☐ Meriwether	166 ☐ John	188 ☐ Lacey
123 ☐ Douglass	145 ☐ Wallace	167 ☐ Hurley	189 ☐ Ripy
124 ☐ Mikels	146 ☐ Thornton	168 ☐ Thornton	190 ☐ Wisdom
125 ☐ Cates	147 ☐ Dalton	169 ☐ Beckman	191 ☐ Hardy
126 ☐ Wildman	148 ☐ Gordon	170 ☐ Paige	192 ☐ Taylor
127 ☐ Taylor	149 ☐ Claire	171 ☐ Gray	193 ☐ John
128 ☐ Macomber	150 ☐ Dailey	172 ☐ Hamilton	194 ☐ Jackson
129 ☐ Rowe	151 ☐ Shaw	173 ☐ Belmont	195 ☐ Griffin
130 ☐ Carr	152 ☐ Adams	174 ☐ Dixon	196 ☐ Cates
131 ☐ Lee	153 ☐ Sinclair	175 ☐ Roberts	197 ☐ Lind
132 ☐ Dailey	154 ☐ Malek	176 ☐ Walker	198 ☐ Bishop

SILHOUETTE SPECIAL EDITION, Department SE/2
1230 Avenue of the Americas
New York, NY 10020

Please send me the books I have checked above. I am enclosing $_____ (please add 75¢ to cover postage and handling. NYS and NYC residents please add appropriate sales tax). Send check or money order—no cash or C.O.D.'s please. Allow six weeks for delivery.

NAME _____

ADDRESS _____

CITY _____ STATE/ZIP _____

Silhouette Special Edition